REVOLTING

YOUTH

Also by C.D. Payne

Youth in Revolt
Civic Beauties
Cut to the Twisp
Frisco Pigeon Mambo
Young and Revolting
Revoltingly Young

REVOL

Y

BROADWAY BOOKS

New York

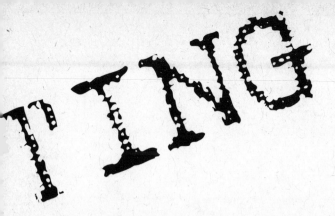

THE FURTHER JOURNALS OF
NICK TWISP

C.D. PAYNE

BROADWAY

All Rights Reserved
Published in the United States by Broadway Books, an imprint of The Crown Publishing Group, a division of Random House, Inc., New York.
www.crownpublishing.com

A previous edition of this book was originally published in 2000 by Aivia Press. It is here reprinted by arrangement with Aivia Press.

BROADWAY BOOKS and its logo, a letter B bisected on the diagonal, are trademarks of Random House, Inc.

Book design by Jennifer Ann Daddio

Library of Congress Cataloging-in-Publication Data
Payne, C. D. (C. Douglas), 1949–
Revolting youth : the further journals of Nick Twisp /
by C. D. Payne.
p. cm.
1. Twisp, Nick (Fictitious character)—Fiction.
2. Teenage boys—Fiction. 3. Diary fiction. I. Title.

PS3566.A9358R48 2009
813'.54—dc22
2009006424

ISBN 978-0-7679-3234-9

PRINTED IN THE UNITED STATES OF AMERICA

1 3 5 7 9 10 8 6 4 2

TO JOY

REVOLTING YOUTH

FEBRUARY

SATURDAY, February 20 — No, I haven't abandoned my impulse toward labored introspection. I've simply been too busy coping with the distractions of sudden wealth to write in my journal. It's fortunate for New England asceticism that Henry Thoreau didn't win big in the stock market while camping out at Walden Pond.

Like me, Hank would probably be making countless expeditions with his future Trophy Wife (Sheeni Saunders) to the big city (Santa Rosa, California) in search of luxurious household furnishings for his rented bachelor digs. Carlotta Ulansky (my 14-year-old feminine alter ego) is inclined toward the comfortably overstuffed, but Sheeni insists on the rigorously tasteful. She has replaced Granny DeFalco's spine-crunching old couch with a sinuous sofa of hand-woven wool (color: eviscerated celadon) fashioned by brooding, socially conscious Finns. Upon this taut perch this afternoon we successfully performed our 31st act of sexual union. Now a casually tossed mauve linen pillow conceals a small, telltale moist spot.

For the sake of statistical texture in my future autobiography— tentatively titled Nick Dillinger Unmasked—I've decided to keep a running total of my sexual experiences (excepting only solo acts, already too numerous to count). This should prove invaluable to future sociologists studying the amorous habits of oversexed, alcoholic fiction writers. Perhaps I'll keep track of my beverage consumption as well, though I fear the inexorable binges of middle age may muddle the count. So far at any rate my lifetime cocktail total is up to four.

Back to sex. I've found that one of the nicest aspects of sexual intercourse is that delicious moment when one is maneuvering one's clammy nakedness atop one's submissive love—heart fluttering, senses tingling, be-condomed T.E. (Thunderous Erection) honing in on its target like a laser-guided smart bomb. I asked Sheeni if girls enjoyed that moment of exquisite anticipation as well.

"I hardly think so, Nickie," she replied. "We're usually paralyzed with fear that the dolt is going to stuff it up our bladder or something."

All in all I'm glad I was born a male, even if lately I do spend a good part of my time dressed as an elderly Italian widow. Yes, homely Carlotta continues her role as a one-girl fashion harbinger of the long-delayed "Mussolini Revival."

Ten minutes later. My journalistic ruminations were interrupted by the sounds of ear-piercing howling. Carlotta rose from her lacquered teak computer desk and strolled into the living room where her obese maid, Mrs. Flora Ferguson (née Crampton), was beating Sheeni's ugly black dog Albert with the New York Review of Books.

"What's the trouble, Mrs. Ferguson?" inquired Carlotta.

Breathing even heavier than usual, my maid paused to compose her reply, causing me to wonder—as I often do—if paying her by the word would speed up her speech. "Sorry, Miz Carlotta . . . I didn't mean . . . to interrupt your writin'. . . . I think this damn dog . . . done piddled on your . . . brand new davenport!"

Feigning alarm, I studied the familiar stain in question.

"Damn!" exclaimed Carlotta. "This sofa cost over $3,500. It was custom ordered from Helsinki."

"That so?" remarked Mrs. Ferguson, impressed. "And it don't . . . even recline!"

Albert looked up at me imploringly as I replaced the linen pillow.

"That dog has got to learn," said Carlotta sternly. "Mrs. Ferguson, you may resume your administration of discipline."

Sighing heavily, she followed my orders. Albert took it like a man. As chief bill-payer in the household (and presumed leader of the pack), I am trying to establish my unchallenged dominance over the rebarbative beast. No one likes to be number two (just ask Sheeni's wanna-be boyfriend Vijay Joshi), but hierarchies must be imposed. They are civilization's only defense against chaos.

SUNDAY, February 21 — The day dawned surprisingly spring-like, which Sheeni interpreted as a sign from God to skip church. We rendezvoused at the downtown Ukiah donut shop for a leisurely perusal of the New York Times and furtive, under-the-table grope. Carlotta hoped this would lead to a quick return home for my 32nd you-know-what, but Sheeni suggested instead a joint expedition on our matching new 21-speed Italian mountain bikes. At a nearby deli staffed by swarthy Middle Eastern men in bloody aprons, we purchased two curried eggplant sandwiches (My Love is experimenting with vegetarianism). She deposited this aromatic package in the streamlined, graphite-reinforced basket mounted on her handlebars. In my basket she placed a small but surprisingly weighty (and noticeably more aromatic) black dog.

"Darling," I pointed out, "it appears your dog Albert would prefer to ride with you. As you can see, he's growling at me."

"He's only clearing his throat, Carlotta. I fear he may have a touch of the ague. An outing in the fresh air cannot help but prove restorative. And sweet Albert belongs to both of us. He loves you very much."

"And do you love me very much?" I couldn't help but ask.

"On a morning this glorious, I love nearly everyone," she replied, swinging a lovely leg over her saddle and powering off in a demandingly high gear. Sighing, Carlotta adjusted her brassiere (containing two jumbo-sized foam shoulder pads, a $20 bill, and a condom) and puffed after her. Albert hunkered down in his basket and glared at me.

We had gone barely two blocks when vile Vijay Joshi emerged from a side street on his modest red mountain bike—once the object of considerable Twispian envy, believe it or not. The morning sun glinted crudely off his plated Taiwanese chrome as Vijay pedaled toward us. He glanced with calculated indifference at my satiny Milanese metalwork and peered longingly down the fluttering neckline of Sheeni's official Wart Watch T-shirt. I felt the need to distract him from this latter activity by crashing into his rear wheel.

"Carlotta! Look where you are going!" he shouted, swerving toward a municipal oak tree and unfortunately just missing it.

"I believe I have the right of way," she replied. "Heavens, you nearly injured darling Albert."

"Do be careful, Vijay," called Sheeni, circling back.

"In this country one keeps to the right-hand side of the road," Carlotta pointed out.

"A dictum you might well observe yourself!" he replied.

If looks could kill, the roadside would be littered with two fresh corpses.

"May I inquire, Sheeni, if you and your reckless chum are cycling to any particular destination?" Vijay asked.

"We have aspirations of reaching Lake Mendocino, Vijay. Would you care to join us?"

4

"Yes, indeed," he replied eagerly. "I understand that lake is one of the scenic delights of your county."

The nerve of that creep. Imagine inviting oneself along on a private bicycle excursion. So much for my eagerly anticipated afternoon interlude of bosky lakeside lovemaking. How frustrating. And how unfortunate that one's desire for sex is inversely proportional to one's opportunities for love-making. I hope those gigantic logging trucks are running on Sundays. Perhaps we'll be lucky and encounter one piloted by a reckless, immigrant-loathing skinhead.

2:15 p.m. Picnicking on a grassy ridge overlooking Lake Mendocino. At Sheeni's suggestion, Vijay is lunching on Carlotta's curried eggplant sandwich. As My Love reasoned, "There are only two sandwiches, Carlotta had a tremendous breakfast, and Vijay is a lifelong vegetarian."

"A lifelong grasping reactionary, you mean," I muttered, suddenly conscious of an urgent rumbling from my empty stomach. I thought back to some of my lapsed Cub Scout foraging skills. Perhaps a grilled salamander would hit the spot.

"Vijay, how is your poor sister?" asked Sheeni, sharing her sandwich with Albert.

"Apurva is quite distraught. The tumult is unceasing. That is why I excused myself from my father's house today. I have never seen him so angry."

"It's unfortunate your neighbors are such gossips," sighed Sheeni.

Some nosey spy has reported to Mrs. Joshi that a staggeringly handsome youth, oddly blindfolded and gagged, was seen on more than one occasion entering and leaving her daughter's bedroom window at night. That was when the tandoori hit the fan.

"How has Trent reacted?" I asked, nibbling a stalk of grass like a dustbowl famine victim.

"He's crushed," said Sheeni. "His parents are accusing him of breaking his word."

"But he didn't," I insisted. "He neither saw Apurva nor spoke to her."

"Perhaps not," agreed Vijay, "but your friend Trent Preston has wantonly violated her chastity. And that is quite a serious matter to my parents."

"Chastity is such a Eurocentric concept," commented Sheeni. "I fear, Vijay, that your country, during its prolonged colonial occupation, may have imported too many Victorian novels. And what is your tiresome father going to do?"

The pretentious twit replied in French. I exchanged glances with Albert as our two lunch-mates conversed in the language of Voltaire and Jean-Paul Belmondo. We were both clueless.

"What did you say?" Carlotta demanded.

Sheeni translated. "Vijay says his father is adamant. He's sending Apurva back to India to live with his brother's family until a suitable marriage partner can be found." She sighed. "Bad news, I fear, for my old childhood sweetheart Trent."

And even worse news for Nick!

"But you needn't worry, mon cheri," said Vijay. "I'm not going anywhere."

That's what you think, Buster, I thought, contemplating a calamitously uncontrolled descent by my adversary over a 200-foot cliff that I knew we must pass on the route back.

8:35 p.m. Vijay still lives. He refused Carlotta's invitation to pause and admire the view. The fellow is such a philistine. He probably regards majestic stands of towering redwoods as so much marketable timber. Speaking of fine wood craftsmanship, My Love and I are curled up together in my new Royal Leisure solid walnut bed under Granny DeFalco's once-musty quilt (since scientifically sanitized). Fortunately, we share a mutual passion for postcoital journal writing. Sheeni, I regret to say, is presently recording the details of a phone conversation she had late this afternoon with Trent Preston. He is "most upset" that Apurva is being banished to India, but details beyond that Sheeni insists she is not at liberty to divulge. I'd peek at her journal, but she writes in an impenetrable (so far) cipher. I wonder if the library has any books on code-breaking? I'm alarmed that Trent feels the need to call up his former girlfriend for solace. Why isn't he pouring out his heart to his swim team buddies? Or to Sonya "The Refrigerator" Klummplatz? I know for a fact she's keenly interested in all aspects of his love life.

"Nickie, I'm ravenous!" Sheeni announced, snapping shut her journal. "Have you anything in the larder for a small supper?"

"You name it," I replied, powering down my state-of-the-art laptop computer. "We could microwave a great lump of Mrs. Ferguson's high-caloric meatloaf."

"That's what I like about you, Nick," she said, reaching for my robe. "You may have the best stocked refrigerator of any teen on the planet."

MONDAY, February 22 — Carlotta confided to Sonya Klummplatz in clothing technology class that her rival Apurva soon may be banished to India. Thrilled to her considerable marrow, Sonya wrote out a note of commiseration, which Carlotta slipped to Trent as he was entering the boys' locker room for swim practice. The guy looked extremely stressed and profoundly miserable, especially after perusing Sonya's note.

"What are you going to do?" whispered Carlotta.

"I don't know," sighed Trent. "We're terribly desperate."

Fabulous, thought Carlotta, patting his tanned muscular arm in sympathy. She yields only to vengeful François in reveling in the suffering of Sheeni Saunder's erstwhile boyfriends.

7:12 p.m. Sheeni declined an invitation to come over this evening, saying she intended to "wash her hair and reread Flaubert."

I fail to see how either of these activities could be preferred to energetic teen intercourse. Yes, My Love and I have some small issues in this department, relating chiefly to frequency and reciprocity.

Considering our age and hormone levels, I believe that three times a day is by no means excessive, even if it entails blowing a small fortune on condoms. Sheeni, alas, rarely can be maneuvered into bed more than once or twice a week. She says we're too young to "wallow in carnality." She's afraid we'll burn out on sex and end up "jaded, disinterested, and passionless" by age 20. I seriously doubt that, subscribing instead to that age-old teen maxim, "Use it, baby, or lose it."

We also appear to have severely discongruous oral expectations. Speaking frankly, I am no slouch in this department, and can state without exaggeration that I have licked, sucked, and tongued virtually every square inch of My Love, not excluding the divine crack between her perfect ass (she didn't seem to mind, though afterwards she refused to kiss me for three days). Sheeni says making love with me is like perfuming oneself with a strong liver paté and climbing into bed with a "pack of famished Pekinese."

As for my needs, Sheeni explains that she cannot divorce the act of fellatio from its political implications. She feels that women have been prostrating themselves at the feet of men for eons, and that it is time to take a stand against female oppression. Therefore, although she delights in the mutual exchange of pleasure, that particular act must remain off the menu. "Trent was very understanding," she assured me when I at last worked up the nerve to broach the subject. "He is quite progressive in his views for a rural youth, as I also expect my future French husband will be."

How I hate that unknown, potentially unfulfilled Frog!

TUESDAY, February 23 — My best pal and landlord Frank "Fuzzy" DeFalco threw up in Mr. Tratinni's physics class today.

He is in emotional turmoil because his long-distance girlfriend Heather recently dumped him for a surfer in Santa Cruz. Fuzzy was sent with a note to Nurse Filmore, while Mr. Tratinni desperately paged Janitor Bob, who remained aloof and disinterested as usual.

Later at lunch Carlotta discussed the situation with the troubled hirsute teen, who slumped listlessly in his chair and refused all nourishment.

"I'm so depressed," groaned Fuzzy. "Every time I think about Heather making it with that guy my stomach flips into back-flush mode. If this keeps up, I might actually be able to make the wrestling team—in the featherweight division."

"You'll get over it," Carlotta assured him, keeping an anxious eye peeled on Sheeni and loathsome Vijay lunching together at the next table over. (To quell vicious rumors, My Love insists on drastically curtailing her public appearances with Carlotta.) "It's probably just a Valentine's Day fling," I continued. "Girls get desperate when they have to spend that overhyped holiday alone. So what does this surfer creep look like?"

Fuzzy sighed. "I'm told he's very good-looking, is a great athlete, and has a wonderful outgoing personality that has made him a beloved figure among the young and hip Santa Cruz surfing crowd."

"Oh, dear," said Carlotta.

"I hope the fucker wipes out on his board and gets eaten by a shark."

"It's tough, Frank," said Carlotta soothingly. "I know you feel jealous and upset. But it'll pass. It's just your genes."

"My jeans? It's Heather's jeans I want the guy to keep his damn mitts out of."

"Our genes control our behavior," I explained. "We're all programmed to get out there and multiply as much as possible. Your genes took one look at Heather and said: 'Wow, fabulous breeder chick!' So now your genes are pissed because they got aced out of the action."

"That's dumb," said Fuzzy. "Then why wasn't I trying to knock her up?"

"Simple, guy. Your rational mind realizes a pregnancy at your age would be a disaster. But make no mistake, your genes would have been thrilled. And hers too. That's why kids our age are so sloppy about birth control. We're at the prime childbearing age, and our bodies know they'll never again get such great odds for genetic immortality."

"OK, Einstein," said Fuzzy. "So why am I throwing up?"

"It's obvious. Your genes are trying to make you sick of Heather. So you'll snap out of it and score another good breeding prospect."

"You mean . . . ?"

"Yep, Frank, long-distance phone sex with Heather is not the answer. It's time you found a local girlfriend."

"Hmmm," ruminated Fuzzy. "Sex anytime I want it."

"It's genetically predestined, guy," Carlotta said. "Go for it!"

"OK, but you've got to help me."

"Me? How?"

Fuzzy looked around and lowered his voice. "I've been helping you dodge the cops, dude. So you have to help me hook up with a new chick."

"OK, OK. I'll see what I can do."

Swell. I'm supposed to find some sexy girl to go out with a not-very-attractive, unpopular, klutzy wanna-be jock who ranks in the 99th percentile for body hair. Oh well, at least Fuzzy's parents have money. That should help.

7:15 p.m. Sheeni dropped by "to study" as Carlotta was finishing up dessert (custard-drizzled cherry crisp) with Mrs. Ferguson and her dim offspring Dwayne Crampton.

"Why do you dine with your domestic staff?" asked Sheeni,

after Dwayne had washed the dishes, My Love had pocketed 75 cents from him in accumulated Albert dog-walking fees, and he and his mother had departed in their wheezing old Grand Prix.

"I have to," I sighed. "Mrs. Ferguson gets very testy when I ask them to take their meals in the kitchen. She refuses to set two tables. You have no idea what it's like to sit here night after night and watch Dwayne devour thousands of dollars worth of groceries with his mouth open. Not to mention his constant suggestive allusions to his dearth of underwear. And speaking of things disgusting, why did you let Vijay paw you like that in the cafeteria at lunchtime?"

"It's to counter all those rumors," Sheeni explained. "This entire tiresome town is gossiping about us."

"OK, so what if we are lesbians," I said, nuzzling her perfect ear. "What business is it of anyone except us?"

"You know how people talk," she said, pushing me away. "We have to be careful. Don't forget you're a fugitive from the FBI."

"My genes don't want to be careful," I whispered, sliding a hand up her enticing thigh.

"I know all about your genes," she replied, removing my hand and opening her physics textbook. "They manifest drives of a remarkable primitiveness—even for a Twisp."

10:30 p.m. All we did was study, believe it or not. What a waste of privacy and expensive mood lighting. Sheeni wouldn't even let me put on my latest Frank Sinatra CD, preferring to bone up on the hydrogen atom without romantic musical accompaniment. Later, as Carlotta was walking Sheeni home, we ran into Vijay (we seem to be doing that a lot lately). He reports his father has bought the plane ticket. His sister Apurva leaves for India on Saturday.

Damn! Now I have to dredge up new girlfriends for Fuzzy and Trent.

. . .

WEDNESDAY, February 24 — Fuzzy is feeling better. He reports he only threw up once today—in wood technology class when someone mentioned they were thinking of laminating up a surfboard. No trips this time to Nurse Filmore. Mr. Vilprang tossed some sawdust on the splatter and made Fuzzy clean it up himself. To distract my pal from his troubles, Carlotta suggested over lunch that we meet this evening after dinner for some minor-league breaking and entering.

10:30 p.m. As arranged, Fuzzy was lurking in the bushes outside my father's rented modular house when my sociopathic alter ego François Dillinger rolled up on my bike just after eight.

"Nick, is that you?" he called, blowing on his hands in the frigid darkness.

"Of course it's me, Frank," I whispered, wheeling my bike out of sight under the carport. "Who else would be sneaking around out here in the boonies with a ski cap pulled down low to obscure his features?"

"Are you sure your dad's not here?" Fuzzy asked nervously as I fiddled with my keys by the side door.

"Relax, Frank. He's at that public hearing in Willits. I read about it in the newspaper. As PR spokesman for the timber company, he has to explain how their proposed massive clear-cutting will actually benefit the forests. He won't be back for hours. Hey, my key doesn't work. Looks like my dad changed the locks."

More parental "don't exist" messages for Nick.

"Damn! What do we do now, Nick?"

"We look under the mat."

Sure enough, a cursory search turned up a shiny brass key.

The first thing we noticed inside was the smell.

"Sheesh, what died?" asked Fuzzy, shining his flashlight around the chaotic living room. "It smells like someone's soaking an entire football team's worth of sweat socks in old cat piss."

"My dad never was much for housekeeping," I said, switching on my flashlight and leading the way toward Dad's "study" (the spare bedroom). "You see anything you want, Frank, just take it."

"No thanks, Nick. There are some seriously major cooties in this place. I can't believe my mom used to sneak around with your dad. That is so gross."

As expected, there in the middle of Dad's cluttered desk sat my trusty PC clone. It beeped a friendly greeting as I flipped it on, and its ancient hard drive rattled into life. Lots of new files, but thank God my journal was still there. I slipped in a floppy and started the download. Nick's traumatic adolescence had not been erased!

While my old computer churned at its glacial Reagan-era pace, I snooped through Dad's stuff. Alas, no lovingly framed, tearstained photos of his runaway son. Just piles of boring timber reports and some wadded-up currency.

"Here's a hundred-dollar bill for you, Frank."

Cooties or no, Fuzzy pocketed the cash. François slipped the rest into my wallet as overdue child support.

"How are you getting on with your dad, Frank?" I inquired.

"All right, Nick. We try not to acknowledge each other's existence."

"A sensible accommodation."

After my journal was copied onto the floppy, I took the precaution of erasing it from the hard drive, then uploaded a file from another floppy.

"What's that?" asked Fuzzy.

"It's a little looping program I wrote. Next time anyone turns on the computer it will scramble a few files, display an onscreen animation of a guy mooning the user, and flash 'Thanks a pants-ful, geezer!' in vivid electric type."

"Cool! Can we see it now?"

"Sorry, Frank. It's a special treat just for my dad. I only wish he had a color monitor to get the full, horrifying effect."

THURSDAY, February 25 — Carlotta's long-simmering gym-class crisis came to a head today. Boorish Dwayne was snapping Carlotta's bra straps in world cultures class when a student aide arrived with a note summoning me to the office of Miss Pomdreck, my aged guidance counselor.

"Oh, there you are, Carlotta," she said, when I appeared at the door of her cinder-block walled office. "I trust you have obtained a note from a local physician confirming the diagnosis of . . . what is your affliction?"

"Ossifidusbrittalus syndrome, Miss Pomdreck," I said, wincing as I took a seat beside her battle-scarred metal desk. "I'm afraid I haven't been well enough to face the trials of yet another medical exam. But perhaps in a few more weeks . . ."

"I'm sorry, Carlotta. I can't postpone this matter any further. I've given you several extensions already. I can only stretch the rules so far. Miss Arbulash is adamant in demanding an immediate resolution of your gym status."

Miss Arbulash is Redwood High's celebrated lady bodybuilder gym teacher.

"Er, why is Miss Arbulash so interested in me?" I asked.

"She says you have a remarkably boyish frame for a girl. She believes you would be a natural for acquiring significant muscle mass."

"But I don't want any muscles," I protested.

"Frankly, I don't see the fascination either, but Miss Arbulash is not one to be denied." Miss Pomdreck called up Carlotta's records on her computer. "OK, I'm taking you out of seventh-period study hall and moving you to girls' gym. You start tomorrow."

"Very well," I sighed. "Shall I give you the name of my next of kin for when I collapse and die on the gym floor?"

"No one will be collapsing, Carlotta. Miss Arbulash can be demanding of her girls on the weight-lifting machines, but I'm sure she'll make allowances for your frailty."

Not when Carlotta drops her towel, lady.

"Whatever you say, Miss Pomdreck." I made no move to leave.

She looked at me over the tops of her old-lady glasses, virtually identical to my own. "Is there something else, Carlotta?"

"Miss Pomdreck, I'd just like to say that you do a wonderful job helping students with special needs on your limited resources. You're a legend in the school."

"I try my best, Carlotta."

"Yes, and I was just thinking how much more you could do if you had your own discretionary funds."

"Discretionary funds, Carlotta?"

"Yes, private monies you could dip into to assist needy students or for other uses. Funds that would be separate from the school's, that you could administer entirely on your own."

Miss Pomdreck was clearly intrigued. "I suppose such a theoretical monetary influx could be of immense benefit to my work."

"Miss Pomdreck, if you permit me to speak frankly, I am in a position to make such a contribution."

"Really, Carlotta?" she said, observing with interest as I rummaged through my purse for my checkbook. "And what sort of modest figure were you thinking of?"

I clicked open my pen. "I was thinking of $5,000."

Stunned, Miss Pomdreck sat back in her chair.

"Think how much good you could do, Miss Pomdreck. It would warm my heart to help in this small way. And such a sum would entail no financial hardship on my part."

"Yes, Carlotta, I've heard it bandied about that you'd come into some money. Well, I really don't know what to say!"

"Say yes," I smiled, starting to write out the check. I paused. "Of course, there is one thing. I shall have to be excused from gym."

Miss Pomdreck studied the row of numbers on my check. "I'll explain things to Miss Arbulash. I'm sure she'll understand, Carlotta."

"Good," I said, signing the check with a flourish. "You've been wonderfully understanding, Miss Pomdreck. I knew I could count on you."

Miss Pomdreck slipped the check into her purse. "We'll keep this a private matter between us, Carlotta."

"Of course, Miss Pomdreck. You can rely on me."

Well, I dodged another close call. I don't know what I would have done if Miss Pomdreck had proved resistant to bribery. I might have been forced to drop out of school, thus terminating my formal education (such as it is) at age 14. What a blow to my literary ambitions—not to mention the world of letters.

FRIDAY, February 26 — Carlotta spent most of her clothing technology class this morning buzzing from table to table trying to stir up some romantic interest in Fuzzy DeFalco. The only person willing to pursue the topic was star-pupil (and teacher's pet) Gary Orion, busy embroidering the hem of his velvet bolero pants.

"Fuzzy DeFalco," he said, trying to place the name. "Isn't he that boy with the shag-carpeted body? What is he—Italian?"

"He claims to be," sniffed Sonya Klummplatz. "He took Carlotta to the Christmas dance, and now she's trying to unload him on somebody else. It's because she knows Trent Preston's girlfriend is leaving the country."

"I am not interested in Trent," Carlotta retorted.

"Yeah, I hear you're stuck on mystery person S.S.," commented Gary.

Time to change the subject. "Say, Gary, are you planning on wearing those pants to school?" inquired Carlotta.

"No way, girl. They're going in my hope chest—for when I move to San Francisco with mystery person T.P."

"Dream on, guy!" sneered Sonya.

4:30 p.m. ANOTHER STUPEFYING DISASTER! Carlotta got the bad news from Miss Pomdreck, who stopped me in the hall as I was following terminally despondent Trent Preston into eighth-period art class.

"Oh, there you are, Carlotta," called my guidance counselor. "I've worked out a nice compromise with Miss Arbulash."

"Compromise?" I asked uneasily.

"Yes, you are officially excused from gym class. She only requests that you assist her that period with a few unstrenuous administrative and locker-room duties."

"Locker room?" I mumbled, stunned. "The girls' locker room?"

"Of course, Carlotta. You start on Monday."

"But, but . . ."

"Now, no arguments, miss. It was all I could do to get her to agree to this arrangement." She leaned closer and confided, "The woman can be quite headstrong."

Later, on the walk home from school, Fuzzy couldn't believe I wasn't "totally thrilled" by my "awesome luck."

"God, Carlotta, it's like every guy's ultimate dream—a free pass to the girls' locker room. Five days a week for the entire semester!"

"Great! And what do I tell Sheeni? She's in that gym class too."

"Cool. You'll get to see her naked."

"I see her naked now, guy."

"Oh, yeah, I forgot. Well, now you can check out the other girls for me. Maybe sneak in a camera. This is better than ditching your parents and getting rich on Wart Watches. Hell, this is like winning the Super Bowl!"

He's right, of course—if I can somehow finesse my way through all the land mines. Maybe Sheeni will be understanding. After all, it's not like I'm deliberately trying to put myself in a situation where I can ogle 35 naked teenage girls.

SATURDAY, February 27 — Sheeni was not that understanding when we met for coffee and donuts at our favorite downtown spot. Prior to her abrupt departure, My One and Only Love declared that I was a "sick and ghoulish degenerate," a "Peeping Tom of the lowest sort," and a "repulsive deviate" exhibiting all the "textbook symptoms" of a "depraved and predatory sexual dementia."

That doesn't seem very charitable—especially considering that Carlotta had sprung for the donuts.

11:25 p.m. When I returned to my lonely rented bungalow, Carlotta received her second unpleasant shock of the morning. There on my sinuous sofa, surrounded by her hastily packed luggage, in an advanced state of emotional distress, daubing her immense dark eyes with a silken handkerchief, sat Vijay's beautiful 16-year-old sister.

"Apurva!" Carlotta exclaimed.

"Good morning, Carlotta," she replied, wiping her nose. "Your maid kindly let me in. I am not going back to India. I've run away from home."

"But how did you get away from your father?"

"There was a crisis at his office. A fortuitous virus is attacking all their computers."

The door to the kitchen swung open, and Mrs. Ferguson

shuffled in with two cups of tea and a plate of her famous glue-your-lips-together sticky pecan rolls. She set the tray down on the coffee table, smiled consolingly at Apurva, and turned to me. "I cleaned . . . the house . . . Miz Carlotta . . . And washed . . . your sheets. . . Lordy! . . I don't know what . . . you do . . . in that bed!"

Carlotta stifled a blush. "Uh, thank you, Mrs. Ferguson. You can take the rest of the day off—with pay."

"Why thanks . . . Miz Carlotta. . . And good luck to you . . . Miz Apurva . . . Don't let . . . those bastards . . . push you around."

"I shan't," smiled Apurva, sipping her tea.

When Mrs. Ferguson had departed, Carlotta got down to brass tacks.

"Apurva!" I exclaimed, "what are you going to do?"

"Well, naturally I've been thinking it over. My situation appears to be one of extreme desperation. Carlotta, have you ever read The Diary of Anne Frank?"

"Uh, no, but I think I saw the movie. Why?"

"I've been reading it this week. A most inspiring book. I hope my mother remembers to return it to the library. Taking the brave Miss Frank as my model, I thought perhaps I could reside in your attic. You could supply me with simple meals and perhaps a book or two now and then. I could repay your kindness when I get a job or my sensational diary is published." Apurva looked at me expectantly and sipped her tea. "Are you thinking it over, Carlotta?"

I wasn't thinking it over. My lips were stuck together. I raised my napkin to my face and discreetly worked things free. "Apurva, I have no attic. The roof's too shallow."

"Oh . . . Then how about your cellar?"

"No cellar either. This is California. We just have crawl spaces."

"Oh dear. That is inconvenient. Well, what if I were to stay out of sight during the day—perhaps in a closet—and then we could cuddle together at night? I've noticed your bed is large enough for two. In India girlfriends often pass the night together in this sisterly way."

François was intrigued, but Nick knew he could never begin to explain such an arrangement to Sheeni. Nor, considering the hair trigger on my erectile response, was the proposed cuddling likely to remain "sisterly" for long.

"I'm afraid not, Apurva. We Americans are much too sensitive to the homoerotic implications of such accommodations. No, what you've got to do is marry Trent Preston."

Apurva nearly dropped her teacup. While my flustered guest was regaining her composure, Carlotta excused herself to answer the telephone in the bedroom. It was My Love, breathless with excitement.

"Carlotta, Vijay just called me in a fit. His sister has disappeared!"

"Er, what sister is that?"

"Apurva, of course. Is she there with you?"

"Certainly not. I barely know the girl. She's probably with Trent."

"Everyone's looking for Trent. Vijay's parents have notified the police."

The police! Just the element of society that fugitive Nick Twisp was trying to avoid.

"Carlotta, did you really pay $5,000 to try to get out of gym class?" My Love asked.

"Of course I did, Sheeni. I'll show you the damn canceled check when I get it back from the bank."

"Carlotta, I've been thinking about your situation. I may have a solution if you are in fact not a voyeuristic pervert."

"What?"

"Have you ever been in the girls' locker room?"

"No, Monday will be my first visit. And I'm not going to blind myself, if that's your idea."

"Carlotta, that locker room is pretty funky. If you were to tell Miss Arbulash that you're highly sensitive to mold and mildew, she'll probably agree to let you stay in the gym. Just promise not to look at me. I'd feel you were spying."

"OK. I'll look at Sonya Klummplatz instead. I've always wanted to see her in gym shorts."

"Carlotta, you are seriously deranged. Shall I come over tonight? We could play Scrabble."

"Sheeni, every time we play Scrabble it's a horrible slaugter."

"Oh, all right. We can practice our irregular French verbs and go to bed early."

"Uh, I can't. Not tonight. I, uh, promised I'd go over to Fuzzy's. He's still a mess about breaking up with Heather."

"All right. Then I'll just have to help Vijay hunt for his sister. Good-bye!" Click.

In a space of five minutes two attractive chicks offer to sleep with me and I have to decline both proposals. Damn!

12:35 p.m. Trent Preston is seated beside Apurva on my sofa with his jacket draped over his head. No, he's not shy. The idiot is trying not to break his promise never to see or speak to Apurva again. Negotiations were now entering a delicate phase.

"Carlotta, can you tell Apurva that I love her with all my heart, but I've never thought of getting married in high school?"

Apurva squeezed his hand. "I understand, darling. You'd be throwing your life away marrying me. We're both much too young."

"Trent, you're not seeing the big picture here," said Carlotta. "If you don't marry Apurva, she'll have to return to India and marry some stranger. Do you want that?"

"I'd hate it, but arranged marriages are part of their cultural tradition."

"Forget cultural traditions," I replied, exasperated. "Forget throwing your life away. If you love each other, why not get married? It's not that big of a deal!"

"It's a very big deal," insisted Trent.

"I agree," said Apurva. "Darling, can you breathe in there?"

"Carlotta, can you assure Apurva that I'm fine?"

"Listen," I said. "Half the marriages in this country end in divorce. So it's not like you're making a lifetime commitment here. OK, if down the road things don't work out, what of it? In the meantime, you've enjoyed some quality companionship and great sex."

"But what would we live on?" asked Trent. "I'd have to quit school and get a job."

"You wouldn't have to quit school," Carlotta replied. "I need a chauffeur. You could come work part-time for me."

"But you don't have a car," Apurva pointed out.

"I don't have a car because I don't have a chauffeur. OK, so I'll buy a car."

"You could rent mine," suggested Trent. "I have a late-model Acura."

Note to myself: In my next life emulate Trent and select parents with money.

"But where would we stay?" asked Apurva.

"You could live with me," I said, thinking out loud. "I've been contemplating getting a nicer place—maybe a larger house with a separate apartment for you young marrieds. Apurva, can you cook?"

"Of course, Carlotta. All properly-brought-up Indian girls can cook. But I would not wish to deprive Mrs. Ferguson of her position."

"Don't worry about that, Apurva. She'll be leaving me soon anyway when her husband gets out of jail. You could do the cooking and still go to school."

"I wouldn't have the funds to continue at my Catholic school," she said, thinking out loud. "And I don't think the nuns would wish to teach a married student."

"You could transfer to Redwood High," Carlotta pointed out. "You could sit next to your husband in class and cheer for him at swim meets."

They both liked that idea, I could tell.

"And your dog Jean-Paul could live with us and Albert. Think how much fun those two dogs could have playing together."

Albert looked at me and curled his lip.

Apurva smiled at my loathsome dog. "It is true that I would miss my darling Jean-Paul if I were married to some unknown and possibly cruel person in India."

"But where could we get married?" asked Trent. "You have to be 18 to get married without your parents' permission."

"That is true," conceded Carlotta, "in 49 of the 50 states."

In my more love-sick and desperate moments I had researched this topic thoroughly.

"And what is the exception?" asked Apurva.

"The very place where I propose to send you—there to marry and honeymoon at my expense. I'm speaking, of course, of the enlightened state of Mississippi."

Alas, not even in that compassionate and progressive state can 14-year-olds marry on their own. Sheeni and I will just have to stifle our matrimonial desires.

2:30 p.m. On the road to the Bay Area in Trent's posh Acura. Our driver at last was persuaded to come out from beneath his jacket, break his vow, and propose marriage to Apurva. She accepted with alacrity. While I made an emergency run to the ATM, Trent took the precaution of smearing mud on his license plates. We are now traveling south on secondary roads so as to elude the cops. So far so good. Apurva's riding shotgun next to her hubby-to-be. Carlotta's in the back seat studying the Hammond Road Atlas.

"OK, here's the plan," I announced. "You fly into New Orleans and take the bus to Biloxi. That's on the gulf and probably scenic, as long as you face toward the water. They should have fairly balmy weather this time of year. Be sure to sample the shrimp gumbo."

"Sounds good," said Trent. "There's only one thing."

"What's that, darling?" asked Apurva.

"How do you think they'll react down there to, uh . . . mixed marriages?"

"Good point, Trent," said Carlotta, "I hadn't thought of that." I consulted my map. "OK, we switch to Plan B: You fly into Memphis and take the bus down to Oxford. That's a college town in the northern part of the state. They should be slightly more liberal up there."

"Perhaps they'll have a nice Indian restaurant," said Apurva. "It might appease my mother somewhat to know that I ate strictly vegetarian meals on my honeymoon."

"I wouldn't get your hopes up, Apurva," said Carlotta. "Until now you've just been in California. You're about to experience the real United States."

5:40 p.m. Oakland International Airport. Smooth sailing so far. We ditched Trent's Acura in Berkeley in a neighborhood where Cal students often park. With any luck, it will still be there (with most of its hubcaps) when they get back. We rode BART to the airport, and secured two seats on an evening flight to Memphis. I paid for their round-trip tickets by check ($1,537.84!), and even managed to suck another $300 out of an ATM in the boarding lounge. Slipping an imposing $800 wad to the bride-to-be, I promised to wire more money to them at their motel if they ran short.

"Oh, Carlotta," gushed Apurva, "how will we ever repay you for your kindness?"

"Yes, Carlotta," said Trent, "why are you being so incredibly nice to us?"

Why, Trent? Because I want you permanently out of Sheeni's life: once and for all, nailed down, no ifs, no buts. And for that I'm willing to do anything short of murder. And don't push me too hard on that point either.

"It's nothing," replied Carlotta, modestly. "It's just that sometimes destiny needs a little helping hand. And please don't mention my assistance in this matter to anyone back in Ukiah."

An announcement was made that boarding of the plane was about to commence.

"OK, kids," said Carlotta. "You know what to do. Go to the courthouse in Oxford on Monday. You'll have to get a blood test, but that shouldn't be any problem. Don't let them give you any flak. If worse comes to worst, try offering bribes. Remember: no holding hands in public around anyone who looks like a redneck. They take miscegenation pretty seriously down there. And if you have any trouble, give me a call."

"I feel everything will be fine," said Apurva, happily clutching Trent's arm. "We'll go shopping for my boy tomorrow. He's getting married and he doesn't even have a toothbrush!"

"Good idea," said Carlotta. "OK, you kids have a good time. And, Trent, don't think about things too much. Just do it."

"Just do it," he repeated. "Right. Live in the present. Tomorrow will take care of itself."

"That's the spirit," said Carlotta. "That attitude has helped men get through their weddings for centuries. If you have to brood about something, think of all the fun you'll have on your honeymoon. You're a lucky guy."

At least on this point I was being sincere. A week in a Mississippi motel with sexy Apurva on someone else's nickel—the guy leads a charmed life.

After hugs all around, the happy couple bounded up the boarding ramp, and forlorn Carlotta was left to figure out how to haul herself back to Ukiah.

Five minutes later: I got the shock of my life while hailing a cab for the crosstown trip to the bus station. Parked at the airport curb was an Oakland black and white—with my evil stepdad Lance Wescott behind the wheel. A married man and so-called "officer of the law," he was flagrantly checking out Carlotta's butt.

SUNDAY, February 28 — It was after 11 p.m. when my bus rolled into Ukiah and nearly midnight when my second overpriced cab ride of the night brought me to my humble abode, which turned out to be not quite as lonely as I'd anticipated. Stretched out in my bed, under Granny DeFalco's quilt, in her preferred sleep apparel (none) was the Person I'd Most Like to Hijack to Mississippi: Sheeni Saunders.

"Hi, Nickie," she said sleepily. "What took you so long? How's Fuzzy?"

"Uhmm, he's feeling better," I replied, hastily disrobing. "What a nice surprise, darling. I thought you were mad at me."

"I don't handle rejection well, Nickie. You should know that by now."

I hopped into bed and embraced her. "I wasn't rejecting you, darling."

"Nick, did you floss and brush?"

I hopped out of bed. "Be right back. Don't go away."

Sheeni slipped on my robe and followed me into the bathroom. "Nickie, no one's seen any sign of Apurva and Trent. All the parents are in a tizzy, including mine for some reason. Everyone's afraid they might have done something desperate."

I paused in my flossing. "You mean like get married?"

"No, silly. They're much too young for that. Everyone's worried they might do something extreme like make a suicide pact."

"I doubt that, Sheeni. Guys as good-looking as Trent don't off themselves. What would be the point? They're probably holed up in a motel in Willits or somewhere. They'll come home when they run out of money."

"You really think so, Nickie?"

I spat out my toothpaste and rinsed my brush. "Of course, darling. They're two reasonably sensible kids. They'd have been fine if their parents hadn't interfered."

"Speaking of which, Nickie, my parents are expecting us at church tomorrow."

"Then we'd better get cracking at the next item on the agenda."

8:45 a.m. It's weird. When Sheeni and I (finally) went to sleep last night, we lay on opposite sides of the bed, but when we awoke we were totally entwined—as if our limbs had been methodically and magically knit together. Sheeni threatens to make me wear latex pajamas, lest these unconscious nocturnal clinches grow too intimate and she winds up expecting our first gifted child. (My genes would be thrilled.)

The phone rang; I laboriously untangled an arm to answer it.

"Carlotta," said Fuzzy, sounding excited. "Have you read today's paper?"

"Not yet, I've been engaged in more important activities."

"Like what?"

"I'll give you a hint, Frank. You used to do it with Heather."

"Is Sheeni there?"

"She's here."

"Damn, Carlotta. You have to find me a girlfriend!"

"I'm working on it, guy. What's in the paper?"

"Go read it!" Click.

9:35 a.m. The alarming story was splashed all over the front page. A homegrown computer virus is wreaking havoc among local businesses and spreading like an infectious plague across the Internet. Most ominous, concerned officials have labeled this destructive new pest the "Geezer" virus.

"Nickie, are you or are you not taking me out to breakfast?" demanded Sheeni, freshly bathed and fully dressed to her usual pulse-quickening effect.

"In a minute, darling. I'm reading about a new computer virus."

"Oh, I heard all about it from Vijay. It's driving his father nuts at work. Vijay fears that it and his sister's tumultuous love life may finally push his father over the brink."

I flipped to where the story continued on an inside page. "Listen to this, Sheeni: Experts describe this latest virus as a simple looping program devised with a brilliant and diabolical twist."

It wasn't a brilliant twist, you nitwits, it was a bug in my program!

"Well, I for one needn't worry," remarked My Love. "No virus can infect my French-language portable typewriter. That is all the technology any serious writer requires."

2:45 p.m. Carlotta was somewhat preoccupied throughout breakfast, our stroll to church, Rev. Glompiphel's feverish sermon (title: "Is There a Virus in Your Soul?"), and a heavy midday meal at Sheeni's house in the company of her Bible-thumping parents. It didn't help that Mr. and Mrs. Saunders spent most of the meal speculating on the fate of poor Trent. They feel strongly that the town's "most promising youth" has "gone astray" ever since he broke off his attachment to Sheeni and was "ensnared" by "that foreign girl."

"Of course, ultimately it's all the fault of that horrible boy Nick Twisp," averred Sheeni's 5,000-year-old mother, slicing Carlotta a generous wedge of lemon meringue pie. "Don't you think so, Carlotta?"

"Er, I don't quite see the connection, Mrs. Saunders," I replied, polishing my fork in anticipation. The woman may be a Blight on Earth, but she does have a knack for desserts.

"It's very simple," explained Sheeni. "If Nick hadn't come along last summer, I would still be going out with the handsome and honorable Mr. Preston. And Apurva would be safely at home burning her incense and worshiping her pagan gods. Isn't that right, Mother?"

"Watch your smart mouth," she retorted.

Sheeni and I exchanged glances. We'd heard that line before.

5:12 p.m. My house was just searched by a Ukiah policeman! I'm still a nervous wreck. The Law arrived in the company of Mr. and Mrs. Joshi, who demanded to know if I was harboring their runaway daughter. I said "Don't be ridiculous," and let them poke through all my cupboards and closets. It was all I could do to restrain Albert, who has nearly as much difficulty with authority figures as I do. At least the cop was polite, and Apurva's mother did apologize on her way out for their "rude intrusion." Snubbing Mr. Joshi, I promised I would call her immediately if I heard from her daughter.

"I'm just as concerned about Apurva as you are," I lied. "Of course, this country is no place to try and raise children with the proper values."

"That is exactly what I told my husband!" Mrs. Joshi exclaimed.

"You're so right," I agreed. "If I were you, I'd send that nice son of yours right back to India—before he's corrupted too!"

6:25 p.m. As I was taking the garbage out to the alley I ran into Redwood High's most celebrated gridiron mediocrity, Bruno Modjaleski, who dropped his garbage can with a deafening clang while studying Carlotta's chest.

"'Lo, Carly," he leered. "You're lookin' good, babe. Was that the cops I just saw at your house?"

"Uh-huh, Bruno. I was forced to call them. Some nosey neighbor is always spying on me!"

8:45 p.m. Enough studying for now. I don't see why physics is so obsessed with the hydrogen atom. Seems to me it properly falls under the jurisdiction of the chemistry department.

I've taken the precaution of deleting all traces of the ill-fated "Geezer" program from my computer. All I can figure is Dad must have carried an infected floppy to his computer at work. The guy should stick to typewriters.

It suddenly occurred to me that Dad and Vijay's father are employed by the same company. I don't see how they could have avoided having some contact with each other. Do you suppose they ever figured out that that familiar-looking coworker was the guy they once met in Dad's muddy driveway for hand-to-hand combat?

No call from Apurva and Trent. I wonder how they're getting on in Dixie? I'd pay a sizeable sum to be a fly on the wall of their motel room tonight. Come to think of it, maybe Sheeni's right. Perhaps I am a demented voyeuristic pervert.

Confession time: I'm not planning on moving or hiring a chauffeur. I expect when all the recriminations die down, Trent and Apurva will go live with his parents. God knows, I don't want them hanging around here with Sheeni and me. They may have a special reason to sponge off Mom and Dad. Before we left for the airport, thoughtful Carlotta slipped Trent one dozen condoms—all of which I had punctured with a small pin. Not very nice, I admit, but their genes will thank me, and I need some insurance against a parentally imposed annulment.

MARCH

MONDAY, March 1 — I just heard on the radio that the governor of California switched on his computer this morning in Sacramento and was mooned by a diabolical virus. That will teach him to have the second-lowest per-pupil expenditure for public schools of any state in the nation. Had I been properly educated, I might know how to write a bug-free computer program.

Enough with the incidentals. We shall now fast-forward to the seventh period, when—composing herself for the ordeal ahead—Carlotta clutched her books to her artificial chest and crept into the girls' gym.

OK, you ask, just how buffed is the industrially tanned Miss Arbulash? Let us simply note that when she talks, the muscles of her face bulge and ripple. And they compose the least developed region of her body. Seldom has a sleeveless, skintight silver leotard been asked to fit a form such as hers. Even the gleaming brass whistle dangling on a chain around her horselike neck seemed larger than life.

Massively intimidated, Carlotta somehow managed to blurt out her story of mildew hypersensitivity, while My Love hovered with feigned disinterest a few steps away.

Miss Arbulash methodically swept her muscular eyeballs over my quaking form. "Are we boycotting gym today, Sheeni?" she boomed in a resonant alto.

"Er, no, Miss Arbulash," replied My Love, retiring to the locker room.

"So, Carlotta Ulansky, you are allergic to mold," she sneered, inspecting me from all sides. "Miss Pomdreck seems to think you're a walking basket case. How many hours of aerobic exercise do you perform each week?"

I tried to think. Did sex count?

"Uh, none." I didn't dare look into those fierce blue eyes.

"Are you taking any herbal or protein supplements?"

"Er, no."

"So, you have abdicated responsibility for your body and are letting doctors convince you that you are a sick person."

"I'm really, really allergic to mold, Miss Arbulash."

"Well, this is your lucky day, Carlotta. We had an impetigo outbreak last week. I had the locker room disinfected from top to bottom. They cleaned the air ducts over the weekend and installed an ozone purifier. It's like a hospital surgical room in there."

"Oh," I gulped, "that's, uh, nice."

Miss Arbulash dumped my books and purse on a shelf, then handed me a clipboard. "We're doing circuit training this week."

"Circus training?"

I imagined exotic gymnastics involving lumbering elephants.

"Circuit training, Carlotta. Your job is to make sure every girl does her allotted reps on each machine."

By now my fellow classmates were drifting out of the locker room in their gym shorts and T-shirts. They didn't seem too happy to see Carlotta, still in street clothes and holding what they (rightly) interpreted as a symbol of cardiovascular tyranny.

"Whatsamatter, Carlotta?" called Janice Griffloch, a zit-plagued wanna-be thespian I had once anonymously fixed up with Trent Preston. "Got your period?"

Miss Arbulash blew her whistle, signaling for the tortures to begin.

Circulating meekly among the reluctant exercisers, Carlotta was the subject of much sotto voce abuse.

"Sucking up to ol' Elbowgash, huh?" whispered my friend Sonya, puffing away on an overloaded treadmill.

Not a good attitude. Not good. Carlotta dialed Sonya's speed UP a notch.

I drifted over to where My Love was working out on the butterfly station.

"That's very good for the bust," Carlotta commented approvingly, awarding Sheeni a dozen extra reps on my chart.

"You are going to burn in a lake of fire," hissed My Love, rotating on to the stair-climbing machine when Miss Arbulash blew her whistle.

Next, I counted the weightlifting reps of tall Barb Hoffmaster, who with each crunch appeared to be chanting under her breath, "Pet dyke, pet dyke, pet dyke."

What's that supposed to mean?

The only person not emanating overt hostility was Sonya's pal Lana Baldwin, a rather plain girl I knew only from her hillbilly accent and spectacularly incorrect answers in business math class. She smiled at me while skiing on the cross-country machine. So Carlotta adjusted her incline lower and added another quarter-mile to her total.

Eventually the workout came to an end: Miss Arbulash harangued her pupils for their lackluster performance, they stared at their shoes in transparent indifference, then everyone (including Carlotta) was sent to the locker room.

"Uh, I'm also allergic to steam," a desperate Carlotta pointed out.

"It's only water vapor," replied Miss Arbulash, handing me a plastic whistle. "I want you to keep things moving in there. Blow your whistle if there's any horseplay."

A teenage youth's first impressions of the girls' locker room: battered grey lockers, blue and white tile floor, water-stained ceiling, clouds of billowing steam, noisy chatter, chlorine odor, human odors, warm moistness, waving towels, brassieres, bare backs, bare legs, bare buttocks, panties, breasts, nipples, sullen stares, pubic hair, pounding heart, feelings of trespass, panic.

Struggling to gain control of my whirling mind, I attempted rational thought. "Oh look," Carlotta noted to herself, "Barb Hoffmaster is not a natural blonde."

I prayed my glasses would fog. Perversely, they refused.

Sheeni, naked as a clam, pushed rudely past me on her way to the showers. "Voyeuristic pervert," she hissed.

"Pet dyke. Pet dyke," someone whispered behind my back.

I couldn't turn around. My motor system had shut down from sensory overload.

Lana Baldwin dropped her towel and smiled at me again. I noted that she was plain only from the neck up. Thinking selflessly of my lonely pal, I wondered if she found body hair attractive on men. She bent over to dry her cute little feet. She had an extraordinarily pink anus. I considered blowing my whistle and sharing this discovery with the group. Then thought better of it.

"So that's how you put on a bra," I thought, learning something new. (Carlotta had been hooking hers together and stepping into it like a skirt.) Naked Sonya drying herself off. Yes, fat girls require more towels; it's only logical. Discreet gliding on of armpit scents. A spritz or two of perfume. Hasty yanking on of clothes to allow more time for critical hair fussing and makeup application. Shoving and elbowing before the too-small mirrors as the seconds tick down. Angry eruptions of hair spray. Moans of despair as the ringing bell touches off a final mad scramble.

A withering glance from My Love as she slams her locker door on Carlotta's hand. I feel no pain. I follow the departing hordes into the gym, gather up my books, and stumble down the corridor toward art class—a small plastic whistle still clutched in my now-throbbing hand.

I had lived through the longest seven minutes of my life. And I get to do it all over again tomorrow.

4:25 p.m. Needless to say, Fuzzy was in Carlotta's face the entire walk home from school.

"Were you like really in the girls' locker room? God, that is so incredible!"

"It's no big deal, Frank. It's only gym class, not backstage at Radio City with the Rockettes."

"What was it like? Tell me!"

"Well, it was very much like the boys' locker room—only with less towel-snapping and more lace."

"Oh man, Carlotta. I used to wonder why a smart guy like you was running around dressed like a chick. Now I know it was a true stroke of genius!"

"Yeah, well personally I'm sick of it. You don't know how lucky you are being able to walk into a restroom and unzip in front of a urinal like a normal person."

"Well, anytime you want to switch, Carlotta, I'll put on that dress and take over your locker-room duties."

"I'll keep that in mind, Frank."

8:45 p.m. I was grappling anew with the hydrogen atom when the phone rang. It was Apurva calling collect from remote Mississippi. She reported excitedly that in eight hectic hours they had passed their blood tests, secured a license, put two "modest gold rings" in layaway (requiring more cash from Carlotta), outfitted Trent with essentials, and made an appointment with a judge on Thursday afternoon. They can't get married sooner because the state imposes a three-day waiting period to permit sober reflection and allow inflamed premarital passions to cool. Married folks in Mississippi, it seems, have not acted impulsively.

"Did they ask you if you had your parents' permission?" I inquired.

"Not at all, Carlotta. They seemed more interested in knowing if we had the $35 for the license."

"They probably wondered why you waited so long to get married."

"I sometimes wish my dear Trent was not so handsome. The clerk informed him privately that if things didn't work out with me, she was available and willing."

"How is Trent?"

"Fine. My darling looks ravishing in his new sports jacket. The waitress at the Chinese restaurant wrote her phone number on his napkin. Do you know, Carlotta, if my parents are very upset?"

"Not too bad," I lied. "They figure you're with Trent somewhere."

"I know they'll like my darling, once they get to know him."

"I'm sure of it," I lied. "He's a charming guy. What's Oxford like?"

"It's a pleasant small town with many historic buildings. We took a long walk after dinner. Parts of it remind me of India."

"How's your motel?"

"Quite comfortable. I told Trent not to worry. Large insects are common in subtropical regions. They are not necessarily a sign of poor housekeeping."

"Are the natives friendly?"

"Oh, very friendly. We have encountered no prejudice, although some reactions can be perplexing. I told an elderly woman by the ice machine that I was Indian, and she asked if I was getting rich on casino gambling."

Again thanking me profusely for my generosity, Apurva gave

me the name and address of their motel. I promised to wire additional dowry cash first thing tomorrow, wished them sweet dreams, and hung up. The phone rang immediately.

"Voyeuristic pervert."

"Sheeni, that's not fair. I did everything humanly possible to stay out of that damn locker room."

"You mean you did everything humanly possible to stare as brazenly as possible at Lana Baldwin's naked ass."

"I wasn't staring at anyone. I was doing my best to avert my eyes."

"Well, just make sure Carlotta has her wig glued on tight tomorrow."

"Why?" I asked, alarmed.

"I shouldn't be spilling the beans, but the rumor is that Barb Hoffmaster and Janice Griffloch are leading a plot to toss Carlotta in the shower."

"Thanks for the warning, darling. I have just one thing to say."

"What?"

"You have by far the best body of anyone in your gym class."

"Voyeuristic pervert!" Click.

So much for paying someone a sincere and informed compliment.

TUESDAY, March 2 — Much of the front page of this morning's newspaper was given over to sensationalist accounts of the further depredations of the "Geezer" virus. All over the world irate computer users are being mooned and their valuable files scrambled. Yesterday's banner headline in the New York Daily News: "Thanks a pantsful, Geezer hacker!"

I suppose I should worry about this, but I have far too much on my plate already. People should just learn to back-up their files and avoid promiscuous network coupling. Abstinence: you preach it to your kids, now try it with your computer.

Only two weeks to go until Sheeni's fifteenth birthday. While Carlotta was cutting clothing technology class to wire money at my bank, she also transferred a large wad to her checking account in preparation for Sheeni's costly natal-day celebrations. It should come as no surprise to anyone that My One and Only Love is a Pisces.

At lunchtime Candy Pringle and other do-gooder senior girls passed out lengths of yellow plastic ribbon for students to tie to their lockers, backpacks, and cars to demonstrate their concern for Trent's safe return. I was not pleased to see that Sheeni and Vijay were wearing matching yellow armbands as they dined together. All of Trent's swim team buddies have shaved their heads (and reportedly their pubic hair as well) in solidarity with their missing pal. As you might expect, the school is abuzz with Trent and Apurva rumors—some of the more improbable ones having been initiated by Carlotta herself.

In business math class Carlotta chatted up friendly Lana Baldwin, who said, "Heck, they all talk like this back in Nitro, West Virginia." She confessed she doesn't have a boyfriend. It's no wonder, considering the way she dresses. The average male student in the school simply has no idea what's going on under her dowdy tweed jumpers and sloppy pullovers.

After that class Carlotta's Ossifidusbrittalus syndrome flared up again, and Nurse Filmore excused her from the balance of the school day. I hope her cheerful presence was not missed in the girls' locker room.

8:10 p.m. I just had another long phone conversation with Apurva. She reports they have purchased their wedding rings, which they are now wearing to get a feel for married life. So far so good. Today they toured Rowan Oak, Nobel laureate William Faulkner's lavish 1840s-era home set on 21 magnolia-strewn acres. They admired his antique Underwood portable typewriter, inspected a small stable he built with his own hands, and peered into the smokehouse where he cured his own bacon. I wonder if the Nobel Prize selection committee is impressed by these sorts of extracurricular author activities? Should I be nominated, I must remember to show them Carlotta's recently completed black A-line skirt.

This proximity to Great Literature evidently excited Trent's poetic imagination. Apurva was eager to share his latest work, titled "Diet of Worms."

> Bitter memories
> Compose my breakfast,
> Sprinkled lightly with
> Longing and regret.
>
> Lost friends
> Nourish at midday
> With their absence
> And neglect.
>
> Faded dreams
> Sustain at night—
> A solemn feasting on
> Ambitions deferred.

Somewhat more intelligible than his previous "futurist percussion" efforts, but not pointing to a very positive state of mind as marriage looms. And what, I wondered, was on his dessert menu— angst a la mode? Carlotta politely agreed with Apurva that it was a "brilliant effort," but suggested—as one girl to another—that she splash on a little more perfume before retiring this evening.

"And how are things going in that department?" Carlotta couldn't help but ask.

I could sense Apurva's blush from 2,500 miles away. "Very

well, Carlotta. Somehow I feel I can discuss these things with you. We've been reading more books on the topic. My darling Trent has been hunting for my G-spot."

"Any luck?" I asked, intrigued.

"Not so far," she admitted. "But the search has been most stimulating."

WEDNESDAY, March 3 — I nearly gagged on my donut when I opened this morning's newspaper. There above the fold on page one was a full-color, highly unflattering photo of my father—in handcuffs. He's been arrested by the FBI!

Working around the clock, federal computer experts had followed the trail of the Geezer virus back to a suspicious PC clone located amid "squalid conditions" in a "rundown" modular home on the outskirts of Ukiah. The creator of the most insidious virus in computing history has been found: alleged super-hacker George W. Twisp.

Scanning the news article, I once again experienced that all-too-familiar scrotal rhumba. The story reported that because of the "sensitive nature" of Mr. Twisp's employment, officials are speculating he may be an "eco-terrorist" sent by "radical elements" to "infiltrate and disrupt" the timber industry.

My father, an environmentalist? The guy has never recycled a can in his life!

9:30 a.m. A worried Fuzzy Defalco cornered Carlotta by her locker just before homeroom this morning.

"Yes, Frank," I assured him, "I've seen the newspaper."

"What are you going to do, Carlotta?"

I lowered my voice. "What can I do? It's out of my hands. Don't worry, Frank. We're safe."

"But, Carlotta, the last guy they nailed for cooking up a virus got five years in the federal pen."

"Yeah, I know," I said, closing my locker. "Most parents deserve a little jail time—for neglect and emotional abuse—but five years is pretty extreme, even for my dad."

"Are you going to confess?"

"Don't be delusional, Frank. You know me better than that."

12:50 p.m. As Vijay was absent from school, Sheeni (now wearing yellow ribbons on both arms) consented to join Carlotta for lunch. I could tell My Love had seen the news reports and was determined to get to the bottom of things.

"I never realized Nick's father was such an expert on computers," she observed, munching the middle of her sandwich in her endearingly infantile way.

"Sheeni, for being a sophisticated person of the world, you eat a sandwich like a three-year-old."

My Love chose to ignore this remark. "One might even describe the Twisps as a one-family crime wave. Soon another member of the clan may find himself behind bars—for criminal peeping."

"It was all an accident," I whispered. "There was a bug in my program."

"I might have known Nick was behind all this. It's obvious the fellow has unresolved Oedipal issues."

"Nick was not trying to send his father to prison."

Sheeni gazed at me, applied her sensual lips to the soft underbelly of her sandwich, bit down, and masticated with arresting grace. Her luminous azure eyes bored into the very center of my being.

Carlotta began to sweat. OK, maybe she's right. Perhaps my subconscious has been plotting a terrible revenge. A tough break for Dad, but what an insight to share with my future analyst.

4:35 p.m. The rest of the school day was uneventful except for girls' gym, where Carlotta again performed her slave overseer duties and nude ablutions monitoring. Alert to locker-room treachery, she positioned herself by the exit door to the gym—

one hand poised on the doorknob, emergency whistle clamped firmly between her teeth. I was admiring the classical proportions of Lana Baldwin's naked torso when a half-dozen towel-swathed girls, led by Barb Hoffmaster, made a feint toward the showers, then suddenly whirled and bolted toward me.

"Get her!" they screamed, their towels flying and breasts flopping.

"FLEEEEEEEE!" screeched Carlotta's whistle, as I dashed into the gym just ahead of the thundering herd. "FLEEEEEEEE!"

Miss Arbulash looked up from where she was discussing treadmill belt alignment woes with Janitor Bob and two of his low-IQ student assistants. The fellows dropped their wrenches and stared open-mouthed.

"What's going on here?" Miss Arbulash demanded.

Carlotta's pursuers skidded to a stop, squealed in surprise, clutched at themselves, turned, and scuttled back into the locker room.

They never laid a glove on me.

And an outraged Miss Arbulash gave them all a week's detention for attempted hazing of her valued assistant.

Later, on the walk home from school, Carlotta informed her pal Fuzzy that he had a date on Friday night with Lana Baldwin.

"Lana Baldwin!" he exclaimed, incredulous. "She's the mousiest chick in our class. And she talks weird."

"She can't help it. She's from West Virginia."

"How come she eats lunch with all the fat girls?"

"Well, she's buddies with Sonya Klummplatz. But don't hold that against her. And don't kid yourself, guy, she's hot."

"Really?"

"I'm talking illegal Chinese firecracker—from the neck down, of course. And she's very nice. She doesn't know you from Adam, but she's agreed to the date on my recommendation. So be nice to her."

"Wow, Lana Baldwin. I hear she's not too bright. Even Sonya says that."

"Frank, do you want to discuss astrophysics or get laid?"

"'Nough said, Carlotta.' Nough said."

7:05 p.m. My father made the national news! Carlotta, Mrs. Ferguson, and Dwayne were glued to the tube as Dad was shown being dragged in front of a federal judge in San Francisco to hear the many and diverse charges against him. Bail for the alleged Geezer hacker has been set at a whopping $2 million dollars.

"I hope when . . . the man gets . . . through forkin' . . . that pile over," commented my maid, "he still has . . . the $179 he . . . owes me . . . in back pay."

"Looks like your former employer may be cooling it in the slammer for quite a while," noted Carlotta uneasily.

"I always knew Nick's pop was lots worse than mine," said Dwayne. "That Nick had no cause to be so stuck up."

(For that remark Carlotta slipped the crusty spareribs pan back into the oven to blacken for an additional 45 minutes.)

In a totally superfluous and prejudicial aside, the reporter concluded her segment by noting that the FBI also was searching for the suspect's teenage son Nick, wanted on a host of unrelated charges. They even flashed a photo of me that was almost as unflattering as Dad's.

9:52 p.m. No studying tonight; I'm too much on edge to worry about the hydrogen atom.

Apurva was even more excited than usual when she telephoned collect for her nightly check-in chat.

"Carlotta, we saw my father on television!" she exclaimed.

Welcome to the club, girl.

"Really! Your father?"

"Yes, he was being interviewed about my old friend Nick's father. Did you know he was behind the disruptive computer mischief that allowed me to escape?"

"Well, I know he's been charged. So what did your father say?"

"He said Mr. Twisp was quite the master criminal and computer whiz."

"But I'd heard the guy didn't know the first thing about computers."

"Oh, no. Father was quite insistent on that point. He was very well spoken. I'm happy to see my disappearance is not causing him to neglect his work duties."

Damn. Mr. Joshi is proving to be even more of a deceitful slimeball than his son. It really is time to put some skinheads on my payroll.

Then Apurva asked Carlotta to referee a small premarital dispute. It seems Trent has requested that she wear a sari tomorrow for their wedding, but as a modern American bride Apurva would prefer to get hitched in a dress.

"What should I do, Carlotta?" she inquired.

"I think you should compromise: you wear the dress and Trent can wear the sari."

Much laughter in Dixie. "Oh, Carlotta, you're so amusing," chuckled Apurva. "It's almost like something my old friend Nick would say."

Time to get serious. "I think you should wear a sari, Apurva."

"Really?"

"Sure. Trent could marry millions of girls in dresses. But you should go with what makes you special."

"I hadn't thought of that. All right, Carlotta, I'll be a traditional bride. I'll wear my best sari and all my gold jewelry."

Gold jewelry! Hey, why haven't those undisclosed assets been made available for pawning?

THURSDAY, March 4 — Wedding day at last. Or is it? The ringing telephone blasted me awake in the middle of the night.

"My marriage!" wailed Apurva. "It's off!"

Rats and damnation. I rolled over and sat up.

"What's the matter, Apurva?" demanded Carlotta.

"That Trent Preston! He's a monster!"

Why me, God? I looked at the clock. 5:37 a.m.

"OK, Apurva, calm down. Give me some facts here. What's going on?"

"It happened at breakfast. Trent was looking at me peculiarly. I thought perhaps I had some grits on my face. Then he said he couldn't marry me."

"But why?"

"I don't know," she wept. "He, he said he doesn't know me."

Damn. Leave it to Trent to start his wedding day with an existential crisis.

"OK, Apurva. Let me speak to Trent."

"He's not here."

"Where is he?"

"I don't know. He's, he's walking somewhere. I can't marry him anyway. He doesn't love me!"

"OK, now don't make any rash decisions. Stay where you are. When Trent comes back, make him stay there too. I'm on my way."

"You're, you're coming here?"

"As fast as I can. Everything will be OK."

"Everything is horrible! I wish I were dead!"

"Just sit tight, Apurva. Leave everything to me."

Imagining it was Trent Preston's head, I pummeled Granny DeFalco's old goose-down pillow. I should never have let that wishy-washy poet out of my sight!

8:45 a.m. On the road to San Francisco airport. I'm booked on a 9:20 flight to Memphis if Bruno Modjaleski can whip his father's big Chrysler through backed-up rush-hour traffic with sufficient terrifying recklessness to get me to the airport on time.

"I told you we should have taken my chopper," said Bruno, powering up the freeway shoulder at 80 miles per hour and dodging concrete abutments with just inches to spare.

"I am not riding 150 miles on your motorcycle in the middle of winter," replied Carlotta, her short but eventful life passing repeatedly before her eyes as she braced again and again for impact.

Giant truck dead ahead!

"I can't look!" I screamed, covering my eyes.

Violent lurch as Bruno swerved. "Relax, babe. God, you're worse than Candy."

In case you're out of the Redwood High gossip loop, Bruno recently dumped parakeet-loving Mertice Palmquist to get back together with head cheerleader (and former love) Candy Pringle. He accepted Carlotta's offer of $100 in cash for a fast trip to S.F. because gorgeous and popular Candy is not what anyone could term a cheap date.

10:32 a.m. Carlotta risked life and limb to reach the airport on time, only to discover that all flights had been postponed because of unsettled weather back east. Even worse, Bruno insisted on extracting another slobberingly intimate kiss as a bonus for getting Carlotta there in one piece. I really don't see how Candy stands it.

While chewing through an overpriced airport breakfast, I noticed that a wall-mounted TV in a bar across the corridor was carrying another news report on my father. Then they showed that same unflattering photo of me. Such high-profile media exposure is not helpful to a fugitive from the law. Realizing I had no choice, I abandoned my eggs, found a pay phone, and dialed Ukiah.

"Good morning, Mr. Joshi. This is Nick Twisp."

"Nick Twisp! You dare to call me, you young scoundrel? I shall alert the FBI!"

"Mr. Joshi, you know my father had nothing to do with that virus."

46

"It was traced to his computer."

"My father has zero computer knowledge. You know th.

"I shall testify otherwise. He deserves to go to prison. A you as well!"

"Mr. Joshi, I know where your daughter is."

"Where? If you have any decency at all, you must tell me!"

"OK, I'll tell you where she is—as soon as I hear that my father has been released and all charges against him dropped."

"Why should I trust you? How can I be certain you know where she is?"

"Right before Apurva left home she was reading The Diary of Anne Frank. She hopes your wife returned it to the library."

He gasped. I hung up.

Sure, it might spring Dad from jail. Big deal. But what happens when Vijay blabs to Sheeni that Nick Twisp is involved in Apurva and Trent's disappearance?

2:45 p.m. Flying through wintry turbulence. When you buy an airline ticket at the last minute, you not only get to pay full fare, they sadistically assign you to a middle seat. Presently Carlotta is squeezed between two businessmen, who from their size and girth might be traveling donut salesmen. The bulkier of the two is wearing a Wart Watch. My business partners (Kimberly and Mario) and I appreciate the business, but don't adults realize they look ridiculous wearing a novelty product professionally marketed to disaffected teenagers?

With each bounce and jolt, meaty elbows tenderize my well-bruised flesh. So much for trying to type on my laptop. In case the plane ices up and carries us all to a fiery death, let me note a few final words: Sheeni darling, I did it all for you. See you in heaven (I hope they don't speak French). Love always, Nick.

P.S. I sneaked a closer look at the man's Wart Watch. It's a goddam knock-off!

6:30 p.m. Blizzards in Mississippi? Apparently so. I hope the their parkas on. Memphis was snowed-in, so ⁚ted to Jackson. Miraculously, the plane did not most wish it had just to see the look of terror es' faces. Now the airline is busing us north to ⁚out conditions on an ice-slicked Interstate. I ⁚pped $50 to the driver to drop me off in Oxford, should we make it that far in the unrelenting storm. Carlotta needless to say had packed for the tropics. At least it's a torrid 95 degrees in this overheated bus. I'm trying to store up excess heat in case I actually have to step out into the frigid, driving snow.

9:10 p.m. Never have I been happier to see two silent, estranged, unmarried teens. The last four miles of the journey I made squeezed in beside the driver of one of the all-too-few snowplows in Mississippi. The good news is I have nearly regained sensation in my hands and my feet are beginning to thaw. The bad news is the motel is jammed with stranded travelers, so Carlotta will be bunking with her pals. Perhaps if Apurva ever comes out of the bathroom where she has locked herself, we can figure out the sleeping accommodations. I for one am exhausted!

FRIDAY, March 5 — I slept as a buffer between Apurva and Trent in the king-size bed. Of course, Carlotta had to retire in her robe, wig, bra, and full makeup. My roommates were similarly well-swaddled for enforced blizzard bundling. G-spot hunting was off the agenda, though several times during the night I found myself with a fairly spectacular T.E. from sudden Apurva proximity. If I'd never met Sheeni, I'm sure I'd be panting to marry Apurva myself right now. Maybe Trent should get his thyroid checked.

The snow finally stopped sometime during the night. When we awoke, I got my first real view of Oxford, Mississippi. The icy vista outside our window looked just like those postcards you see of wintry Vermont.

Inside, the atmosphere was even frostier. Carlotta invited

morose Trent to dine with her in the crowded motel coffee shop, while miserable Apurva drank her lonely cup of motel tea back in the room.

"This whole trip was a mistake," sighed Trent, neglecting his grits and ignoring our waitress's blatant eyelash fluttering. "I should never have come here."

I sipped my coffee. "So what's the problem, guy?"

"I just don't know this person, Carlotta. This person I'm supposed to be marrying. And she doesn't know me. I realized it yesterday while writing a love poem."

Great. Trent flubs a rhyme or two so the wedding's off.

"Apurva and I are strangers, Carlotta."

"Hardly strangers, Trent."

"Do any of us really know anyone, Carlotta? Is there such a thing as true intimacy between people?"

What on earth does intimacy have to do with marriage? I considered administering a vicious head-slap, but resigned myself to a philosophical debate. I dunked my donut and plowed ahead.

"Trent, everyone has those feelings. Of course, we're all locked inside our own skins. People who have been married for 50 years feel that way sometimes. They look across the breakfast table and suddenly wonder who the hell is that old fart?"

"I have to feel a profound connection, Carlotta, before I can marry someone."

"Trent, you're a very fortunate person. You've won the lottery, guy. But you can't even see it."

"What do you mean?"

"Trent, think of the odds of your ever meeting Apurva. She came from halfway around the world, to our small out-of-the-way town. From a totally different culture. Yet, somehow, you two made a connection. A deep and intense connection. You can't deny that."

"I suppose not."

"And she's a wonderful person. Intelligent and kind—she lights up every room she walks into. And she has a generous heart—full of love . . . unselfish love for you."

"Yes, I think she does love me."

"You're so fortunate, Trent. You have a chance to do something truly noble."

"What, Carlotta?"

"Make a difference in a person's life. You know what will happen to Apurva if you don't get married. She'll be shipped back to India and get shackled to some stranger."

"She might be happier in the long run."

"You don't believe that for a minute. That's a coward's voice talking. Apurva will always love you, Trent. She's committed herself to you. That is her destiny. OK, you're both young, but these feelings don't change. You must do what you know is right."

"And what's that, Carlotta?"

"Make Apurva happy. Save her from the nightmare you know she faces. Do what's honorable and right. Be a man, not a wimp."

Trent sighed and wiped away a tear. "OK, Carlotta. You're right. I guess I'll marry her."

I slammed down my coffee cup.

"That's not good enough, Trent! Apurva will never marry you if she feels you're at all reluctant. Love is a delicate thing, Trent. You've injured her deeply. Now you have to win her back."

"I'm so mixed up, Carlotta. I've, I've been thinking of Sheeni."

Flushed out into the open at last!

"OK. Well, Sheeni's a special person too. We both know her very well. She's quite exceptional."

"She is, Carlotta."

"But let's face the facts here, Trent. Enduring love requires constancy. Right?"

He stared at his plate. "Very much so."

"And do you believe Sheeni ever will commit her heart and soul to you?"

"Probably not."

"And do you have faith in the strength and endurance of Apurva's love for you?"

"I've never doubted it for a minute. Not really."

"So why are we sitting here indulging in these boring head games?"

"You're right, Carlotta. I'm very fortunate to have Apurva in my life."

"Well, you don't have her at the moment, Trent. But here's a suggestion: I'll stay here and order another donut. And you go back to the room and convince Apurva that you're the luckiest guy in the world."

"What if she doesn't believe me?"

"Just turn on the charm, Trent. God knows you've got enough to spare."

10:45 a.m. The wedding is back on. Well, sort of. The happy couple is willing, but the town is virtually paralyzed under a foot of snow. Now an icy wind is blowing the stuff into impassible drifts. No one seems to possess so much as a snow shovel. Court has been canceled, but Carlotta managed to establish phone communication with a county clerk, who is trying to locate a judge. I told her it was urgent because Grandma Preston back in Cleveland was hanging on by a thread in intensive care just waiting for news of her grandson's wedding.

Carlotta found a deck of cards in a drawer next to the Gideon Bible. To kill time and keep Trent's mind occupied while waiting for the clerk to phone back, we've been playing hearts. I love to slap the dreaded queen of spades on the bridegroom-to-be. The guy's a terrible hearts player. It probably doesn't help his concentration that Apurva is toying with a lock of his golden hair.

12:20 p.m. We have a two o'clock appointment in Judge Randolph Marulle's chambers (if we can make it there—it's started snowing again). To prepare for the crosstown hike, we slogged next door to a hardware store and bought their last three pairs of black rubber boots (size XXXL). The giant boots are big enough to shod a rhino, but we've lashed them to our calves with duct tape.

At least the weather has resolved the bridal raiments issue. As Apurva owns no wool saris, she has bundled up in all her warmest dresses and sweaters, attractively accessorized with two pairs of jeans and the rhino boots. Examining herself despairingly in the motel-room mirror, she declared she was "the ugliest bride in history." Trent kissed her, told her she was beautiful, and said he did not intend to spend his honeymoon nursing a wife with pneumonia. The guy sure can be charming when he wants to be.

7:10 p.m. The deed is done. Sheeni Saunder's childhood sweetheart is officially scratched from the dating market. I did have a bit of a scare at the beginning. Judge Randolph J. Marulle turned out to be one of those loquacious, serious-minded jurists who like to pry. The first thing he did was remark on the youthfulness of the bride and groom. Where were their parents, he wanted to know, and did "you kids" realize the seriousness of such a "momentous step" as marriage? So Carlotta took him aside, explained that the parents were at the bedside of a terminally ill grandmother, and stressed that both families wanted the baby to be born legitimate. The judge glanced at Apurva, shivering in 14 layers of clothing, and decided to get on with it.

Carlotta gave the bride away; the beaming court clerk served as the other witness. It was all over in less than five minutes. The bride and groom whispered "I do," 14-karat gold rings were slipped successfully on nervous fingers, the judge declared them husband and wife, lips met in a binding kiss, the clerk flashed her

Polaroid camera, and Carlotta breathed an immense sigh of relief. I only hope my own wedding to Sheeni goes as smoothly.

After the ceremony Carlotta treated the newlyweds to a festive wedding supper at Shanghai Dixie Palace, the only restaurant we could find that wasn't shuttered in the reborn blizzard. Oh well, I like Chinese food and you can't beat the prices. Our convivial waiter even served us a bottle of Mississippi sparkling chablis without checking our IDs. A feast to remember even if it was vegetarian, and the bill (including tip) came to less than $40.

9:50 p.m. As our motel is now even more clogged with stranded travelers and partying Ole Miss students, no amount of pleading was able to free up another room. Yes, diary, it appears that we are about to experience a Wedding Night for Three.

SATURDAY, March 6 — Carlotta's friends refused even to consider her offer to sleep in the bathroom or out in the hallway. Reflecting the altered circumstances, we negotiated a slight shuffling in the bed order. Carlotta was moved to an outside position, and Apurva slept in the middle next to her husband. Lots of breezy banter as we settled in, but one could sense their lack of privacy chafed on the newlyweds. Carlotta thoughtfully pretended to fall immediately to sleep, but I don't think things progressed very far on the other side of the mattress beyond a mild snuggle and possible furtive grope. Oh well, it's not like anyone had come to that crowded bed a dewy-eyed expectant virgin.

As I lay there in the dark wondering if Carlotta was the only person in the room with a spectacular T.E., I tried to distract myself by imagining what Sheeni would say if she knew I was honeymooning with her former boyfriend. I pray she never finds out. I wondered how Fuzzy back in Ukiah was getting along on his first date with Lana Baldwin. Why, I asked myself, do people go to such bizarre lengths to couple with others when that fairly peculiar physical act is all over in a few minutes? Of course, you can blame the crazed single-mindedness of our genes. My genes, I knew, had been alerted that alluring, fecund Apurva lay just an arm's length away. And why, they clamored to know, wasn't I doing anything about it? If my genes were in an uproar, one can only imagine the consternation among Trent's. His biological destiny had been sanctioned by the state, he had golden genes to die for, his goal was within reach, yet somehow someone had called a time-out on the field.

3:05 p.m. Memphis airport. Boarding for my flight to San Francisco is supposed to commence in 20 minutes (I've heard that before). Snowplows have cleared the runway and crews are de-icing the plane. Anxious to escape further honeymoon chaperone duties, I managed to bribe the motel manager's son into braving a trip to the airport in his four-wheel-drive SUV.

Carlotta hopped out of bed pretty early this morning—announcing to her groggy companions that she would be back with breakfast in exactly one hour—no more, no less. While I slogged through the snow in search of an open donut shop, I hoped and presumed that marriage consummation was underway back at the motel. It is true that I detected a certain slackening of tensions upon my return. Too bad our culture doesn't believe in throwing open the window and hanging out the bloody sheet.

Apurva wanted to call her parents, but Carlotta advised them both to wait until they return on Wednesday (Trent has a vital swim meet with Willits on Friday).

"You only get one honeymoon," I pointed out. "Don't spoil it by involving a bunch of hysterical parents."

Leave-taking with the newlyweds was quite wrenching, as you'd expect. Not a dry eye in the house, but sharing someone's wedding night can be such an emotionally bonding experience—especially if you're paying for the entire affair.

· · ·

SUNDAY, March 7 — It was sometime in the middle of the night when Carlotta finally dragged her weary carcass through my front door. She dropped her bags and shuffled into the bedroom. There, lounging impatiently under Granny DeFalco's quilt, was My Love—naked as a clam and primed for conversation.

"Nickie! Where have you been?" she demanded, switching on the lamp.

"Oh, hi, darling. Boy, am I exhausted. Do you mind if I skip the flossing tonight?"

"Nickie, you've been gone for three days! You left darling Albert unattended!"

"Well I left a note for Mrs. Ferguson," I replied, collapsing fully clothed on the bed. "Maybe I'll skip brushing too."

"Nickie, don't lie to me. I know you were with Trent and Apurva. I heard all about it from Vijay. Where are they?"

I fished through Carlotta's purse and handed My Love a Polaroid photograph. She stared at it in disbelief.

"What the fuck is this?"

"They're married, Sheeni. I tried to talk them out of it, but they wouldn't listen."

All the color drained from my darling's face. "But they're too young to get married!"

"Not in Mississippi."

"Mississippi! How did they get to Mississippi?"

"Same way I did. By airplane."

"You paid for their tickets!"

"No way, honey. They were already there when they called me. They were destitute. So I went there to see if I could talk them into coming home."

"Why didn't you call me!?"

"They made me promise not to tell anyone."

Sheeni stared in horror at the photo. "What's she wearing? She couldn't possibly have gotten married looking like that! My God, what's that on her feet?"

"It was cold there, honey. They were having the Blizzard of the Century."

"But, why!" she cried. "Why did they get married?"

"Beats me. Don't tell anyone, but I think Apurva may be, you know, in a family way."

Sheeni pulled away as I tried to embrace her. She tossed the photo back at me and curled up in a ball, facing the wall.

"When did they do it?" she asked, burying herself in the quilt.

"Friday."

"Mississippi, huh? Then it's not a real marriage. It doesn't count in California. It's not valid in civilized regions."

"They are legally married, Sheeni. And I am very, very tired."

No answer. I stood up and started removing my clothes. I could hear muffled sobbing from under the quilt.

I switched out the light and got into bed. I stared up at the ceiling and listened to My Love cry bitter tears for another man. I no longer felt like sleeping. Eventually, she rolled over and faced me.

"I've been in love with Trent since I was five years old. Do you know why I broke up with him?"

"I assume because I came along."

"Don't flatter yourself. It's because you can't spend your whole life with someone you met when you were in kindergarten. It's just not done."

"Oh."

First time I heard that rule.

"Is that all you can say?"

"Sheeni, I love you. I will always love you. And I don't give a damn that we met in junior high school."

She slid her arms around me and pressed her soft warm body against mine.

"Oh, Nickie, I want you to make love to me . . . now . . . without a condom."

Thrilled, François kissed her. "Isn't that rather reckless, darling?" I asked.

"It's reckless and it's necessary."

And so, diary, I joined at last with My Love as nature intended—secretions undammed, flesh against flesh, being to being. After a gloriously unfettered sensory implosion, we fell asleep in each other's arms—as entwined as two people could ever be.

Hours later I awoke with an arm pinned painfully under 112 pounds of exquisite girl. Extracting the mangled limb, I lay awake in the dark and thought about what Sheeni had said. Some of it was pretty awful, but at least she finally confessed to loving someone. Too bad it had to be Trent. Still, her heart clearly does embrace the concept of love. That means she is theoretically capable of loving other people (me, for example). And she did have unprotected sex with me. Pretty shocking, but I'm not exactly sure what it all means, except that my genes are thrilled. Here's another question: Does some of it stay in there or does it all dribble out on the sheet?

10:45 a.m. Sorry, God, church was just not on our agenda today. I microwaved some frozen tamales, and we breakfasted in bed with the Sunday paper. My dad, I'm semi-happy to report, has been sprung from jail. Authorities now believe the virus was planted on his computer by "technologically sophisticated eco-terrorists." The page-one article noted that former suspect George W. Twisp has divulged to police that "a large sum of money and many valuable items" had disappeared recently from his home. What a liar!

While Sheeni took a leisurely hot bath, I made a call to keep my half of the bargain.

"Hello, Vijay," I said, "let me speak to your father."

"Who is this?"

"None of your fucking business."

Mr. Joshi came on the line. I gave it to him short and sweet.

"Your daughter is honeymooning with Trent in the South. She'll be home on Wednesday." Click.

Bet I made their day.

2:35 p.m. Sheeni just left in a huff because I refused to divulge Trent's exact location in Mississippi. My Love expressed a desire to phone the twit. As if a guy needs to interrupt his romantic honeymoon to take a call from a former girlfriend, even if all she claimed she wanted to do was "wish them both hearty congratulations." I suggested she send them a card. I know etiquette is on my side on this issue, and I was making that exact point when Sheeni slammed the door.

Still somewhat jet-lagged, Carlotta sat in the sun on the back porch and watched Fuzzy and Lana wash Granny DeFalco's cherry 1965 Ford Falcon. It will be his to drive in 14 months and 23 days (he's counting down the hours to his sixteenth birthday, when he can get his license). For now he has to content himself with driving his car in and out of the garage, and revving the engine to impress chicks. From the boisterous way they were squirting each other with the hose, I gathered that things had not gone too badly on my pal's first date.

8:40 p.m. The Weather Channel reports another big storm is headed toward the South. Looks like I got out just in time. With any luck, the newlyweds may be holed-up in that motel all week with nothing to do but exhaust their supply of defective prophylactics. Surely that elusive G-spot has been located by now.

MONDAY, March 8 — School today was abuzz with rumors of a Preston-Joshi merger. Half the girls in my classes looked like they were in shock and the other half appeared to be in deep mourning. Heartsick Sonya in clothing technology class was totally out of control.

"If Trent married that girl," she declared to Carlotta, "I'm going to kill myself. Right after I murder you."

"What did I do?" I asked, alarmed.

"You introduced me to him. You got my hopes up, girl."

"Well, meet me in the cafeteria at noon and I'll introduce you to my neighbor, Bruno Modjaleski. He's a fabulous kisser."

"Bruno Modjaleski is a pig," she retorted. "Besides, everyone knows he's going with Candy Pringle. And I very much doubt he ever kissed you."

"Want to bet $50?"

"You're on, pimple toes."

Sheeni was pretty frosty toward me in physics class. I wasn't sure if she was pissed at me, attempting to quell vicious rumors, preoccupied with the hydrogen atom, disturbed by rumors of my bet, or simply anticipating future Carlotta snubbing in gym.

Another traumatic embarrassment in the cafeteria. Of course, with Candy Pringle snacking on a slimming cheerleader's lunch in the chair beside him, Bruno had to deny everything. Carlotta turned a violent shade of scarlet and was forced to pay off Sonya right on the spot just to shut up her big fat mouth. What a humiliation, especially with you-know-who yucking it up with Vijay at the next table over.

Fuzzy questioned my sanity on the walk home from school.

"Carlotta, why are you spreading it all over school that you made out with Bruno?" he demanded.

"I'm not, Frank. It just seemed like an easy way to make fifty bucks. And why aren't you walking Lana home?"

"Her brother gives her a ride. They live way back up in the hills somewhere."

"Perhaps they're trying to re-create their West Virginia milieu. So how was your date?"

"Great. We had pizza downtown. Then we walked to the Little League park and smoked a joint in the visitors' dugout."

"Where'd you get the reefer?"

"From Lana. We smoked one in the Falcon yesterday too. It was awesome. I thought my brain was going to explode."

"So she has a great body and access to powerful hallucinogenics. I told you I can pick them. What base did you get to?"

"Well, I'm sort of working up to holding her hand."

"Frank, you'd only known Heather for three hours when you made it to home base."

"True, but Heather ran a pretty fast offense. Did Lana say anything about me?"

"She said you were tons of fun and really smart."

"Cool. When did she say that?"

"This afternoon in the locker room. You might call it the naked truth."

Fuzzy punched Carlotta in the arm.

"Brute! How dare you strike a woman!"

"Yeah, well just keep your filthy eyeballs off my chick."

5:45 p.m. Carlotta received another unexpected blow when she walked in her front door. The table was set for five. Making themselves at home were my new cook and chauffeur. Bored with being snowed in and worried about their parents, Trent and Apurva had decided to bail on their honeymoon. Already Apurva was in the kitchen showing Mrs. Ferguson how to make vegetarian meatloaf. Trent was petting Albert on the sofa and listening politely to dim Dwayne boast how his dog Kamu could "bite the head off" Apurva's dog Jean-Paul.

8:05 p.m. Our next shipment of Wart Watches had better sell out in a hurry. Trent eats like he's at the training table of the Chicago Bears. Marriage in general seems to be good for the appetite. I only pray Apurva was eating for two. All through the meal I could sense Trent was wondering why Carlotta insists on dining with repulsive Dwayne. Hey guy, I don't like the cretin any more than you do.

Serving seconds on dessert, Mrs. Ferguson was dumbfounded to discover that Trent and wife somehow had visited Memphis without touring Graceland.

"And what is Graceland?" inquired Apurva.

Mrs. Ferguson staggered back from this blow.

"It's Elvis Presley's home," explained her husband. "It's now open to the public."

"You have . . . heard of Elvis . . . ain't ya?" asked my maid.

"Certainly," replied Apurva. "He's that heavyset singer who died many years before I was born."

If Apurva regards Elvis as ancient history, I can only imagine what she thinks of Frank.

After dinner Trent took Carlotta aside and requested a $100 advance on my first month's car rental. I paid him in cash and told him to park the Acura out of sight in the alley behind the garage. Then Apurva helped me move my stuff out of the bedroom, which Carlotta is graciously giving up (but only temporarily!) to the newlyweds. Believe it or not, I'll be bedding down tonight on the sofa in the living room.

Oh well, I keep reminding myself that at least Trent is married—just as those aging Vietnam War protesters make the best of things by reminding themselves that at least Richard Nixon is dead.

10:20 p.m. Thank God Sheeni didn't call or come over. I did have one visitor: Bruno Modjaleski, who knocked on my front door to apologize for being a lying weasel.

"I'm sorry I cost you the fifty, Carly. But I'm going to make it up to you."

"Good," replied Carlotta, folding her arms over her nightgown and not letting him in. "I could use the money."

"Yeah, I decided to pay you back with $50 worth of kisses."

Before I could slam the door, the brute grabbed me and made his first installment right there on the front stoop. A fate worse than death (especially the ass grope) and I didn't even get it down on video to show Sonya.

TUESDAY, March 9 — Another unfortunate development, diary. Let me begin by noting that I am a sound sleeper. This is why I did not hear the key turn in the lock sometime around midnight, nor hear the person enter. The room was dark and their view into the living room (where Carlotta was sleeping) was partially screened by the new entertainment center cabinet extending out from the wall to form a de facto entry foyer for my tiny home. I surmise that the person proceeded quietly down the hallway to the bathroom, where they removed their garments. Ever-useless Albert, locked in the kitchen, raised no alarm. They then tiptoed across the hall to the bedroom, where—while attempting to slip beneath the covers—they encountered the lightly clad voluptuous form of a sleeping female. Waking in surprise, Apurva leaped to what for her might have been a logical conclusion and shouted, "No, Carlotta, this is not right! No!"

Her husband woke up; Carlotta jolted awake and dashed into the bedroom just as angry Trent switched on the light. Everyone gasped. On the other side of the bed was My Love, coming to the traumatic realization that she was standing nude in a room with her former childhood sweetheart and his new wife.

Time slowed way down to drag out the shock and horror as eyes met eyes around the room.

"Sheeni!" Trent expostulated.

Apurva moved her lips, but no sounds emerged.

Carlotta's mind spun like a slot machine, but nothing came up.

At last My Love broke the impasse. She folded her arms over her nakedness and walked silently from the room. Open-mouthed, Trent and Apurva gazed questioningly at Carlotta.

"Er," Carlotta mumbled, "she must have, uh, come to the wrong house . . . by mistake."

A moment later My Love had tossed on her clothes and fled out the front door. I grabbed Trent's raincoat off a hook, threw it on over Carlotta's nightgown, and hurried after her down the darkened sidewalk.

"Sheeni! Wait! Stop!"

My Love turned, hit me in the eye with a small metallic object, and stomped on.

I picked up the discarded key and hurried after her.

"I'm sorry," I said, catching up with her. "I'm really sorry."

She did not slow or look at me. "I have never been so humiliated."

"I know, darling, it's, it's . . . regrettable."

"Don't call me 'darling.' You are such a scumbag. How can I face them ever again? How can I face anyone in this damn town?"

"Sheeni, could we slow up here?"

Still declining to look at me, My Love quickened her pace. "You say you love me, but you never tell me anything. I've had it with your deceptions."

"Sheeni, they just showed up a few hours ago. How was I supposed to tell you? I had no idea you were coming over. I mean, I was trying to do you a favor."

"Don't make me laugh."

"I was! I was trying to help out your old boyfriend. I gave up my bed to them, for Christ's sake. And I don't even like the guy!"

Sheeni slackened her pace. "This entire evening has been a disaster. I had a fight with my parents. So I sneaked out of the house . . . looking for solace."

Carlotta put my arm around her shoulder. "What was the fight about, darling?"

"Trent. What else? Oh, Nickie, I'm so embarrassed. You have to think of something to tell them—so they won't think I'm a . . ."

"Yes, I know. OK, darling, I'll give it a shot."

Sheeni stopped and we embraced in the shadows beneath a street tree. "Oh, Nickie, Trent really is married. I can see that now."

Well I should hope so.

"Yes, Sheeni darling, and we're two underage minors out past the curfew on a school night on a street that's well-patrolled by cops."

My Love grabbed back her key, gave me a quick kiss, and darted off into the night. I sneaked home, observed the light was off again in the bedroom, and retired to my lonely sofa. I had six hours to manufacture a plausible explanation for the events that had just transpired.

8:20 a.m. "I'm gay," Carlotta announced.

We were breakfasting uneasily around Granny DeFalco's old yellow chrome dinette.

"We gathered as much," replied Trent, gazing intently at his Cheerios.

"We value that you are able to share that with us," added his wife, also avoiding eye-contact.

"It's a shame there are so many unenlightened people in this town," said Trent, pouring a second helping of cereal. "We appreciate your need for discretion."

64

"Thank you for being so understanding," blushed Carlotta.

"And Sheeni too?" ventured Apurva.

"Yes, of course," I replied. "She's known since she was in kindergarten."

Trent put down his spoon and flashed Carlotta a tremulous smile. Sensing I was messing profoundly with his world view, I sipped my instant coffee and pressed on.

"But she's not ready to tell anyone yet. In fact, she asked me to make up some kind of plausible lie for what happened last night. As if I could."

"She must be very disturbed," said Apurva. "I do feel sorry for her. But it is also a great relief to me. I have spent too many hours worrying that my darling Trent was not entirely over her."

Trent patted her hand. "Don't be silly, honey."

"Carlotta," said Apurva, "once again you have made me very happy."

And once again I have made Trent perfectly miserable. What could be better than that?

11:15 a.m. Sheeni cornered Carlotta this morning in the hall-way outside physics class.

"Carlotta," she whispered, "what did you tell them?"

"Mostly the truth," I lied. "I said you had a fight with your parents. That you had heard about the storms back east and were under the impression that Carlotta was still in Mississippi. So you let yourself into my house with the key I had given you to take care of Albert. End of story."

"Carlotta, you're a genius."

Thus noble falsehood triumphs again over evil truth.

"I do my best, Sheeni."

"Where are they now?"

"They went to see Trent's parents. They invited me to come along, but I declined the pleasure."

I have enough parental problems without taking on Trent's.

1:30 p.m. Giving up her accustomed seat at the Shunned Loners' table, Carlotta accepted an invitation from Sheeni and vile Vijay to eat lunch with them. The latter adopted a transparently insincere cordiality in pumping Carlotta for details about his sister's wedding. I said it was a simple but moving ceremony that was a testament to the Southern Way of Life.

"I think everyone should get married in Mississippi," added Carlotta, glancing at Sheeni. "I only wish they'd lower the age limit even more."

My Love rolled her eyes.

"What I can't understand," said Vijay, "is how that ruffian Nick Twisp heard about it?"

"I'm sure I wouldn't know," replied Carlotta. "Perhaps you should ask your sister."

"I'm not certain I'll be permitted to speak to her," said Vijay.

"Vijay's father is threatening to banish Apurva from the family," explained Sheeni.

"That is so unfair," said Carlotta. "Doesn't he want to see his grandchild?"

Vijay dropped his potato-and-peas samosa.

"Of course, I may be speaking prematurely here," I hastened to add.

3:05 p.m. Within 20 minutes it was all over the school that the next generation of Trent Prestons was on its way. My volatile friend Sonya did not take the news well. In gym she "accidentally" dropped a large barbell that dented the maple floor and came within an inch of pulverizing Carlotta's left foot. I can't let my guard down for a second in that class. Not even when Lana Baldwin bends over to draw her pink lace panties up her still-damp thighs.

5:30 p.m. Feeling a trifle overstimulated, Carlotta had planned to retreat to her humble bathroom to attend to a private matter, but I arrived home to find my living room occupied by Trent,

Apurva, and one-and-a-half sets of overwrought in-laws. I had never seen my former employer (Mr. Preston) so red-faced. The two mothers-in-law were sharing my box of tissues. Apurva had a box of her own. Trent was clutching her hand and seething inwardly (I recognized the signs from my father). I could sense that many ugly and hurtful things already had been said. But then that's what parents are for.

Mrs. Ferguson shuffled out from the kitchen. "They didn't want . . . no snacks . . . Miz Carlotta . . . I done . . . made the offer."

"Thank you, Mrs. Ferguson."

"They stayin' . . . for supper? . . . I'm makin' . . . Hawaiian ham loaf."

"Uhmm, I'll let you know." Carlotta turned to the somber gathering. "Well, don't let me interrupt. If you need anything, I'll be in the bedroom studying."

"Just a minute, young lady," boomed Mr. Preston. "This discussion concerns you as well."

Damn, trapped like a rat. Sullen Trent made the mumbled introductions; no one offered to shake hands. Carlotta reluctantly took a seat in the only unoccupied chair.

Mr. Preston proceeded in his prosecutorial manner. "I understand you have extended offers of employment to my son and his wif—I mean, Apurva."

"Oh . . . Did I?"

"And how much do you intend to pay?" he demanded.

Put on the spot. Now I remembered why I disliked parents so much. They do get in your face. I thought back to Rev. Glompiphel's recent wage proposal to Carlotta for a position as rectory domestic slave. "Uhmm, how about $100 a month—each?"

Mr. Preston frowned. "Miss Ulansky, are you aware of this state's minimum wage laws? And what do you intend to offer in terms of health benefits, dental coverage, workman's compensation, and pension plan?"

Pension plan! Good grief, they're teenagers! We're concerned about living, not retiring. And how many of those costly perks had he extended to his erstwhile employee Nick Twisp? Exactly none, as I recall.

"Uh, I, I hadn't thought of that," mumbled Carlotta.

I excused myself to answer the telephone in the bedroom. It was my sister Joanie calling from Los Angeles with cataclysmic news.

"Nickie, you and Dad have been all over the TV down here!"

"I know, Joanie. It was just a big misunderstanding. They let Dad go."

"Nick, Kimberly saw one of the reports!"

I collapsed on the bed.

"Damn! Did she tell Mario?"

"Yes, and I think they're going to the FBI."

My mind reeled. Well, that's one way for my business partners to welsh on future Wart Watch royalties—fink on me to the feds.

"Nickie, why don't you turn yourself in?"

"I can't, Joanie. Thanks for the warning. I'll keep in touch."

Trying to keep my panic under control, I immediately called Sheeni.

"Meet me at the lunch counter in Flampert's Variety Store in 15 minutes."

"But, Carlotta, we're about to sit down to dinner."

"Fifteen minutes!" I insisted. "It's vitally urgent."

Grabbing my bank books and laptop computer, I ducked out through the kitchen.

"I'm stepping out for a moment, Mrs. Ferguson," I informed my maid. "Can you wipe down everything in the house I might have touched?"

She paused in mashing the potatoes. "Everything?"

"Yes, if you will. Your son can help. Please do your best."

"OK, Miz Carlotta . . . but where . . ."

I didn't stop. On my way out the back door I reached behind the washing machine and pulled out my emergency backpack, loaded with essentials and ready to go. (A precaution all teens would be wise to take.)

8:42 p.m. I'm writing this in the front seat of Fuzzy's Falcon inside my garage. I've plugged my laptop's 12-volt adapter into the cigarette lighter socket. I hope my pal won't object to this modest battery drain. The car still smells faintly of controlled substances, but so far I have observed no consciousness-altering effects.

The plan is to hide out here for the night (assuming I don't freeze to death; My Love declined to let Carlotta spend one last night at her house). Thankfully, I have my sleeping bag and heat-conserving Mylar space blanket in my emergency pack.

I figure if the cops descend on my house, I can slink away up the alley before anyone notices. I got a scare about an hour ago when a car squealed into the driveway. I sneaked a peek out the grimy garage door windows and was relieved to see it was only Mr. Joshi in his rad Plymouth Reliant. He slammed his car door and strode toward the house. A moment later the noise level inside went way up. I hope the neighbors don't call the cops.

Sheeni was most upset when I told her the news at Flampert's. We had an urgent, whispered conversation over grilled cheese sandwiches and bad (even for Flampert's) raisin chiffon pie.

"Carlotta, this is disastrous! Who will take care of darling Albert?"

"I'm facing ten years' imprisonment by the California Youth Authority and you're worried about a dog?"

My Love looked stricken.

"OK, Sheeni, he's a very nice dog. Trent and Apurva can take care of him. Darling, you have to help me get my money out of the bank tomorrow."

"I told you to move your funds offshore. Mine are totally untouchable."

Like Latin America's smarter drug lords, My Love stashes her money (a 15 percent rake-off of my Wart Watch royalties) in an extremely circumspect bank on the Cayman Islands.

"Sheeni, can you go to my bank first thing tomorrow and withdraw all of my funds? You're a signatory on all the accounts."

"I can't, Carlotta. No way. It's too dangerous. Just call them up and tell them to wire the money into my account. I'll give you the number."

"But, Sheeni, I need money now!"

"Sorry, Carlotta. I'm in enough trouble as it is. My parents will kill me when they find out who you really are. They'll positively murder me."

"Sheeni, let's run away together. Let's be wild and rebellious like your hero Jean-Paul Belmondo."

"Sorry, Carlotta. Life as a runaway homeless teen is just not in my plans."

"Sheeni, if you love me, you'll go away with me. You hate it in this town! And we've got money."

My Love shook her head. "I can't make any decisions now. I'm too upset."

And so we parted (for how long?) outside of Flampert's. I longed to take her in my arms and never let her go. But all we could do was shake hands, say "good night" like two casual acquaintances, and walk away.

9:35 p.m. Apurva's parents peeled out about ten minutes ago. As far as I know, all Prestons remain inside. Perhaps Trent's parents are planning on bunking on the sofa. I trust everyone isn't waiting for tardy Carlotta to return. It looks like dinner was served quite a while ago (I could see Dwayne washing the dishes through the kitchen window). I hope Apurva's mother was not too appalled by Mrs. Ferguson's animal-laden Hawaiian ham loaf. I could use a nice slab of it myself right now. Fortunately, I'm keeping hunger at bay with handfuls of high-protein trail mix from my backpack.

I wish Carlotta were in there to help the newlyweds stand up to parental browbeating. Apurva has a will of iron, but Trent is such a milquetoast. Who would ever guess it to look at the guy?

Life is so unpredictable. It's hard to believe that a few hours ago my biggest problem was trying to figure out how much to pay my chauffeur. Now I'm living out of one bag and have a relentless FBI hot on my trail.

Oh well, at least Trent is married. That's one good reason to postpone further contemplation of desperate suicidal acts.

WEDNESDAY, March 10 — If I were one foot shorter (or Fuzzy's Falcon one foot wider), I might have passed a halfway comfortable night. No cars in the driveway except Trent's Acura. Looks like the senior Prestons finally bailed.

As Carlotta was hitting the road with her getaway burdens, a gate opened across the alley and out bounced a large garbage can gripped in the strong but uncoordinated arms of you-know-who.

"'Lo, Carly," leered Bruno. "Big party at your place last night, huh?"

"Bruno, can you do me a favor?"

"Sure, babe. You want it on the lips or down lower this time?"

By now I had learned simply to ignore his lascivious queries.

"Bruno, do you know Trent Preston?"

"Yeah, but I ain't gonna wear no yellow ribbons for the guy."

"Can you give him this message when you see him: Make yourselves at home; the rent is paid until July?"

Bruno's lips moved as he tried to squeeze Carlotta's message into his 12-megabyte brain, probably in the process erasing something vital like Joe Montana's lifetime passing stats.

"Will do, babe. Want another installment on the fifty?"

"No thanks," I replied, hurrying away. "Don't forget my message."

"OK, babe," he called, mentally undressing me one last time. "Keep it shakin', girl!"

Carlotta breakfasted on a selection of farewell donuts at my favorite spot downtown. I sat in the shop's least conspicuous corner and read the newspaper 47 times while waiting for the bank to open. No news of Nick Twisp manhunt breakthroughs, though a brief article on page three noted that former Geezer suspect George W. Twisp was considering filing a multimillion dollar wrongful-arrest lawsuit. Such a monetary award, I reasoned, could only balloon his child-support responsibilities. Go get 'em, Dad!

Her resolve fortified by five cups of strong coffee, Carlotta thoroughly cased the entire downtown area before cautiously entering her bank. No obvious police-types in sight. I walked purposefully up to a teller window, stated my business, and was bounced immediately to the branch manager, Mr. Mince, who asked me to take a seat beside his desk. Carlotta did so, though my heavily loaded backpack required her to hunch uncomfortably forward. If worse came to worst, I was hoping it might stop a bullet.

The banker examined my records. "So, Miss Ulansky, you wish to withdraw all $709,000?"

"Yes, sir. In cash."

He smiled. "You have an armored truck parked outside?"

"No, sir. I'll just stuff it in my pack."

Mr. Mince's sparse eyebrows zoomed up into his forehead's stratosphere. "Miss Ulansky, it would take at least a week for us to procure your funds in currency. And I cannot recommend withdrawing such an amount in that manner. Have you spoken to your financial advisors about this?"

"Certainly," I lied. "OK, how much can you give me in cash right now?"

He considered my request. "We might be able to manage $20,000."

"Fine, I'll take it," I replied, handing him a slip of paper. "The rest you can wire to this account."

He frowned his severest banker frown. "Miss Ulansky, I trust you realize this Caribbean institution is not federally insured."

"I know. Can I please have my money?"

Mr. Mince sighed, excused himself, and walked over behind the counter to confer with the head teller. Much talk, much head-scratching, many nervous-making glances in my direction. I could feel my panic rising with each passing second. Eventually the banker returned—empty-handed—to his desk.

"I'd like the $20,000 now," I insisted.

"We'll have it in a second," he smiled. "They're counting it out now. You know, Miss Ulansky, we'd hate to lose you as a customer. I trust you're not dissatisfied in any way with our service."

"Uh, no."

"Good. Then I hope you'll reconsider closing your accounts. We have some very attractive rates on our CDs at the moment."

The guy was stalling. I could sense it now. I tried to stay calm and think what Sheeni would do if she were here.

"Mr. Mince, I have directed you to transfer my funds to an institution of my choosing. If this is not done immediately, I shall be facing dire financial consequences for which you and your bank will be held responsible. Do I make myself clear?"

"Perfectly. I'll see to it at once."

Another drawn-out conference with the head teller. Damn. The vibes were bad, very bad. What price $20,000? Ten years in jail?

A shoot-out with the cops? Now Mince was on the phone! Total panic. Time to bail. I eased myself out of the chair and walked as nonchalantly as I could toward the door. Tellers and customers turned and stared. I could no longer feel my legs. My heart was thumping wildly. I pulled on the door handle. It wouldn't budge. Locked! Mince must have pushed the silent alarm. Wait, maybe not. I pushed on the door. It opened. I was outside on the street. Sunshine. Traffic noise. Sirens! No, it was just the pounding in my ears. I was 10 feet along. Now 20 feet. Someone called my name. I turned. Mince! On the sidewalk pursuing me! I tried to run.

"Miss Ulansky!" he called again. "We have your money now. It's ready."

I stopped. "Oh, uh . . . OK . . . Can you, uh, bring it to me out here?"

"I hardly think so, Miss Ulansky," he replied, offended. "We don't conduct business on the street."

10:12 a.m. The bus is supposed to arrive in 18 minutes. Still no cops in sight. Maybe the feds are waiting until I get out of town, so there won't be any heavy police action around large civilian populations. Taking no chances, I stuffed the $20,000 (in crisp new $100 bills) into a vinyl and leather money belt I purchased at a surplus store. François wanted to check out their impressive handgun display, but I figured he'd be stymied by the damn waiting-period requirements. Boy, the NRA really dropped the ball on that one.

The bulging money belt under Carlotta's black dress is not that comfortable—or flattering. I just checked out her appearance in the bus station ladies' room mirror. She looks like a slight, skinny chick with bad hair, peripatetic boobs, and love handles. To look at her you wouldn't suspect she has $87.13 in her wallet, $3,000 in standby road cash concealed in her backpack, and a modest fortune double-security-strapped to her midriff.

12:45 p.m. On the road south. I just ditched my female alter ego in the bus's tiny restroom. Out the small back window went Carlotta's $13.99 miracle-fiber bouffant wig. Out went her ugly black dress, shawl, and orthopedic shoes. Out went her brassiere and their insincere stuffing. Out went the geeky glasses and discount earrings. Out went her purse and budget cosmetics. Off in the midget-sized sink came her unalluring makeup. Nick Twisp is back! I went to the restroom a girl and returned a guy. And my seatmate, a garrulous old lady on a coast-to-coast one-woman anti-Mormon crusade, never noticed the difference. She picked up again right where she'd left off.

4:45 p.m. Layover in Modesto. Can't write much. My laptop batteries are low and I'm too depressed. Every mile traveled takes me farther from My Love. Sheeni, darling, I miss you!

THURSDAY, March 11 — 2:26 a.m. Los Angeles bus station. The bus had a breakdown on the Grapevine (nearly giving me a heart attack; I feared it was a ruse by the cops), delaying our arrival by three hours. The neighborhood is too scary to venture out in, so I guess I'll camp here until morning. Very tired. Lots of lowlifes loitering about. Glad Carlotta isn't here to get pestered and harassed. Can't believe Jack Kerouac enjoyed all those marathon bus trips. I feel like a zombie!

11:10 a.m. I dozed off on a bench in the bus station and woke up sometime later with something tugging on my arm. An emaciated guy in a dirty Hawaiian shirt was attempting to steal my laptop. Fortunately, I had locked it to my wrist with a set of handcuffs François talked me into buying at the Ukiah surplus store. I kicked the guy in the shins, he dropped the computer and ran. God, I despise criminals—another good reason to stay out of jail.

After a dreary breakfast at a downtown greasy spoon, I hailed a cab and gave the driver the address of Paul Saunders.

"Is that in Beverly Hills or Bel Air?" he asked.

"I have no idea," I replied. "Probably the more affordable of the two."

Paul, it turned out, lived in affluent Bel Air. The driver left me off in front of a posh hilltop mansion. Wow, I thought, Sheeni's brother must have really hit it big in the music business. The house was white-painted adobe with an Aztec-stepped roof, elaborate iron grillwork, and a soaring entry colonnade that looked like it might have been transplanted from a suburban Macy's store. All the junipers in the front lawn were modeling exotic haircuts. I walked up to the great carved teak door and clanged the bronze dragon clapper. From somewhere inside came the faint sounds of multiple dogs yapping. Eventually, the door opened.

"You are no one," said an oddly coiffed young Asian woman (the maid?) in a shimmering off-the-shoulder yellow sarong.

Now I was receiving "don't exist" messages from complete strangers.

"I am Nick," I replied. "I'm here to see Mr. Saunders."

"Paulo is down by the pool," she answered, pointing east. "Eight, two, zero, three."

Did L.A. types—always trendsetters—now speak in numbers? Mildly befuddled, I wandered east around the side of the house and came to a locked iron gate. Nobody's fool, I punched in eight, two, zero, three. The gate clicked open.

I followed my nose down a narrow terraced canyon and came to a hidden Shangri-La of tall eucalyptus trees overhanging a lushly landscaped black-bottom pool. Gaps here and there in the verdant foliage afforded glimpses of distant smog-girdled Los Angeles. Sheeni's older brother, in shorts and sandals, was smoking a joint and varnishing the wooden paddle of an ornate Venetian gondola, made of brightly colored inflated vinyl.

"Hello, Nick," he said, offering me a toke.

Dumping my pack and laptop, I helped myself to a massive drag. Ferocious brain-cell popping immediately commenced.

Trust Paul to have the Real Stuff. I plopped down beside him on the pool's "natural" sandy beach. "Did Sheeni tell you I was coming?"

"Why should she have to do that?"

Oh right. I remembered that my life was an open book to Paul. I decided to avail myself of his prescience. "Paul," I said, passing back the joint, "can you tell me if the cops are closing in?"

He took a drag and considered the matter. "No more than usual, Nick. Far as I can see."

I celebrated this good news with another massive puff. The doors of perception were banging open with a vengeance.

"Paul, this is a terrific spot!" I exclaimed, gazing about. "And it's all yours!"

It wasn't. He and Lacey, he explained, were just renting the pool cabana.

"What pool cabana?" I demanded, bogarting the joint.

"The architect would be pleased to hear you ask that," he replied, setting down his paintbrush and standing up. "Come this way."

Suddenly conscious of every grain of sand under my feet, I struggled as best I could to follow him. He strolled over to a section of sheer canyon hillside, pulled aside a possibly artificial bush, and pointed to a small opening in the rock. "After you, Nick."

Handing him the rapidly diminishing joint, I got down on my hands and knees, and crawled through the narrow opening. My host followed sans spliff. To my amazement, we were standing in a small but expensively furnished cave, illuminated by slender skylights disguised as natural fissures in the rock. Only a high-priced professional decorator, I suspected, would have dared to employ that much faux leopard skin upholstery. Even the lamp-shades matched.

"Paul, you live in a cave. How quaint!"

"Well, Nick, like a lot of things in this town it's fake."

"But so convincing!"

And what an ideal hideout from the cops.

7:52 p.m. I spent the afternoon passed out on Paul and Lacey's narrow daybed—the only sleeping accommodations in their tiny one-room designer cave. The two must do an inordinate amount of intimate cuddling—no doubt a wonderful pastime, but how does Paul ever get any rest? When I came to, Lacey (more gorgeous than ever) had returned from her job as hair stylist to the stars and was dishing up delicious-smelling takeout from a half-dozen paper cartons.

"Hi, Nickie!" she exclaimed, pressing herself to me as if intending to impart a chest rubbing on my shirt. "Long time no see, guy!"

"Except on TV," added Paul.

"Yeah, Nickie," she sighed. "Sorry about your misunderstanding with the cops."

Virtually speechless, I mumbled something in reply. Nothing gooses the nervous system like a hug from Dad's old girlfriend. She inspected my head.

"What's happened to your hair, Nickie? If I didn't know better, I'd say you'd been wearing a wig—for months."

How did she guess? "Uh, it must be from my baseball cap. What's for dinner?"

"It's totally Thai!" she replied. "Let's eat."

We dove in. I was famished.

"I love your cave, Lacey," I said.

"Thanks, Nickie," she replied. "We're only here temporarily. The Krusinowskis don't use their pool much in the winter, so they're letting us rent the cabana for a few months until we get settled. I get a little claustrophobic in here sometimes. Paulie, it's still nice out. How about some fresh air?"

"Sure, love." Paul pressed a red button next to a light switch. The entire front wall of the cave split apart and motored back, revealing a stunning view of the underwater-illuminated pool and the lights of the city twinkling in the distance.

"Too much," I exclaimed. "This Mr. Krusinowski must have money to burn. What is he—a bigshot movie producer?"

"Not exactly," replied Paul. "He manufactures truck springs in Hawthorne."

"I cut all of the Krusinowskis' hair," Lacey noted proudly. "They love my work."

"Who was that Asian woman who answered the door?" I asked.

"That would be Connie Krusinowski, their daughter," replied Lacey. "Lovely little thing. Cute figure now too. She has major hots for Paulie."

"She's just a kid," laughed Paul.

"Paulie, she's 18. That makes her one year younger than me. And, Nick, she's not Asian, she's Polish."

"I don't think so," I said. "The person I saw was Asian—maybe Korean. She had straight black hair and an accent too."

"If you ask me the accent's a bit much," observed Lacey. "But Connie never does anything halfway."

Sensing my confusion, Paul filled me in, "Plastic surgery, Nick. It's one of the major industries down here."

"Lots of girls want to look Asian now," explained Lacey. "It's a very popular look. And almost everyone's been augmented. I hate it because people look at me and just assume I went way overboard. But I'm totally natural. Can I help it if I was built this way?"

Well, I could see how a certain skepticism on that point might be excused.

FRIDAY, March 12 — My first night in a cave, where our early ancestors dwelt for eons during the first great vogue for leopard fur. After performing my bedtime ablutions in the cabana's lilliputian bathroom, I set up my air mattress and sleeping bag in an adjoining cave that houses the pool filter machinery and heater. Pretty cozy, if you don't mind moderate chlorine poisoning. I'm hoping the caustic fumes will prove beneficial to my skin.

When I emerged from my lair this morning, Connie Krusinow-ski in jade-green pajamas was paddling about the pool in the inflatable gondola. She steered its lofty prow in my direction and studied me with her great almond-shaped eyes—one brown, one blue.

"Hello," I said, feeling a bit like a trespasser. "Nice morning for a row."

"My eyes. They do not match."

"Oh really? I hadn't noticed," I lied.

"My contact lens. It has fallen into the water."

"Well, accidents can happen. I'm, uh, Nick. We met yesterday. I'm staying with Paul and Lacey. You have a very nice place here."

"I am a stranger in Venice. The secret ways of the canals are known only to Paulo, my brave gondolier. Where is Paulo?"

"Paulo Saunders? I was just going to crawl into his grotto to see if anyone was awake."

"Tell Paulo that a lady awaits. Tell him that the rising wind bears the scent of the sea."

Not quite. I recognized that aroma. Someone in a nearby cave was frying bacon.

10:47 a.m. After a hearty breakfast, Lacey departed for work, I washed the dishes in the toy-like sink, and Paulo rowed his flirting, half-dressed passenger around the pool. Since it was too late in the morning to reach Sheeni (or Fuzzy) at home, I dialed my sister on the cabana's faux granite phone for an emergency update. Joanie would be out of town attending flights until Sunday, reported her adulterous live-in boyfriend, Dr. Philip Dindy, PhD.

"Are you planning on making her work all through her pregnancy?" I inquired.

"I was not aware that Joan has divulged any such status to you," replied the chinless hairsplitter. "And besides, what possible business could that be to a juvenile delinquent like you?" Click.

François reminds me that it may be time to add homicide to my rap sheet.

6:35 p.m. I had a pleasant day helping Paul on his rounds. We toured through the most exclusive westside neighborhoods in Paul's ratty old Nissan pickup, stopping at one fabulous home after another to waltz right into the backyard and clean the pool. Paul was very nice about showing me the tricks of his trade. He thinks it's important for us artsy types to have some marketable skill to fall back on while we're waiting for the world to recognize our genius. He's a musician, but he recommends pool-cleaning for writers too. For example, he pointed out that it would be an easy matter to sneak your screenplay into the stack by the pool. Then, who knows, somebody influential might actually read it.

Best of all, being a pool-cleaning slave is pretty easy. It's a simple matter of sweeping out the crud, checking the filter, and tossing in some toxics. And you might get lucky and find a diamond earring or two amid the disgusting muck in the filter. You also get to chat up Beautiful People, some of whom may be reclining by their pool in a state of near undress. We encountered one such sun-worshiper today in Brentwood. Pretty cool, but let's face it: Once you've been the attendant in a high-school girls' locker room, the sight of a leathery middle-aged woman with her top off is not that big of a deal.

On the way back to Bel Air we stopped for groceries and birthday cards for Sheeni. I hope mine reaches her in time. No time to shop for a gift, but at least I have shown my regard by wiring $689,000 into her personal account. If that's not love, I don't know what is.

7:05 p.m. Someone has searched through all my stuff! I went into the pool-filter cave to change my shirt, and discovered my backpack was not as I had left it. Everything had been gone through, but nothing appeared to be missing. I counted my backpack emergency stash—all $3,000 was still there. My laptop also had been tampered with, but its contents are protected by a password. If the FBI is on to me, why don't they just move in for the arrest? Or do they first prefer to induce acute paranoia in their victims?

10:20 p.m. After trying for hours, I finally reached Sheeni at home. So far My Love has seen no signs of the feds, but she reported that two Ukiah cops had a long conference today with Miss Pomdreck in her office.

"Damn, maybe they're checking into that $5,000 check from Carlotta."

"Could be, Nickie. You know bribes really should be paid in cash."

"I'll remember that next time, darling. How are Trent and Apurva?"

"They're still at your house, Nickie. They were astounded by Carlotta's sudden disappearance. The whole school is buzzing with rumors about you. No yellow ribbons this time though. Sorry, Carlotta, you just weren't that popular. Oh, and Trent told me he hopes Carlotta was not offended by his father's rudeness."

"Well, Mr. Preston was rather brusque. Is Trent back in school?"

"He's back—and with Apurva. They're such dreadful role models. All the couples going steady want to get married now. Candy Pringle is researching package deals on flights to Mississippi."

"We could go too, Sheeni. Your brother says he can help me get a fake ID. And you'll be legally old enough in a few days."

"Don't make me barf!"

Crestfallen as usual, I moved on.

"Sheeni, did you get my money?"

"It's safe, Nickie. It's totally untouchable. And don't worry. I searched your house to make sure you didn't leave behind anything incriminating."

"You broke into my house? When?"

"This morning. I cut physics class. And I didn't break in; I used my key."

"I suppose you also snooped through Trent and Apurva's things."

"I may have. That woman has no style at all. She wears cotton underwear from Kmart—with polka dots! I can't believe Trent fell for her."

"Sheeni, they're married."

"Well, they are until they run out of money. I don't think the parents are planning on supporting them."

Damn. More parental disappointments for Nick—and they're not even my parents.

"Yes, Dolores, the wolf may soon be at the door. Sorry, I have to go now."

Clearly, one of Sheeni's jailer parents had entered the room.

"Sheeni, darling, I love you."

"Ta-ta, Dolores. Do keep in touch."

More worries. I think it's a very bad sign that My Love is violating Trent's privacy. A very bad sign!

SATURDAY, March 13 — Another glorious day in La-La Land. When I emerged from my den, Connie Krusinowski was traipsing down the path in an off-the-shoulder silk kimono.

"Hi, Nick," she said, dumping an armful of plush towels on a large flat rock.

"Oh, hi, Connie."

Both eyes were brown this morning. The exotic accent and aloof manner had disappeared.

"Want to take a hot tub with me?"

"Sure, Connie. But I don't see a tub anywhere."

"You're not supposed to, silly." Connie touched the rock with her toe. A motor energized, and the rock swiveled aside to reveal an inviting pool of steaming hot water. Connie slipped off her robe and stepped into the bubbling water. Spectacularly well-developed, she was blonde from the waist down. I hastily shed my clothes and unbuckled my money belt (advertised as "waterproof," but I decided not to chance it). Due to circumstances beyond my control, I was obliged to enter the pool with my back to her. She didn't seem to mind.

"You know how many calories I had yesterday, Nick?" she asked, bouncing up and down in the whirlpool jets. "Six! I ate one black olive."

"That's very commendable, Connie. Are you on a diet?"

"I'm always on a diet, Nick. I have a 19-inch waist. I'm much thinner than that fat cow Lacey. Do you like my breasts?"

François felt a candid response was called for here. "I do, yes. They're very nice."

"They should be. They cost $6,800. Dr. Rudolpho is such a genius. Of course, it's always good to get a second opinion—even if you are just a horny teenage boy. I saw you on TV last week."

"Oh?"

"I think we may be kindred spirits because your life is even more of a mess than mine. And we're both terribly in love with members of the Saunders family."

"So you were the snoop who went through my stuff!"

"I had to, Nick. I'll do anything to win Paulo's love. Just as you would walk over flaming hot coals for his sister Sheeni."

"Yes, I suppose I would. Is that why you became Asian?"

"Uh-huh. I read in a magazine that all Caucasian men are fascinated by Oriental women. What do you think?"

"I think you're pretty fascinating."

"Thanks, Nick. And thanks for the flattering erection. I just wish Paulo felt the same. Why do you suppose he's so stuck on Lacey?"

"Well, she's beautiful, outgoing, fun to be with, refreshingly unaffected . . ."

"Unaffected, huh? Now there's an overrated quality!"

3:45 p.m. On my way to East Los Angeles with Paul after lunch I mailed a letter to Trent. It contained one sheet of brown paper (blank) wrapped around ten crisp $100 bills. That should keep the newlyweds in groceries for a while. I only wish some anonymous donor would underwrite my future marriage to you know who.

After dropping in on a musician pal, Paul drove me to meet Mr. Castillo, the document specialist. He was a friendly white-haired man who conducts his business out of a single-car garage behind his modest stucco house.

"A new identity," he said, wetting his pencil. "Making a fresh start. That's nice. And what name have you decided on?"

"Nick Dillinger," I replied, spelling it out for him.

"How about a nice middle name too? No extra charge."

Sure, why not? "OK, uh, Sinatra."

"A man with musical taste," Mr. Castillo commented approvingly to Paul. "And how old would Mr. Nick Sinatra Dillinger like to be?"

I replied without hesitation, "Eighteen."

"Eighteen. A very nice age. Me, I would like to be 35, but 18 will look very good on you—especially in a few years. And what birthday would you like? We have 365 to choose from."

"December 12." If it was good enough for Frank, it's good enough for me.

"Very nice, Nick. Not too close to Christmas, but in the holiday spirit. We'll have your driver's license ready in two days. That will be $200 in advance."

"Two hundred dollars?" I asked, shocked. "That seems like a lot of money for a fake ID."

"There's nothing fake about it," Mr. Castillo replied, smiling.

"All of our materials come straight from the DMV. The governor himself couldn't tell the difference. And what else will you be needing? A birth certificate? A Social Security card? Maybe a nice U.S. passport so you can visit all those Dillingers back in the old country?"

Mr. Castillo talked me into the whole package for an even grand. I fished the hundreds from my money belt, he snapped a couple of instant photos with an oversized camera, shook my hand, and said, "Welcome to America, Mr. Dillinger."

What a relief. May I never hear that despised name Twisp ever again!

11:30 p.m. Since Paul and Lacey are being so nice in letting me hide out in their cave, I made dinner again (a streamlined version of Mrs. Ferguson's famous Okie pot roast). The petite cabana kitchen is a challenge: just a two-burner hotplate and a microwave. Still, I didn't hear any complaints from my hosts. After washing up, I accepted an invitation from Connie to go hear Paul and his new trio at a small club out in the Valley. Her flashy red Mercedes convertible roadster only seats two, so the invitation wasn't extended to Lacey, who was dead on her feet anyway from having spent the entire afternoon giving Brad Pitt's executive assistant a total makeover.

On the drive out to the Valley I filled in Connie on the events of the past few weeks.

"Sounds good, Nick," she said, powering her fabulous rod through a red light. "The way I see it you only made two crucial blunders."

"What?" I demanded, alarmed.

"Number one: You got Trent married."

"But that was the whole point!"

"So you say. Nick, my Paulo is very intelligent. Is your Sheeni smart?"

"She has enough brains for 12 normal people."

"Paulo too. OK, you know what he says? He says people only want what they cannot have."

"That sounds rather defeatist."

"Maybe, but there's a lot of truth in it. First Sheeni had Trent and then she dumped him. She didn't want him anymore. So you go and get the guy married to Apurva. Now—boom—he's someone she cannot have."

"That's right," I affirmed, "because he's married."

"That doesn't stop anyone, Nick. You think I would stop throwing myself at Paulo if—God forbid—he should marry Lacey? A marriage license is just more gasoline on the flames."

"I don't know if I agree with any of that, Connie."

"Nick, you're a clever guy, but really you should run these schemes by a woman first. It's a good thing you met me."

"OK," I sighed. "What was my other blunder?"

"Giving Sheeni all your money."

"But she's only safeguarding it for me temporarily."

"Uh-huh. Nick, would it come as a surprise to you if I told you that women are attracted to men with money?"

"I suppose not."

"That's right. It's because we're looking for good providers—guys who can take care of all the children we're probably not going to have."

"But you're attracted to Paul. He's not rich."

"I can afford an artsy intellectual, Nick. I'm already loaded. I know my babies aren't going to starve."

"Oh, right."

"So in Sheeni's mind you've just gone from being a lover with money to a leech without money. From being an asset to a liability. Now she has this big problem: you want your money back."

"You're damn right I do."

"Good luck, Nick. You're going to need it."

The club was a small Van Nuys storefront that had been

remodeled (with sledgehammers and wrecking bars?) into an intimate jazz venue. I was too upset by what Connie had said to pay much attention to the music, which was complex, cerebral, intense, discursive—everything except engaging. But the sparse audience of trendy Valley jazzophiles dug it in their laid-back way. Paul blew his horn, a thin black man massaged the electric piano, an older fellow with a goatee achieved cosmic fusion with his drums, and François gulped down three glasses of an expensive merlot procured through the force of Connie's glamorous charisma. Bill Gates should tip like she does. My spirits revived slightly on the ride home when my driver let François nuzzle her perfumed ear.

"More proof of Paulo's theory," she commented. "Nick, you want me because you cannot have me."

"Hardly," I slurred. "I want you because I am drunk, miserable, lonely, and sought by every police jurisdiction in the state."

"You're kinda cute, Nick. But I'm not into incest."

"How do you figure that?"

"Do the calculations, guy. If all goes as we hope, you'll soon be my brother-in-law."

I suppose she's right, but it sure didn't feel like a sister's ear that François was nibbling.

SUNDAY, March 14 — By the time I crawled out of my sleeping bag everyone had departed for parts unknown. Not even a donut in sight. I wandered out into the blazing sunshine, and found the hot tub occupied by a stocky middle-aged bald guy exhibiting nearly as much body hair as my pal Fuzzy. He didn't seem surprised to see me.

"Hi, Nick," he said. "The water's a perfect 104 degrees. Hop in, kid."

"OK." I shed my clothes and slipped into the swirling water. It felt good, though I hoped I wouldn't turn the same color of well-done corned-beef as my companion's barrel chest and protruding gut.

"I'm Bernard Krusinowski," he said, extending a meaty paw. "Call me Bernie."

I shook his hand. "Nick Twi—uh, Dillinger."

"Well, Nick, what do you think of my little patch of paradise?"

"It's very nice, uh, Bernie. It's the nicest pool I've ever seen."

"Would you believe six years ago this was just a washed-out ravine?"

"No way could I believe that."

"Your sister is a beautiful woman, Nick."

I was confused. Was he talking about a Twisp? "Oh, do you know Joanie?"

"Who's Joanie? I'm talking about Lacey. Connie told me you're visiting your sister for a while."

"Oh, right."

"So how come her name isn't Dillinger? I understood she's never been married."

"Uh, she's my half-sister," I lied. "We have different fathers."

"She's just about the most beautiful gal I've ever seen. Gives a mean haircut too, if you don't mind having a professional barber touch things up later. 'Course, my wife Rita likes her too. Thinks she's a mighty nice gal. Respects her a lot. You won't find Lacey hopping into hot tubs with just anybody. I've invited her myself. Just joking around, of course. Turned me down flat. Now I got her brother instead. Can't see much of a family resemblance though. What do you think of my daughter?"

"Uh, she's very nice."

"Got a wild streak in her," he winked. "Just like her dad. Thought her mother was going to die when Connie came back from Mexico looking like a Chinese laundry girl. I told her don't worry, the grandkids will still come out Polish. Yep, she's a wild one."

"She's wild all right," I laughed.

A coarse wet hand locked onto my arm. "Just stay out of her pants, fella," he hissed. "And no more hopping buck naked into this hot tub with her."

I gulped. "Oh, OK, Mr. Krusinowski."

He unclamped my arm and smiled. "Call me Bernie, Nick. Call me Bernie."

11:30 a.m. After exiting the tub as gracefully as I could, I hid out in the cave until Paul and Lacey returned with breakfast croissants and the Sunday Times. I alerted them that their landlord was now under the impression that Lacey and I were related.

"Isn't he the sweetest guy?" asked Lacey. "All those millions, but so down-to-earth. He treats us just like family."

"You especially, dearest, he would enjoy treating like family," remarked Paul, reading the entertainment section.

Lacey ruffled my hair. "Paulie's jealous, Nick. He hates the idea of being possessive, but he's just as bad as the rest of you fellows. Of course, all he has to do is ask me to marry him."

"Don't make me barf," replied Paul, turning the page.

Boy, those Saunders kids sure bring a lot of enthusiasm to any discussion of marriage. And their parents haven't even gone through an ugly, soul-searing divorce.

2:30 p.m. Speaking of body hair, I just made a long-distance call to the reigning North American Junior Champion.

"Nick! Where are you?" Fuzzy exclaimed. "It's like you just disappeared into thin air."

"I had to cut out, Frank. Somebody ratted on me to the FBI."

"Damn, Nick. So that's why the cops were at school on Friday. I thought maybe they were after Bruno for finking out on his public service. Where are you?"

"I better not say, Frank, in case your phone line is tapped. I'm safe for now though. Have you seen any cops around my house?"

"Just Bruno snooping as usual. He better not mess with Apurva, or Trent will deck him. They moved in, you know."

"I know. Will your parents kick them out?"

"Nah, my dad golfs with Trent's dad, and I hear they worked something out. Lana thinks it's pretty cool they got married. They're having sex every single night and there's not a damn thing their parents can do about it."

"How's it going with Lana?"

"Great. I'm already up to base two-and-a-half. You're right, Nick, she's one hot tamale."

"What's the half base?"

"Well, I almost got to third base, but she was wearing a sanitary napkin."

"God, Frank, that's gross."

"I know, Nick, but I was totally high at the time. Lana gets the most awesome weed. Don't spread it around, but I think her father may be a grower."

"What makes you say that?"

"Well, she lives way out in the boonies, she's totally mum on the subject, and she's incredibly well-supplied."

"Frank, I may have found you the world's ultimate girl-friend."

"I know, Nick. If she was beautiful, I'd already be saving up for our tickets to Mississippi."

3:45 p.m. Sheeni just phoned while I was killing time by the pool until Paul and Lacey finished their "nap" in the cave. I took the call on a weather-resistant cordless phone disguised to look like a native succulent.

"Nickie, I have shocking news!"

Instant circulatory arrest.

"What's happened?" I gasped.

"I just found out from Vijay: Trent has resigned from the swim team!"

Alarm waned, confusion waxed. "So?"

"So he was the best swimmer on the team. It's a disaster for Redwood High."

"Sheeni, as I recall you have no school spirit and zero interest in athletics. Why do you care what happens to the swim team?"

"It's all that Apurva's fault. She's ruining his life. He's had to get an after-school job! He's going to be lugging bags of concrete for Fuzzy DeFalco's mafioso father."

"Well, hard work never hurt anybody."

"Nickie, you sound just like a Republican. Trent should be devoting his free time to the further enrichment of his extraordinary mind. This precipitous and premature marriage is a fiasco."

Confusion waned, alarm rewaxed. "Sheeni, quitting the swim team is a small price to pay for a fulfilling marriage with the woman he loves. Trent and Apurva are very happy. You shouldn't interfere."

"Who says I'm interfering? And how do you know they're happy? As I recall, you're 600 miles away."

"Sheeni, darling, you have to accept that they're married. Apurva may already be expecting."

"I don't believe that for a second. Trent was always very careful when—"

"When what?" I demanded.

"Well, he's always been a sensible person . . . when driving, for example."

Yeah, right. Time to change the subject.

"Sheeni, have you set up an account yet for me with your bank?"

"Of course not, Nick. You have to do that yourself. I could request that they mail the paperwork to you, if you like."

"Sheeni, maybe you should just send me a check for the full amount."

"Don't be silly, Nickie. How would you ever cash it? Your money's safe. I'll make sure you get all the interest. Don't you trust me?"

I certainly want to, darling. But so far everything that Connie warned me about seems to be coming true.

9:15 p.m. Connie took me out for dinner at a restaurant on Santa Monica Boulevard that was so exclusive it had no sign, an unlisted phone number, and you had to sneak into it from the loading dock of an appliance store. Needless to say, it was jammed with L.A.'s Celebrity Elite, but Connie managed to secure us a nice table in a prime corner. If that wasn't Tom Cruise dining at the table next to ours, it was his studio stand-in.

"Nick, do try to look older," she said, after our snotty waiter refused to bring her the wine list. "I feel like I'm dining with a child star." Both eyes were dark and her accent was back.

"I haven't shaved for four days," I pointed out. "I think I'm starting to look like Don Johnson."

"More like Donna Johnson," she replied, scanning the menu.

I let her order for both of us; the menu prices had momentarily paralyzed my vocal cords. When I recovered, I recounted this morning's hot-tub run-in with her father.

"Don't worry about Daddy, Nick. He always feels a need to intimidate any male who ventures onto on his property. It's an alpha dog territorial thing. You're lucky he didn't piss on your leg."

"But how did he know we were in the hot tub together? You can't see it from your house."

"Oh, he probably looked at the videos."

"What videos?"

"There are security cameras concealed all over the grounds, Nick.

Daddy likes to review the tapes. I think he's hoping to spot Lacey in the hot tub. But she always wears a bathing suit—the prude."

"You don't mind your father looking at you naked?"

"Why should I, Nick? He used to change my diapers."

"Yeah, I guess."

Still, I wouldn't want my mother ogling me in the buff—especially if I had recently undergone successful augmentation surgery. After I scarfed down my appetizer—two tiny, oddly fragrant pancakes—my companion informed me that they contained the ground-up thoraxes of a giant Yucatan beetle. Yuck, and no wine to wash it down with either. I chugged some of my pricey Swiss sparkling water.

After ascertaining that my entrée was indeed salmon, I asked Connie if she thought her dad was really interested in Lacey.

"I certainly hope so, Nick. Why else do you think I invited those two to come live in the pool cabana?"

"I thought it was so you could heave yourself at Paul."

"Only partly. My larger task is to dislodge Lacey from his ridiculously small bed. And who better to appeal to Lacey's maternal materialism than my wealthy father?"

I was stunned. "Connie, you mean to say you'd break up your parents' marriage to win Paul?"

"Certainly, Nick. Let's face it: My father has reached that age when successful men turn into slobbering bimbo bait. He's exhibiting all the symptoms. OK, if he's destined to make a fool of himself with a younger woman, it might as well be with Lacey. Then, voila, I grab Paulo on the rebound."

"But what about your mother?"

"My mother is a big girl, Nick. She can take care of herself. Believe me, you would not want to meet her lawyers in a dark alley."

• • •

MONDAY, March 15 — The Ides of March (whatever that means) and My Love's fifteenth birthday. Just think, this is the second year of her life in which she has had the pleasure of knowing me. Ours is now a passion with history and depth. If she comes to her senses and we get married this year, she'll be a spry and shapely 65 when we celebrate our Golden Wedding anniversary. By then science will have tinkered around with human genes so we won't be wrinkled and decrepit. I may be making love to Sheeni at the age of 200! Every 50 years we'll have to invite our prestigious friends over for a really big anniversary bash.

To celebrate this momentous day, I decided to defy Connie's alpha-dog dad and share a hot tub again with his nubile daughter. Sheeni, I wish it was your own naked body beside me in the bubbling foam.

"You're still not thinking of me as a sister," commented Connie, observing my underwater promontories. Both eyes were sparkling blue; her accent was taking the morning off.

"It's just that I've never seen a blue-eyed Asian before."

"Damn, I forgot my contacts again. I'm always doing that. It drives the Chinese guys wild at the CIA."

Connie is not a spy. She's a sometime student at the California Institute of the Arts. Not to worry. The fellow student she pays to take detailed lecture notes and write her term papers never misses a class.

"Did I tell you I was thinking of becoming a Negro?" I asked.

"No, Nick, you didn't," she replied, glancing down. "And I'm not sure you're equipped for the job."

I decided to overlook that slur against my manhood.

"I've been discussing it with Paul and Lacey. It looks like it's my only option if I want to go back and be with Sheeni."

"She has a thing for black guys?"

"No, but I can't go back as a woman again. And I can't think of any other disguise that would fool people. Lacey's offered to dye my hair and give me a permanent. Paul says I can darken my skin by soaking in a bath of walnut husks."

"Nick, there's more to being black than being brown."

"I know, Connie, but I did grow up in Oakland. I can sound black. I spent years listening to rap."

"When did you ever listen to rap?"

"Constantly. It was always being blasted out of passing cars."

"I thought so. It's a good thing you met me, Nick. So I can save you from your own stupidity."

"What's wrong with that idea?"

"Just this: Black people are always getting stopped by the police. They're a magnet for cops. You'd be locked up within a week."

Damn, she's right.

4:38 p.m. I know we've been indoctrinated to look down on high-school dropouts, but their academics-free lifestyle may be getting a bum rap. Instead of cramming my brain with arcane facts about the hydrogen atom, I spent another pleasant day driving around and cleaning pools with Paul. We shared a joint in the Hollywood Hills with a sun-loving starlet wedged into a bikini that looked like it had been made-over from a Barbie doll costume. She confided that she had spent well over $8,000 on high-visibility electrolysis—another occupation to consider if I don't make it as an alcoholic fiction writer.

I'm now an officially licensed 18-year-old! I am now of legal age to drive a car, vote, join the Marines, or marry the woman of my choice. What a relief to skip those middle adolescent years—a painful and confusing time, I'm told, for so many teens. Mr. Castillo did a beautiful job validating the existence and citizenship of Nick S. Dillinger. The hologram on my driver's license is flawless. I love flipping open my wallet to gaze upon my new ID. It even has the little pink sticker in the corner advising authorities they may harvest my organs should I perish in a car wreck or (more likely) in a hail of police bullets. I feel like I've finally put my sordid origins behind me, having at last achieved a new, more suitable identity. I almost didn't recognize that upbeat feeling when I pocketed my new documentation. Hey, it's called positive self-esteem!

6:25 p.m. Amazing news, diary! I just checked in with my sister Joanie. Mario hasn't ratted on me to the FBI! Apparently he's concerned that my arrest might invalidate their design copyrights on the Wart Watch and Footborghinis (still in prototype stage). Kimberly's seen the light too. (More proof that money talks.) All this stress on my nervous system was for nothing! Joanie got the good news last Friday and left the details with Dr. Dingy to relay to me in case I called. But somehow my reprieve must have slipped her asshole boyfriend's mind. If she ever decides to marry that turkey (assuming he divorces his present wife), she better not expect me at the wedding.

The bad news is I have to go back to being Carlotta. And just when I thought I had donned my last unflattering brassiere. Long years of leg shaving and boner stifling may loom ahead. Too bad I tossed all her stuff out the bus window. But it may be time for a Carlotta Ulansky image makeover. Connie has offered to take me shopping tomorrow on Rodeo Drive.

8:10 p.m. Something has gone horribly awry. I just dialed My Love to wish her happy birthday and tell her the good news. When Sheeni's 5,000-year-old mother answered the phone, I switched to Carlotta's bubbliest voice.

"Hi, Mrs. Saunders. Sorry I missed church yesterday. Is Sheeni home?"

"Liar!" she screamed. "Voice of Satan! God will strike you dead, Nick Twisp!" Click.

The biggest earthquake yet just rumbled through my scrotum: a brutal 9.7 on the Richter scale.

• • •

TUESDAY, March 16 — After a miserable night, I awoke feeling like a hair ball in the hot-tub drain. It doesn't add up. Where did I go wrong? Too on edge to eat anything. I've strapped on my money belt and loaded up my backpack. I am now ready for instant flight to God knows where.

10:45 a.m. I couldn't take the suspense any longer. I dialed Redwood High in Ukiah and asked to speak to freshman honor student Sheeni Saunders. The secretary said Sheeni couldn't come to the phone because she had just been taken down to the Ukiah police station. More violent internal organ convulsing. I composed myself and asked to speak to Frank DeFalco instead.

"Who is this?" demanded the secretary, suddenly suspicious.

"Polonius DeFalco," I replied calmly. "I wish to inform my nephew of a tragic death in the family."

The secretary hurried off to hunt for Fuzzy. After a nearly interminable wait, my pal came on the line.

"Uncle Polly?"

"Frank, it's me, Nick. Your uncle Polly croaked, remember?"

"Yeah, I figured it was you. Thanks a pantsful, dickhead."

"Frank, what's the matter?"

"I'll tell you what's the matter. The whole school knows I took a chick to the Christmas dance. How am I supposed to explain that to Lana? And guess what? Bruno Modjaleski is looking to pound your ass. I told you to back off on making out with that guy. And all the girls in Lana's gym class are totally out for your blood. They had to bring in counselors for some of them. And Elbowgash is screaming for your scalp."

"Frank, how did the cops find out about me?"

"How should I know? They raided your house early this morning. Trent and Apurva had to show them their marriage license.

Boy, were those two spooked. I think Trent wants to pound your puny ass too."

"Have the cops talked to you?"

"Not yet, but everyone knows I was tight with Carlotta. If they drag me downtown, dude, I'm spilling my guts."

"Frank, you don't have to tell them anything."

"That's what you think. My parents are going to kill me."

"Frank, if you say anything, I'll have no choice but to squeal about Lana's dad being a grower. Don't think your girlfriend won't know where I got the information."

"You're scum, Nick. You're total slime."

"I'm your best friend, Frank. We have to stick together. Don't worry, I'll make it all up to you."

"How?"

"Financially, Frank. Remember, I'm loaded. If you see Sheeni, tell her to call me right away."

"OK, Nick," he sighed. "See you in jail. Maybe they'll stick us in the same cell. Right before they give you the chair!"

Fuzzy had better keep his furry lips zipped. If he blabs to the cops that I'm responsible for the Geezer virus, Dad may be on the hook for several hundred million dollars in computer damages. And I'll be looking at another five years in federal prison.

3:45 p.m. I'm a nervous wreck. I stayed home and hid out in the cave all day. Nothing to keep my mind off my troubles except snooping through Paul and Lacey's personal stuff. Lacey's on the pill (no condoms for lucky Paul), her reading tastes run to boring hair styling magazines, and she owes nearly $12,000 on her credit cards. Paul's few possessions (mostly clothes and music scores) wouldn't fill one suitcase. The guy sure travels light. I found an intriguing photo of Paul as a kid pushing a cute toddler in a stroller. This was written in green ink on the back: "Paul and Sheridan at Oroville Dam." Sheeni's real name is Sheridan! What a revelation to discover that one is passionately in love with a person named Sheridan who once toured dams in a pink sunsuit and bonnet. But how come My Love doesn't go by the name Sherry?

5:15 p.m. No answer at Fuzzy's house. Damn. I tried not to imagine zealous detectives working him over with rubber hoses. As an experiment in masochism I punched in Carlotta's old number. The man of the house answered.

"Hi, Trent," I found myself saying.

"Hi, Nick," he replied calmly.

"I'm surprised you recognize my voice."

"How could I ever forget it?"

I had no idea what to say next.

"How's it going with you, Trent?"

"Not bad. Thanks for the thousand bucks."

"It was an anonymous gift, Trent. It may not have come from me. How's Apurva?"

"She's a bit disturbed by your duplicity, Nick. You really are quite a remarkable liar."

"Well, I do what it takes to get by. Are you getting a divorce?"

No answer.

"Sorry if that was too personal a question."

Still no reply.

"Uh, how's the poetry going, Trent? Written any new poems?"

"Nick, I realize, of course, that all of your actions toward us were undertaken with a malevolent intent, but I would just like to say one thing."

"What's that?"

"Thank you."

"Beg your pardon?"

"I'm very happy to be married to Apurva—despite all the grief of the past few days. It's brought us immeasurably closer. Inexplicably, we owe our happiness to you, Nick Twisp."

"Why thanks, Trent," I replied, sincerely touched. "It's very big of you to admit that."

"And I'd just like to say one more thing, Nick."

"Yes, Trent?"

"I hope the cops nail your sorry butt. And throw you in jail for a long, long time." Click.

Guess the guy's still pissed I turned down his invitation to the Christmas dance.

10:45 p.m. Bravely defying parental strictures, My Love sneaked out of her house and called me at last.

"Sheeni! Did you tell the cops I'm hiding out at your brother's?"

"Of course not, Nickie. I divulged as little as possible. Father was there the whole time as my lawyer. The cops were tiresomely persistent, but I merely stated that I became aware of Carlotta's true identity after Vijay revealed to me that Nick Twisp knew about Apurva's wedding, which only Carlotta had attended. I said I had no idea where you'd gone. My parents aren't buying any of that, but they don't want me to get in too much trouble as an accessory to your many and diverse crimes. Nickie, they've slashed my allowance! And grounded me for months!"

I tried to sound sympathetic. "Uh, that's a shame, darling. What else did the cops ask you?"

"Well, they pestered me about Carlotta's house and who I saw there and who your friends were. Oh, and they were very interested in knowing what you'd been living on—especially this obnoxious cop from Oakland."

"That would be Lance, my demonic stepfather. What did you say?"

"I said I heard that you'd been playing the stock market."

"Quick thinking, darling. Did the cops tell you how they got wise to me?" I told her about Mario's decision to remain clammed.

My Love sounded stunned. "Nickie, why didn't you call Mario in the first place?"

"I didn't see the point. From the way my sister talked, it sounded like he'd already squealed. And squealing seemed just like something Mario would do. Besides, I was afraid the cops might be setting a trap for me by monitoring his phone line."

"Oh, Nickie, this is awful!"

An appalling realization dawned.

"Sheeni! It was you!"

"Nickie, I was petrified! And it was my birthday. I thought surely on my birthday my parents would have to extend at least a measure of leniency. I mean, what better day to make a ghastly confession—especially with the authorities apparently closing in."

"Oh, Sheeni, you didn't . . . "

"I'm sorry, Nickie. Can you ever forgive me?"

"I, I suppose it's not really your fault. I'll just have to murder my sister's boyfriend. He knew on Friday, but never bothered to tell me."

"Nickie, I have to go. If my parents discover my absence, their acharnement will be insuppressible."

"Sheeni, I love you!"

"Nickie, I . . . I . . ."

My heart leaped. "Yes, Sherry, darling?"

"Never call me that name! I hate it!" Click.

A bewildering response, but at least one mystery is resolved. Do you suppose under similar circumstances I might have ratted on Sheeni? I've been considering that question from every angle, and I keep coming to the same conclusion: Not in ten million years.

WEDNESDAY, March 17 — Connie took me out for breakfast at a place in West Hollywood that was famous for its pancake portraits of the stars. I had a full stack of Meryl Streeps; Connie nibbled her one piece of unbuttered toast while I filled her in on yesterday's conversation with Paulo's sister.

"I'm glad to see evidence of such ruthlessness in a Saunders," she commented. "It's very reassuring. I was beginning to worry that my children with Paulo might come out too serene for their own good."

"What's that supposed to mean?" I demanded.

"Nick, sweetie, your Sheeni dimed you to the cops to keep your money."

"She did no such thing. She merely confessed to her parents and they called the police."

"It amounts to the same thing. Did she say anything about giving your money back?"

"Er, no. The conversation was necessarily abbreviated."

10:05 a.m. WE'VE BEEN RAIDED BY THE COPS! I had my stuff ready and was waiting by the pool when Connie came flying down the path in a state of semi-undressed panic.

"Two cop cars, Nick! They just pulled into the drive. Quick, you've got to hide!"

I darted toward the cave, but Connie grabbed me by my shirt.

"Not in the cabana, Nick! It's too well known. Didn't you see it last summer in Architectural Digest? Here!"

She pushed me into the hot tub, told me to duck, and swiveled the rock-cover closed. I was plunged into an all-encompassing steamy darkness. The heat was so overwhelming I couldn't sense if I was entirely underwater. Holding my breath, I whirled around in panic. A tiny pinpoint of sunlight. In its faint glow I could see that beneath the tight-sealing cover was an airspace of several inches. Holding my nose above the scalding water, I took a deep breath as heavy footsteps approached. Muffled male voices. I strained to make out the words, but could only distinguish Connie saying, "Do you handsome fellows have a warrant?"

My heart was pounding, sweat was pouring off my body, but I fought to slow my breathing—I knew that tiny pocket of air could not last long. The insistent heat was unbearable. I felt like a lobster in a pot. Too hot, too hot, too hot—every nerve-ending in my body was telegraphing madly to my brain. I tried to think cool thoughts: ice cream, iced tea, cold showers, frozen shoes, numb toes, Mississippi snowstorms, my father's heart. Minutes, hours went by. Each passing second felt like the last that could be endured. Where was Connie?! Had she forgotten me?! I grew light-headed from the bad air. I knew if I fainted I was done for. I tried to wedge my fingers between the cover and the tub rim for support, but the seal was too tight. Bad air, bad air, bad air—my heaving lungs cried out. Too hot, too hot, too hot. Then a wet shroud of sweltering blackness descended over me.

I came to with the sun in my eyes and something sharp poking me in the back. Sheeni was kissing me. Only it wasn't Sheeni, it was someone else and she wasn't exactly kissing me, she doing something annoying like attempting to blow air into my mouth. I wished she would stop and also stop leaning on me because it just made the rough rocks under my back hurt even more. I pushed her away and struggled to sit up.

"Nick! You're alive!" exclaimed Connie.

"No thanks to you," I muttered, rolling over and expelling several hundred gallons of brackish water.

I knew I would never get in another hot tub. And I seriously doubted if I could ever bring myself to venture anywhere near a bathtub.

12:20 p.m. Los Angeles bus station. Waiting for the bus to San Diego. Things are seriously fucked up. It would have been far less complicated for me simply to have drowned. Turns out the cops weren't looking for me. They nailed Paul this morning in West L.A. for marijuana possession and were raiding his pad to search for Incriminating Evidence. The cops seized my backpack! They poked through my pack, found my $3,000 in emergency road cash, and decided it was drug money. They were going to grab my laptop too, but Connie said it was hers. I guess she couldn't claim the backpack since she doesn't wear boy's underwear.

So now I'm on the run again with just the clothes on my back. Fortunately, I was wearing my money belt, which turns out to be not quite as waterproof as advertised. I now have $17,700 in soggy hundreds, plus a sodden wallet stuffed with sopping fake documentation.

4:47 p.m. On the bus to Ensenada. I'm now in Mexico! I can sort of relax now, assuming you can ever do that in a Third World country. When I reached San Diego, I switched to the Tijuana Trolley for the ride to the border. I admit I was pretty nervous walking through the gate into Mexico, but no one even asked for my ID. You can waltz right into their country and the Mexicans don't even raise an eyebrow! Of course, we gringos stick out like a sore thumb, so it's not like they have a hard time keeping an eye on us.

At the Tijuana bus station I swapped one of my soggy hundreds for a big wad of colorful pesos, and bought a first-class ticket to Ensenada. They have different bus classes down here because theirs is not an egalitarian society, and people of means do not wish to ride with the chickens and the bleating goats. Fortunately, the ticket seller spoke English and understood where I wanted to go. I studied Spanish briefly in the seventh grade due to a scheduling snafu, but all I remember is buenas tardes—and I'm not sure what part of the day you're supposed to say that.

Famous alcoholic fiction writers of the past often journeyed south of the border to soak up local color and get wasted. I'm trying to emulate them and be open to new experiences for my art. My initial impressions of Mexico: lots of dust, not many trees, and are the janitors all out on strike or what? No daycare for peasant toddlers down here. The streets are jammed with brown-skinned tots hustling gum to the tourists. I now have about a six-month supply.

9:15 p.m. As instructed by Connie, I'm now holed up in the Christina Hotel, a modest cinder-block structure in the southern part of Ensenada, one block up from the main road that runs along the harbor (no view though). The Spanish lady (Christina?) in the office wasn't too thrilled about renting a room to someone my age with no luggage and a hunted look in his eyes, but I flashed my fake ID and some real pesos. My room's not bad, except that when I walked in, it smelled like somebody had been having enthusiastic intercourse on the creaky double bed about two minutes before I arrived. I opened some windows to air things out. I have a chair, a wooden table, a small rug on the brown vinyl floor, a TV that mostly works (bad color), a bathroom with rusty metal shower, and the world's smallest kitchenette. The little refrigerator in there runs constantly and sounds like a military helicopter with a bum muffler. It looks like it hasn't been defrosted since way before I was born. I opened a cupboard door under the sink and a gang of tough-looking cockroaches looked up expectantly. I gave them some previously chewed gum to work on in hopes they'll stay put.

After stashing my laptop under the bed, I had a fish taco dinner at a cantina around the corner—all washed down with some strong Mexican beer. Good news—the legal age for drinking down here is 18. It was all I could do to swig down one whole bottle and stagger back to my hotel. I can't believe people drink that stuff by the case.

Ensenada is crawling with blue-haired gringos living it up on their Social Security, so English is spoken widely. The town is bigger than I'd been expecting: a bustling city squeezed between brown scrub-covered mountains and a curving blue bay. A nice place to visit, but would you really want to get a face-lift here?

Now I know how Trent felt before his wedding in Mississippi.

This entire dubious enterprise is taking on a pronounced air of unreality. You meet a girl in a trailer park, and nine months later you're hiding out under an assumed name in a foreign country and waiting to get your face carved up like a slab of meat. How did I ever let Connie talk me into this wacky scheme? What if the doctor botches the operation and I wind up grossly disfigured?

"Scarface Dillinger," they might call me.

With a hideous mug and a moniker like that, I might have to think seriously about making a sincere commitment to a life of crime.

THURSDAY, March 18 — My little refrigerator has been defrosted. I had to unplug it last night to get some rest. Now my kitchenette is a swamp. Oh well, I'm not planning on doing any lavish entertaining here anyway. I had breakfast at a ritzy eatery overlooking the fishing wharf, then exchanged more dollars and bought a long-distance phone card and some T-shirts, underwear, and toiletries at a tourist store. I found a pay phone and called Connie, who was sounding major stressed.

"Were you able to bail out Paul?"

"Not yet, Nick. There have been some unforeseen complications."

"Like what?" I asked. "What's the big deal about a marijuana rap?"

"Well, it's no big deal if they catch you with a few ounces, but Paulo had a whole gym bag full of it."

"He did! What for?"

"Nick, Paulo worked as a pool cleaner. There's no point in having that job if you don't peddle a little dope on the side. People expect it as part of the service. Unfortunately, Paulo has some prior arrests too."

"Paul has a police record?" I asked, flabbergasted.

"Of course, Nick. You can't go on a spiritual quest in this

country without having a few run-ins with the law. So now the D.A.'s talking three strikes."

"You mean . . ."

"Yes, Nick, Paulo could get 25 years to life! That's why the authorities think he's a flight risk and are asking the judge to deny bail. If my father's lawyers do succeed in getting him freed, I hope to God he'll do the sensible thing and run away to Europe with me."

"Connie, that's awful."

"I know, Nick. Paulo's parents flew in last night. They're staying in the guest house. My initial impression of my future in-laws was not favorable."

"And it's not likely to improve. Was Sheeni with them?"

"No, she stayed in Ukiah."

Sheeni's all alone in that big house. I hope she doesn't do anything immature like invite Vijay over.

"How's your hotel, Nick?"

"Uh, it's OK. Is it where you stay when you come here, Connie?"

"I hardly think so, Nick. I asked our housekeeper Benecia to recommend a place for you. Be sure you're back at your hotel by 12:30. The clinic is sending a car for you. And no more trying to chicken out. I know you'll thank me for this. Dr. Rudolpho is a genius."

Yeah, that's what they said about Dr. Frankenstein too.

"Nick, have you decided to take my advice and go with the Aryan god look? Of course, you'd have to lighten your hair and wear blue contacts."

"I'm not sure, Connie. I don't know if looking like a face on a Hitler Youth poster is really my thing."

What a shock about Paul. You find a guy to look up to, a mentor figure who appears to have escaped most of the bullshit of modern life, and he turns out to be a drug dealer. And why didn't he foresee those cops bearing down on him? A brother in the pen and a fiancé on the run—can fate be this cruel to a gifted young intellectual like Sheeni Saunders?

3:50 p.m. I was extremely nervous on the drive up to the clinic. For one thing, I was being conveyed in another one of those big slab-sided Lincolns—a pearlescent silver sedan from the 1960s. Not a good omen. The last time I was in one (Jerry's convertible) I managed to spark a $5 million fire in Berkeley. And let's not forget what happened to JFK in his. At least Dr. Rudolpho's clinic makes a good first impression, giving some cause to hope it's not an entirely fly-by-night operation. A big two-story hacienda is surrounded by a dozen or so adobe bungalows—all set on lavishly landscaped grounds with a sweeping view of the town and the sparkling blue bay. Nobody walking around in bandages, thank God. I assumed all the patients were laid up in the swanky bungalows.

The hacienda was beyond posh, and not a dust ball in sight. They must be running the janitors on double shifts. I was shown into a small waiting room and left by myself. Nothing to read except a pile of glossy magazines called Gorgeous! devoted entirely to nose-job success stories. Hard to believe so many people got shafted that severely by Mother Nature in their nasal equipment. I can only imagine the playground taunts some of those beak disaster cases must have endured. Of course, the whole scene was making me even more nervous. Waiting for a plastic surgeon has got to be at least a hundred times more nerve-wracking than waiting for your dentist.

Eventually a bell rang somewhere and a cute nurse in a white uniform came in to escort me to Dr. Rudolpho's private office. He rose graciously from behind his massive carved desk and shook my hand. I felt reassured immediately. He was a tall outdoorsy fellow (about 40?) with the boyish good looks of Joel McCrea enlivened with a vigorous dash of Randolph Scott. It was all very professionally done with hardly any visible scarring. Is it possible for plastic surgeons to operate on themselves? I speculated that perhaps his surgical training was like barber college—with the neophyte surgeons first working on each other before graduating to the paying public. One of his talented classmates must have been a big fan of old westerns.

With the preliminary chitchat out of the way, Dr. Rudolpho pressed his small but expressive fingers together and launched into a disquisition on aesthetics.

"What humans regard as beauty, Mr. Dillinger, is merely a subtly perceived harmoniousness of features. Your features, for example, lack a vital symmetry. Your chin is recessive, your nose a facial afterthought, your eyes want positional credibility, your lips are too thin, your ears too big, and your hair . . . well, let's not get into that. Is it your earnest wish for me to unscramble these genetic miscarriages and reveal through my art that hitherto elusive underlying order?"

"Not really, doc. I just want to look completely different. I want to walk out of here looking like a totally different person—someone that no one who knew me before would recognize. Can you do it?"

Dr. Rudolpho gazed up at his carved ceiling beams and thought the matter over.

"Oh, and one more thing. I want to look older—at least 18."

"I thought you said you were 18."

"I am 18. I just want to look it. Care to see my ID?"

"No, I'm sure your ID, if not your physiognomy, validates your age. Nick, I could get into serious difficulties operating on a minor without his parents' permission."

"My parents are dead, doc. I'm, I'm on my own. And I've got the money."

"So our mutual friend Connie assures me. What sort of direction would you like to go? I need a little guidance from you."

I handed him a damp picture from my wallet; he studied it with interest.

"Are you sure this is what you want, Nick?"

"I'm positive. Can you do it?"

"I can do anything, Nick. Let's get that straight. OK, we're looking at a rhinoplasty, eyes and lips reconstruction, and inserts for both cheeks, forehead and jaw. The ears we'll have to let slide this time. That will be $10,000, payable in advance."

"No problem."

"Postoperative recovery will require at least a week, preferably two. Our fee is $500 a day."

"Gee, that's kind of steep. Do you offer any budget plans?"

"You can stay in your own hotel. Our nurse will visit twice a day. That's $100 a day."

I blanched. "Do you have any super-saver discount plans?"

"That's as cheap as we go, Nick. Our fee includes all medication and liquid meals. You'll have to drink through a straw for the first few days."

"Does it hurt, doc? I think you should know I experienced some major trauma recently when I got my ears pierced. I don't cope well with pain."

"Trust me, Nick. It won't be too bad." Dr. Rudolpho escorted me to the door. He had the longest legs on anything I'd ever seen not drilling for oil in the North Sea. Even in his loose-fitting white doctor's smock you could tell the guy was all pants and no torso.

"Have a light lunch this afternoon, Nick, but eat nothing after 6:00 p.m. And no liquids after midnight. Our car will pick you up tomorrow morning at 7:30."

"OK. One more thing, doc. Can you do anything about changing my voice?"

"Well, that's not normally in my line of work. The larynx, however, is a remarkably uncomplicated organ. One snip and the timbre of your voice would be altered forever."

"How much would that cost?"

"I'll throw it in on the house."

"Thanks, doc. But I must tell you I'd rather not sound like Andy Devine or Gabby Hayes. I've never contemplated a career as a cowboy sidekick."

"You'll sound fine, Nick. Connie's right. You're a remarkable young man."

Dr. Rudolpho turned me over to the cute nurse for "preliminary processing." A plastic badge pinned to her left breast identified her as "Angel." I wasn't sure if that was her name, her vocation, or a cogent summation of her physical assets. Angel took my weight, measured my blood pressure and pulse (it went up whenever she smiled at me), extracted a hypo of blood from my arm for laboratory analysis, and snapped some "before" photos of my face and head from all angles. She assured me in her endearingly accented English that the pictures would be kept in the strictest confidence, and that I need not fear finding myself splashed across the pages of Gorgeous! magazine.

"I pity the chicas bonitas when Dr. Rudolpho finishes with you," she assured me. "Mucho hearts you'll be breaking—even more than you do now."

Before François could imply that she could operate on him anytime, I was led away by a staff honcho. He took me into a small inner office, where I counted out $10,700 in damp C-notes and signed a slew of forbiddingly worded liability releases in Nick S. Dillinger's fancy new signature. I may emerge looking like the Second Coming of Boris Karloff, but Dr. Rudolpho and minions are legally untouchable.

6:35 p.m. My last afternoon resembling former person Nick Twisp. I took my old face out for one last airing. I strolled into town along Ensenada's main drag. A big white cruise ship had anchored in the bay, and the open-air shops were jammed with souvenir-hungry tourists. The two-year-old gum-hustlers were out in force, but were thronging mostly the older, more affluent-looking gringos. I watched a kid about my age grilling skewers of meat on a sidewalk barbecue made from an old paint can. It smelled delicious, the price was right, but I decided to pass. For all I knew he might have been serving up marinated dog bits.

To stave off scurvy I had a margarita at a fancy cantina that claims (on its cocktail napkins) to be one of the most famous bars in the world. Since I intend to be the one of the most famous alcoholic fiction-writers in the world, I felt it was destiny that had guided me there. I chugged a second margarita for its vital salt, then lurched off to look for a pay phone. My Love wasn't home, but I reached my old pal Fuzzy on the third ring.

"Nick, where are you?"

"Oh, out and about," I slurred. "How's the Nick Twisp manhunt going?"

"The cops worked me over, Nick, but I didn't spill. I just kept telling everybody that I never knew Carlotta was a guy. The cops had the nerve to ask me didn't I feel you up after the Christmas dance? I said no way. I said I only took Carlotta to the dance because I felt sorry for her. I swore the same thing to Lana. I told the cops the only person I knew who was making a serious play for Carlotta was Bruno Modjaleski. So they dragged him downtown."

"The cops interrogated Bruno?"

"For about five hours. They figured he must have known Carlotta was Nick—being so intimately acquainted and all. Turns out one of your neighbors saw him pawing Carlotta on your front stoop. Boy, is Candy Pringle pissed. Bruno hasn't been to school for two days. I think the guy's ashamed to show his face. Good thing the season's over. He might of got tossed off the football team for being a degenerate."

"Frank, did the cops ask you what Carlotta had been living on?"

"Yeah, they asked me all kinds of stuff, Nick. I lied just like you told me. I said I thought maybe you'd been scamming old ladies."

"Gee, thanks, Frank."

"Well, I couldn't think of what to say. I figured you didn't want me to spill about the Wart Watch."

"Good job, Frank. I appreciate your discretion."

"So how much are you going to pay me, Nick? I'm running up a big tab showing Lana a good time. She invited Sonya to the movies on our last date and I dropped over ten bucks at the snackbar."

"Oops, I have to go, Frank. I'll keep in touch." Click.

Still no answer at Sheeni's house. I slipped my phone card back in the slot and dialed the aforementioned Sonya Klummplatz. She was amazed to hear from me.

"Oh God, is it really Nick Twisp himself—in person?"

"The very same, also known as Carlotta Ulansky."

"Oh, Nick, you are so cool. You fooled everyone. God, you're so great. Lana and I think it's neat that all those cops are looking for you."

"You guys aren't mad about gym class, Sonya?"

"Not us, Nick. We both need practice being naked with guys. But Barb Hoffmaster wants to murder you. I think it was just a big put-on—all those girls flipping out and demanding counseling. It was just so they could sue the school for emotional trauma. It's like when they have a bus crash in San Francisco and all those bystanders rush on the bus and start moaning. So I guess you weren't really interested in Trent, huh?"

"Of course not, Sonya. Would I lie about that?"

"And you told the truth about Bruno too. Nick, I owe you $50. Where should I send it?"

"Just hold on to it, Sonya. I may be by to collect it one of these days."

"You can collect more than the fifty, Nick, assuming you don't dig Bruno's manly lips."

"I have no interest in football players of any sex."

"Cool, Nick. My bedroom's off the porch in the back. I'll leave the window unlocked."

Flattering, I suppose, but hardly news to inspire unalloyed delight. Still, it's nice to know someone will be pining away for the late Nick Twisp.

9:37 p.m. Señora Christina's nine-year-old son Guadalupe just knocked on my door to tell me I had a call. I almost hoped it was Dr. Rudolpho phoning to say my operation had been postponed for 24 hours to permit additional patient chickening-out contemplation. Instead it was Connie calling with the latest Paulo update.

"Did the judge let him out of jail?" I asked.

"Not yet. I found out something interesting from the lawyers though."

"What?"

"You know that cops are supposed to have probable cause before they can stop someone and search their vehicle?"

"Right. Did they not have probable cause with Paul?"

"No, Nick, they had it all right. Somebody phoned in an anonymous tip that Paulo might be carrying drugs!"

"Really? Who would do a thing like that?"

"Well, I have an idea. My father's been going way out of his way to comfort Lacey throughout this ordeal. And he might have seen Paulo on a security tape smoking a joint."

"That's awful, Connie. Could your father really be that big of a rat?"

"Well, I don't think he expected Paulo to get in this much trouble. Still, I can't take any chances."

"You told Lacey?"

"No way, Nick. But I'm siccing Mother's lawyers on Paulo's

case. I think she can appreciate the logic of getting Paulo sprung as soon as possible—even if Daddy doesn't."

We then discussed my upcoming surgery and my impressions of Mexico's greatest surgical genius.

"I guess he seems pretty competent," I admitted. "How come his legs are so long?"

"Well, they've been augmented, of course."

"What was he—a midget?"

"Not a midget, but pretty short. Of course, you have to understand, Nick, they can't add to a person's chest or abdomen—I mean in length. So, naturally, the legs wind up a bit long in proportion to the rest of the body. I think he looks quite striking."

"You can say that again—like a human egret. Connie, this is all feeling pretty weird."

"It's just pre-surgery nerves, Nick. We all get it. Just think what an advantage spectacular good looks will be in wooing Sheeni."

She had a point there.

"Does it hurt, Connie?"

"Hardly at all, Nick. They give you wonderful little pills. I know you'll be thrilled. Just think about my breasts."

Sensible advice a guy can relate to—as I scrutinized my old visage one last time in the bathroom mirror. I shall now retire to my lonely bed and think about Connie's breasts, Sheeni's naked form, and the divinely curvaceous white-clad figure of Angel, Dr. Rudolpho's heavenly nurse.

FRIDAY, March 19 — (no entry).

SATURDAY, March 20 — (no entry).

SUNDAY, March 21 — Bandages off eyes. Can now see to type. Feel like survivor (?) of grisly car wreck. Like I went through windshield face first. Terrible sore throat too. Can't talk. Where's Angel with damn pills!?

MONDAY, March 22 — Little pills wearing off too soon. Face feels like vicious sadists are tenderizing it with ice picks. Worse than 10,000 ear piercings. Doctors are such liars!

TUESDAY, March 23 — Woozy from pain and little pills. Throat still sore, face very raw. Can't talk. Angel changed bandages. Man (Joel McCrea?) came by and snipped out "first round" of stitches. Says I'm doing "very well." Says kids my age "heal like earthworms." Told me not to look in mirror. I sneaked a peek. Terrible shock. Look like star of "Night of the Living Dead." Too depressed to write. Need more little pills!!

WEDNESDAY, March 24 — Can now squeak out sounds. Not totally mute as feared. Lips still don't move. Operation a disaster. Everything grossly swollen: black eyes, purple face, hideous blob of violet nose, lips from the black lagoon. Everywhere horrible scabs and Frankensteinian stitches. Monumentally depressed except right after gobble little pills. Angel remains upbeat. Says I'm doing great. Suspect she may be on pills too. She brought chicken taco in addition to mealy liquid dinner. Ate most of it. Wonder if carnivals still hiring sideshow freaks? Pills, I need more pills!!

THURSDAY, March 25 — Not sleeping so much. Angel switched to different color of little pill. Watch TV, but very depressing. Vilest and most-heinous villains still much better looking than me. Hop up to peek in mirror every few minutes. A disaster! Only hope for future happiness is if Sheeni tragically should be struck blind.
Señora Christina's son Guadalupe knocks on door. I open a

crack. He screams in terror and flees. One minute later: Señora Christina knocks on door. Tells me I have phone call. I put towel over head and follow her to office. Call is from despised agent of my misfortune, Connie Krusinowski.

"Hi, Nick, how're you doin'?"

"Frrrrpp."

"Can't talk, huh? Well, I got the whole story from Dr. Rudolpho. You're doing great, guy."

"Hah!"

"Good news, Nick. Mother's lawyers persuaded the judge to overlook Paulo's first prior because he'd been a minor at the time. The Deputy D.A. got intimidated by all the legal muscle brought in behind Paulo, plus she turned out to be a jazz fan. So she agreed to let Paulo cop a plea for possession only. It's all over. The judge gave him a tongue-lashing and six months in the county jail. Pretty awful for Paulo, but he could be out in as little as four months. Guess who's planning on visiting him as often as I can? The good news is Lacey and Daddy are virtually inseparable. If I'd known things were going to turn out this well, I'd have ratted on Paulo myself."

"Grzzz!"

"Just kidding, Nick. Lacey let it slip to Paulo's parents that you'd been staying with them. Did you know they really dislike her? So anyway, they totally flipped out and decided somehow that you were responsible for Paulo's arrest. Isn't that silly? What a relief to put them on a plane yesterday. They had to rush back to Ukiah because Sheeni got arrested."

"Huh!"

"Oh, hadn't you heard? I suppose not. Well, the cops up there had been watching your old house in case you returned. But you'd have to be pretty retarded to do anything that dumb. Anyway, they nabbed Sheeni sneaking into the house during school hours. The fellow who lives there now—what's his name, Trint? Trant?"

"Ent!"

"Oh, right, Trent. It seems he doesn't want to press charges, but his wife was pretty upset. Apparently, it wasn't the first time Sheeni had shown up there uninvited. I told you you never should have gotten that guy married off."

"Grrrrr!"

"Well, there's no point in adopting that attitude. Have you told Sheeni you got your face fixed?"

"Huh-uh."

"Well don't. It doesn't make any sense to go through all that trouble and expense if she's just going to dime you to the cops again. My advice to you is to keep your mouth shut."

"Grrrrr!"

"Sorry, Nick, honey! As if you could possibly do anything else at the moment."

FRIDAY, March 26 — Some of swelling went down last night. My lips starting to move. Can mutter few words. Throat still hurts and voice very low. Look and sound like dead person. Dr. Rudolpho came and removed rest of stitches. Took some photos. Said I was healing even better than expected. Threatened to cut off future visits of Angel with little pills! Had prepaid week gone by already? Felt more like 12 years. Forked over additional $700 to prolong vital ministrations by lovely nurse with magic pill bag.

Face starting to itch like mad. Dr. Rudolpho warned not to scratch, but said I could shave in a few days to lessen itching. Said it could take one full year for swelling to disappear completely and face to take final form. Why wasn't I informed of this fact before? Cannot hide out in crummy Mexican hotel indefinitely. Fast depleting all funds and insanity threatens from tortuous tedium. Also developing obsessive fixation on care giver. Long to press disfigured lips against Angel's luscious red ones. François making very brazen proposals. Nurse just laughs. Little pills responsible for inflamed libido? Even Señora Christina starting to look mucho foxy.

SATURDAY, March 27 — Swelling and purple blotches starting to retreat. Nose no longer resembles rotting eggplant. Very odd to look in mirror and see this stranger staring back. No sign of old Nick in new countenance, except developing Twispian zit on expensive new chin. Seem to have plenitude of lips. Can this be right? Have more lips than Louie Armstrong. Horn-playing gigolos would kill for such lips. Brought up disquieting lip surplus with Angel. She said Dr. Rudolpho always makes his patients "muy kissable." François demands immediate proof. She obliges. Gives sweet peck on lips. What a dish. Tight white uniform and little cap highly erotic too. Wonder if penalties severe in Mexico for rape? Angel laughs when asked about private life. Refuses to discuss possible boyfriends. Again declined François's sincere offer of marriage. Changed my pills to yet a different color. I decide alcoholic fiction-writing is passé. Must keep up with the times. Now aspire to become modern drug-addicted author instead.

SUNDAY, March 28 — Angel brought Mexican pastries and thermos of coffee for breakfast. Said I no longer need liquid meals. Bawled me out for scratching face. Again declined to fix firm date for marriage. Also declined François's request for emergency sponge bath. Asked me if pain was severe. I lied and said yes. She doled out six little orange pills. Told me to take one every two hours. As soon as she left I gulped down four. Face doesn't hurt, but boredom is excruciating.

Loud banging woke me from mid-morning snooze. Heaved carcass off bed and opened door. Surprise visitor Connie Krusinowski swept in. Skintight black silk sheath dress matched her eyes.

"Hi, Nick! Let me look at you, guy."

Connie took my face in her hands and studied it from all angles.

"Very nice, Nick. Not a direction I would have gone, but you have to admire the boldness of Dr. Rudolpho's vision. I told you the guy was a genius. Well, say something, Nick. God knows, you've got the lips for talking."

"Hello, Connie," I rumbled.

"Nick, you sound like a 92-year-old man."

"You should have been here a few days ago. I looked like one too—recently deceased."

"That's why Dr. Rudolpho bans all mirrors from the patient cottages at the clinic. They're too depressing. You get to remain blissfully ignorant of how frightening you really look. Don't scratch, Nick."

"I can't help it."

"Get your things together, guy."

"Why? Are we going somewhere?"

"I came down in my parents' yacht. We've come to rescue you!"

"But I can't leave!" I gasped. "I just paid for another week of nursing visits. I need those little pills!"

"Let me see what you're on."

I produced the two precious orange pills from my hidden stash.

"Just as I thought, Nick. It's only Tylenol."

Tylenol! I'm paying a hundred bucks a day for a continental breakfast and Tylenol!

"You're fine, Nick. Let's go."

"But what about my $700?"

"Chalk it up as a drug deal gone sour, Nick. Come on, let's blow this crummy joint."

Since I had virtually no possessions, it took me all of 30 seconds to pack. Connie stuck a big straw hat on my head to keep the sun off my tender face and pushed me out the door. Parked outside was a little two-door car that looked like a miniature boat. It had simulated wood planking on the sides, a curving prow, a lethal-looking bowsprit, and cute porthole windows. Yachting pennants flew from gleaming metal poles fore and aft; matching brass hub-caps flashed shiny embossed anchors. The interior of the car was done up like the cockpit of a vintage cabin cruiser—all varnished wood, polished brass metalwork, and blue and white nautical upholstery. Connie tossed my stuff in the back seat and explained that her mother's yacht always traveled with its own runabout car. She tooted the horn to scatter the crowd of curious gum-sellers, gunned the engine, and steamed out of the parking lot.

"Did you get my $3,000 back?" I asked.

"Dream on, Nick. The cops have probably blown it already on parties. They never followed up on your backpack though. Good thing there was nothing in it with your name on it."

"No, I made sure of that. But I would like Sheeni's autographed photo back. Did you hear anything more about her?"

"Not a word, Nick. But don't worry. This separation is doing you good."

"How so?"

"Because right now you're what Sheeni cannot have. With any luck your absence is taking her mind off that married boy-friend."

I fervently hoped so.

"Have you thought about a new name?" Connie asked.

"I've decided on Nick S. Dillinger."

"Wrong. You can't keep the same first name. And Dillinger sounds way too suspicious. You have to give the cops credit for some brains, Nick. How about Dick?"

"Too Nixonian. And how would you like to walk around with the name Pussy?"

"I see your point. OK, how about Rick?"

"Rick . . . Rick I could live with."

"Good. What about Rick S. . . . Smith?"

"Too boring. And it sounds made up. I need something manly. And to the point. Something suggesting a raw jungle passion."

"I don't think Rick S. Tarzan would work. Hmmm . . . How about Hunter?"

"Rick S. Hunter. Not bad. Not bad at all!"

Rick S. Hunter—if that's not the name of an oversexed bestselling author, I don't know what is. I can see his handsome visage now, smiling out from thirty million dust jackets. Beloved by his readers, acclaimed by the snootiest critics, and wedded to the glamorous Mrs. Sheeni Hunter. Hey, that works nicely too.

3:15 p.m. I got a job! I've been officially hired on as cabin-boy slave aboard the S.S. Plock, which turns out not to be a boat, but the biggest, most elaborately fitted-out motor home I've ever seen. A self-powered "yacht on wheels," it measures nearly 50 feet long from stem to transom. One side motors out in fore and aft sections, virtually doubling the interior space. Like its little runabout car, the mothership was done entirely in a spare-no-expense nautical style. It must have cost a fortune, but Connie assures me that since it was built to demonstrate her father's beefiest truck springs, the whole thing was tax-deductible. The grand yacht was moored less than 100 feet from the rolling surf in a nice private campground on a scenic peninsula a few miles south of town. Connie pulled in and parked behind it.

"Plock, Bel Air," I said, reading the elaborately gilded letters on its stern. "Shouldn't that be Pluck?"

"Everybody asks that," Connie replied. "Plock is a city in Poland, Rick. It's famous for giving the world generations of notable Krusinowskis."

Connie led me inside, where I oohed and aahed over the exquisitely crafted main salon, paneled in a lustrous tawny-brown hardwood.

"What's this wood?" I asked, running a finger over its satiny grain.

"It's mahogany, Rick. The real stuff—from Cuba. Very hard to get." She led the way up a brass-trimmed circular staircase and through a hatch to a vertigo-inducing roof sundeck (no railing), where Connie's mother and a wiry but muscular older man, flamboyantly tattooed and lacking a right hand, were seated on deck chairs and sipping large margaritas in the warm breeze. Each lap cradled a sleeping Chihuahua. Simultaneously, the tiny dogs snapped awake and snarled at me.

"Ah, the surgery victim," said Mrs. Krusinowski, putting down her embroidery hoop and lifting her sunglasses to scrutinize my face. She was a thin but paunchy fifty, with fading blond hair and still handsome blue eyes. "Well, young man, I hate to tell you this, but your efforts to become a Chinaman have failed miserably. And what's happened to your lips?"

"I wish I knew," I muttered.

"Don't growl at me, young man," she replied. "Connie, your friend sounds like an elephant in heat."

"His lips are still a little swollen, Rita," Connie replied. "That's to be expected. Rick has agreed to work as cabin boy. But everyone has to keep totally mum about his operation. And he won't take less than $800 a week."

"What impertinence!" exclaimed Mrs. Krusinowski. "You'll take $700 a week and like it. Dogo, get that boy his uniform and show him how to make a proper margarita."

"Sure thing, Mrs. K," the tattooed man grunted in a deep, blue-collar twang.

He chugged his drink, passed the snarling Chihuahua to Connie, and led me back downstairs. I couldn't help but stare at his stump, which was tattooed with a bloody dagger and the words "Hell's First Installment." A vividly mottled snake tattoo coiled around his other arm, ducked beneath his "Biggest Little Dog in the World" Chihuahua T-shirt, and wrapped its other end around his neck—the tip of its snake tail just tickling his left earlobe in which a large gold ring dangled.

"Dogo Dimondo," he said, extending his left hand.

I fumbled to shake it. "Rick S. Hunter. What happened to your hand?"

"Hydraulic press," he replied, searching through large drawers under the mahogany chart table. He pulled out a wrinkled navy-blue uniform that looked like something an admiral of the fleet would wear to a Presidential inauguration. I had never seen so many brass buttons. "Too bad, Rick. Looks like it's your size. She tried to get me into it, but I lucked out. My shoulders were too damn big."

7:40 p.m. I look ridiculous in my scratchy uniform, but for $700 a week I'm willing to indulge the fancies of the ruling class. Connie's mother now addresses her two crew members as Dogo and Tojo (short for Admiral Tojo). She explained that she has given me an Asian name to assist my emotional recovery from "your surgical disappointments."

Besides being the chief mechanic, navigator, and driver, Dogo is also an expert cook. The way he slams saucepans around in the lavishly equipped galley, it's hard to believe he's doing it all with one hand. The man does amazing things with baby mussels and unsalted butter. I assisted with the dinner preparations by making the salad and keeping the blenders whirling. I served up an avalanche of margaritas, diverting some of the pale green froth into my own glass for quality-control purposes. Much tastier and more festive than swallowing pills. Perhaps I'm destined for celebrity alcoholism after all.

Connie addresses her mother by her first name. That usually implies some heavy emotional gravy over the dam. I notice they don't have much to say to each other, but no bloody flare-ups as with my mother and Joanie. Maybe rich people don't feel as much need to scream at each other. Connie's mother is a nut for embroidery; all the walls are jammed with expensively matted and framed scenes done in tiny cross-stitches. Many of them, I've noticed, involve painfully cute gamboling Chihuahuas.

9:40 p.m. Guess who got stuck with the washing up? Oh well, all I had to do was stack things in the commercial-grade dishwasher and push a button. So while my companions were up on the roof-deck enjoying the balmy moonlight, I snooped through the rest of the ship. Super posh. In the aft is the Krusinowski master stateroom with its vast built-in mahogany bed and palatial marble-and-mirrored bathroom. Forward of that is Connie's compact but opulent stateroom, then another bathroom done in blue and white tile, then the galley, and main salon. No sign of quarters for the crew. I hope this means what I think it means.

11:15 p.m. It did—partly. When I returned from walking Anna and Vronski, Captain Krusinowski and her first mate were nowhere to be seen. I turned the dogs over to Connie, who put them to bed in their own climate-controlled kennel across the corridor from her cabin (I had assumed it was a closet), then retreated to her room. Unfortunately, a lonely single bed had been made up for the cabin boy on one of the built-in settees in the main salon. I switched off the light, stripped off my uniform, and climbed into bed. A few minutes later Connie slipped out of her cabin. As she made her way forward, I was surprised to discern my visitor was wearing hardly anything worth mentioning.

"Rick, I've been thinking about your lips," she whispered, kneeling beside my settee.

Instant killer T.E.

"Yes, Connie. And I yours!"

"Would you mind kissing me?"

"Not at all!"

Connie leaned forward, I reared up. We met lip-first in the gloom. After a too-short interval, we parted.

"They're very nice, Rick. What a fool I've been."

"Oh, Connie!"

"Yes, I should have asked Dr. Rudolpho for bigger lips."

I put my arms around her bare shoulders and pulled her toward me for a second helping.

"Rick, what are you doing?"

"Making love to you, my darling," purred François.

"Forget it, guy," she said, unpeeling my arms. "Remember, we always want what we cannot have."

Damn!

MONDAY, March 29 — I was wrong, diary. With the possible exception of Anna and Vronski, everyone passed a celibate night. Dogo Dimondo, I discovered, sleeps in a spartan bunk down below in the luggage basement. Barely three feet of headroom and only accessible from the outside. He and I showered (not together) in the campground restroom, while the ladies performed their morning ablutions in the Plock's sumptuous facilities. I successfully shaved my new face. Noticeably less facial puffiness, and the bruises have almost entirely disappeared. Maybe a slight diminution of the lips as well. I love studying my new self in the mirror. Nothing like some expensive plastic surgery to turn a guy into a total narcissist. Well, it keeps me occupied for hours, and as hobbies go it's pretty inexpensive. Some of our fellow campers seem impressed by my new uniform. Several served up crisp salutes as Dogo and I walked back along the beach with our towels.

Dogo made breakfast; I manned the espresso machine. We sat around the mahogany table in our suede-covered captain's chairs and read the English-language Ensenada paper, while Anna skirmished with Vronski for a lamb bone and Connie checked out the satellite reception on the wide-screen, high-definition television that lowers from the ceiling at the push of a button. This lifestyle I could get used to.

Mrs. K studied me over her newspaper. "Tojo, you remind me of someone. Connie, who does he look like?"

Connie glanced over. Her eyes this morning were the same lapis lazuli as her mother's. "I don't know, Rita . . . maybe a white Nat 'King' Cole."

"Nah, that's not it," said her mother. "It'll come to me. I've seen that face before. And don't curl your lip at me, young man."

I wasn't curling my lip. I was trying to suck them in.

11:35 a.m. After breakfast Connie drove me into town in the Plock II. We located a passport photographer's studio on the main drag. There I obtained two instant color photos of my new face. These I've airmailed to Mr. Castillo with a request for a new set of Rick S. Hunter identification papers. I also asked for a forged honor-student academic transcript for my next tenuous venture back into public high school. As down-payment I enclosed two $100 bills from my dwindling stash. (Alas, my money belt is now barely noticeable under my clothes.) I promised to pay the balance when I drop by to pick them up.

I'm hoping Mr. Castillo finds it in his heart to give me a frequent-customer discount. These constant identity changes are a big financial drain. At Connie's suggestion I've ditched Nick S. Dillinger's driver's license, Social Security card, and passport—retaining only his picture-less birth certificate as an emergency ID to get back across the border.

On the way back I asked Connie if her father would be joining us.

"Well, he's supposed to, Rick. My parents usually try to plan some sort of boring family trip for my spring break. But things are going so well with him and Lacey, I'm hoping he'll find a way to cancel."

"Won't your mother be angry?"

"I suppose so. But she can always go back to working on

Dogo. She's been flirting with him for years. He lost his hand in Daddy's factory, and Rita's been trying to reassure him that he's still a complete man. I think she wants to sleep with him to atone for all the guilt she feels."

"Maybe I should cut myself on your blender, Connie. How would that make you feel about me?"

"Depends on what you slice off, guy."

2:15 p.m. Mrs. K had some sort of disturbing phone conversation with her husband and is totally pissed. I can only assume he's been delayed because Lacey is finding him improbably fascinating. Of course, she has a history of falling for older men (my father being a recent gross example). After lunch Mrs. K sent Dogo in the Plock II up to San Diego to pick up some guests at the airport. I gather they were invited by Mr. K without consulting his wife. I hope she doesn't plan on bunking them in the salon with me.

Mrs. K and Connie are taking the dogs for a walk. The cabin boy was left behind to perform slave laundry duty. (I found a large stainless-steel washer and dryer stacked in a closet next to the galley pantry.) Oh well, at least I get the thrill of handling Connie's bras and panties, if not their actual contents. Dogo's underwear I'm finding somewhat less stimulating.

8:40 p.m. Amazing news, diary. When Dogo returned from the airport in the Plock II, who should ease his ungainly, seersucker-clad bulk out the passenger-side door but Sheeni's beetle-browed father! Followed by her 5,000-year-old mother (in shorts!) and then My One and Only Love herself, looking profoundly depressed. My heart seized as Connie made the introductions, but Sheeni listlessly shook Rick S. Hunter's clammy hand without any sign of recognition. Nor apparently did her parents realize they were once again in the presence of alleged agent-of-Satan Nick Twisp.

I was thankful then for Tojo's ill-fitting uniform. The face and voice were different, but under my clothes lurks the same dreary body Sheeni knew all too well. Until I'm reassured I can trust My Love, I'll have to keep it and all of its parts well-screened from her view.

Mr. and Mrs. Saunders have been assigned Connie's cabin; she and My Love are to share the salon; I've been bounced downstairs to bunk with Dogo in the luggage basement. While Connie showed My Love the sights of the campground, I sneaked my laptop down to my glorified slave kennel, then hustled over to the park restroom for a quick mirror fix. I smoothed down my hair and anxiously practiced holding in my lips. The facial bruising was barely noticeable and my chin zit was under control—which was more than I could say for my nervous system.

Mrs. K tried her best to be hospitable, but the presence of two teetotaling fundamentalists and their sullen underage daughter put something of a crimp in the cocktail hour. The regulars sipped their margaritas, the guests slurped down virgin mai-tais. These, as prepared by the cabin boy, were not as chastely rum-free as the term "virgin" might imply. Still, no one complained. By the time Dojo got around to tossing that first great lump of butter into his saucepan, virtually everyone was in a holiday mood. The addition of guests, however, necessitated a new formality in dining. Only five places were set at the mahogany table. Dogo cooked, I served. Later, the domestic staff supped separately on the leftovers.

Mrs. K and Mr. Saunders did most of the work in keeping the dinner conversation going; My Love seemed oddly subdued—refusing even to look at her parents. Sheeni's father profusely thanked Mrs. K for helping rescue their "profligate son" from a "disastrous misstep." Sheeni's mother politely thanked her for allowing them to share once again in such "Sybaritic luxuries." Connie asked Sheeni about Ukiah and school, but received only monosyllabic replies. Could My Love actually be preoccupied with worry over me?

"Tojo, step here into the light," commanded Mrs. K as I was

refilling the coffee cups from a silver pot. "Now tell me, who does this young man look like?"

I blushed and sucked in my lips as everyone looked up to scrutinize my remodeled face.

"He's a very presentable-looking boy," remarked Sheeni's mother, "for a person of obvious mixed ancestry."

"He looks a little like a client I once defended on a child molestation charge," commented Mr. Saunders.

"I'll tell you who he looks like," said Sheeni, glancing shyly up at me. "He looks like Jean-Paul Belmondo."

"You mean that French actor?" asked Connie.

"That's it!" exclaimed Mrs. K. "That's the name I was trying to think of. He's the spitting image."

I hope you like it, Sheeni. As usual, darling, I did it all for you.

TUESDAY, March 30 — No word yet from the tardy Mr. K. Until that lusty magnate decides whether to join us, the Plock remains aground on this sunny, south-of-the-border bayside sand dune. Oh well, I consider it a great stroke of fortune just to be aboard the same grandiose land yacht as My Love, even if so far she hasn't uttered three sentences to mysterious cabin boy Rick S. Hunter. At least today her spirits seem slightly revived. As you can imagine, it's a constant struggle not to take my pouting darling in my arms and smother her with wild Belmondoesque kisses. Last night was slow torture knowing My Love was reclining in an undiaphanous nightgown just a few feet above my own feverish body. The fact that I was wedged like a sardine next to Dogo Dimondo didn't help matters. I felt the strongest compulsion to attend to a private matter, but had to lie there like a lump in my coffin-sized bed while the surf rolled in romantically just a few yards away.

Anna and Vronski are exhibiting a strong dislike for Sheeni's mother. Whenever she approaches, they make an ostentatious show of running and hiding. I feel exactly the same way. She's the only Plock passenger still addressing me as "Tojo." Everyone else seems to be following Mrs. K's lead in calling me "Bondo." At breakfast, whenever I felt an urge to slide a poached egg down her collar or spill coffee in her lap, I kept reminding myself that she's the grandmother of my future children. It's a good thing for her I never had a vasectomy.

2:28 p.m. I just had a long, disquieting conversation with My Love. While I was hitching up the Chihuahuas for their post-lunch constitution, Sheeni inquired if she could accompany us.

"Sure," I rumbled with forced nonchalance, handing her Anna's leash.

My Love was dressed in sandals, jonquil shorts, and that all-too-familiar yellow tube top that had traumatized me at Clear Lake so many months before. We strolled south along the beach toward distant rocky cliffs, where a renowned sea geyser was rumored to spout a stream of saltwater more than 60 feet into the air.

"It must have been pretty here once," Sheeni remarked, "before all those Americans built their tacky beach houses."

"Humans are such a blight," I replied, tugging Vronski away from some drowned sea creature's rotting corpse. "And dogs run a close second."

My Love chuckled. "Aren't you hot in that coat?"

"Not at all," I lied. "I'm getting over a cold. That's why my voice is a little raspy. And Mrs. K expects me to remain in uniform."

"Do you work for them all the time?"

"Just on vacations. I almost didn't make it this time on account of my motorcycle accident, but the bruises are healing nicely ... Anything the matter? You've seemed a little, uh, withdrawn."

"I didn't want to come here. My father insisted. My mother

didn't want to come either. She doesn't approve of the Krusinow-skis, as you may have surmised from her rudeness. Father insisted on accepting the invitation. He's a lawyer and they instinctively suck up to people with money. I think he's hoping to land some of the Krusinowskis' legal work."

"Well, there are worse things than a vacation in Mexico on the beach."

"Not with my parents!"

Anna paused for a leisurely postprandial dog gag and barf.

"How are you getting on with Connie?" I asked.

"She's OK."

We resumed our walk.

"You know she's madly in love with your brother."

"So I heard. Personally, I think it's pathetic that someone would mutilate themselves surgically to try and attract some disinterested person. Don't you agree?"

"Well, I'm not sure I'd call it pathetic," I said, swallowing hard. "Perhaps more like enterprising." I felt a change of topic was called for. "I understand, Sheeni, that you had a recent brush with the law yourself."

My Love gave me a quick hard look. "You seem remarkably well-informed. It was just a misunderstanding—one of many recently. Things have been very crazy lately. My brother was arrested. A close friend of mine got railroaded into a stupid marriage. Another friend had to skip town just ahead of the cops. I haven't heard from him for two weeks."

"You must be worried sick," I said hopefully.

"Not really. He can take care of himself."

"You almost sound like you wouldn't be that upset if he were arrested."

"Well, it might simplify matters if he were."

I tried not to reveal the turmoil those ominous words touched off in my heart.

We never made it to the alleged geyser. My Love was her usual indefatigable self, but the dogs' little pencil legs threatened to give out. We turned back.

"I, I never heard the name Sheeni before."

"My real name's Sheridan. Father's a Civil War buff. A friend when I was little started calling me Sheeni."

"Oh, who was that?"

"A boy named Trent Preston."

More distress for Nick. Someday I hope to uncover some aspect of My Love's eventful life in which that deranged poet has not been intimately involved.

4:10 p.m. When we got back, the Plock was jammed with ogling fellow campers, apparently invited over by Sheeni's mother, much to Mrs. K's evident annoyance. My Love retired to the roof deck with her book; Connie and I retreated to the beachside patio of the campground minimart for cold beers (Connie paid). I squeezed in juice from my little lime wedge and sucked on the brown bottle without mercy.

"How's it going with Paulo's sister?" asked Connie.

"Terrible. She wants to rat on Nick to the cops."

"Really? She said so?"

"In so many words."

"It's to be expected, Rick. But I can see why you're obsessed with her. She's a knockout. A bit on the cold side though."

"Sheeni's a very warm person. She's just pissed at her parents right now. Connie, you've got to help me get my money back from her."

"How?"

"Tell her you spoke by phone with Nick. Tell her I said for her to write you a check for $689,000. So you can deposit it and then forward the money to me."

"OK, Rick. But I'll be amazed if she goes for it."

I finished my beer and belched so explosively that everyone on the patio turned and stared. As if I cared.

"What do you think of our future in-laws?" I asked.

"God, Rick, they suck. How did those two ever produce Paulo and Sheeni?"

"That, Connie, is one of the great mysteries of the age. Another is why your father ever invited them here."

"That's easy, Rick. It's more proof that he ratted on Paulo. Extreme guilt is the only possible explanation. Shall we order some nachos?"

"Connie, I thought you subsisted on one olive a day. Lately you've been eating like a horse."

"There's no need to diet now, Rick. Poor Paulo's in jail and Lacey's practically out of the picture."

"Are you sure you didn't turn him in yourself? Perhaps it was your body's final desperate ploy to avoid starvation."

"I wish I was that devious, Rick. Maybe I should take some lessons from your girlfriend."

9:40 p.m. Some Plock passengers had to eat an expensive, multicourse dinner at a ritzy restaurant up in the hills. But since the Plock II runabout only seats five, the two servants got to remain behind and dine on leftovers from the back of the refrigerator. My Love, needless to say, looked enchanting dressed to go out. Bondo, with his new Gallic blood, stared brazenly at her, but she didn't seem to notice. Connie looked inscrutably exotic in one of her many oriental-theme slinky silk frocks and new-to-me violet eye contacts. Sighing, I watched them drive away, then manufactured two stiff margaritas while Dogo dished up the leftovers. Bad news, diary. Not yet 15, I've already lost track of my lifetime cocktail count.

"Dogo, how did you get to be such a great cook?" I asked, chowing down on his toothsome leftovers.

"CIA, Rick."

"You were a spy! But aren't large eye-catching tattoos somewhat counterproductive for undercover work?"

"Different CIA, Rick. After my accident I went to work for the Ks on their boat. It was a real one—a 42-footer. But Connie gets seasick so they sold it. They sent me to the Culinary Institute of America."

"Really?"

"Yeah, paid for the whole thing. Guess they got tired of my hobo stew and hangtown fry."

"You never made a play for Mrs. K? I think she likes you."

"No percentage in it, Rick. Sure, I'd like to jump her bones. She needs somebody to. But what happens when it's over, when we get sick of each other? Eh? I'll tell you what happens. Dogo Dimondo is out on his ass. And I like this job."

"Do you have a girlfriend?"

"I get my quota, Rick. Chicks go for my stump."

"Beg your pardon?"

"My stump. Chicks are always checking it out. They start wondering what it would feel like."

I put down my fork. "You can't be serious."

"I give it to 'em, Rick. Anytime they want it." He held up his truncated but well-muscled arm. "All the way up past the elbow. That's what they like!"

I didn't finish the rest of my dinner. Just when you start thinking someone is a nice normal guy, he smacks a long one deep into foul territory. Not only that, I have to sleep unchaperoned right next to the fellow.

WEDNESDAY, March 31 — Mr. K is still delayed in L.A. with plant problems. Manufacturing truck springs must be a very delicate operation. Mrs. K said "to hell with him" and gave orders after breakfast for Dogo to weigh anchor. He started up the powerful diesel engine and flipped some toggle switches on the dash. The rooftop satellite dish powered down, the expando slide-outs motored in, the front awning and steps retracted, and the hydraulic stabilizing jacks raised up and locked. Dogo did have to disconnect manually the power cord, water hose, and smelly sewer hook-up. I assisted with these tasks and got a big smear of grease on my uniform while helping attach the towbar to the Plock II.

The original plan was to cruise down the length of Baja California to La Paz, but the campground manager confided to Dogo that some gringo RVers had been waylaid recently by bandits along the more isolated stretches of the highway. So Mrs. K decided to head east toward Mexicali, then travel south through Sonora state toward Guymas on the other side of the Gulf of California. Personally, I would have headed straight back to the Estados Unidos, where you can drink the water, understand the natives, and where the bandits are mostly confined to the urban districts.

Deviate or no, Dogo demonstrated his customary competence in whipping our immense motor home along Mexico's narrow highways. For him a second hand would only be redundant, not to mention sexually confining. Mrs. K occupied the copilot's seat with her dog-theme embroidery; the other passengers made themselves at home in the comfortable, though now less spacious, main salon. Anna and Vronski parked themselves on a padded window shelf and nodded to passing motorists like those plastic novelty figurines. While we glided northeast on Route 3, I did the laundry (tossing in my soiled coat), vacuumed the carpet, cleaned the bathrooms, and served assorted snacks and beverages to the pampered passengers. I suppose this is what is known as a working vacation.

Later in the morning I had a private tête-á-tête with Connie on her mother's bed in the master stateroom. I was still wearing Dogo's yellow rain slicker as a temporary cover-up while my admiral's coat tumbled in the dryer.

"I talked with Sheeni last night, Rick, while we were getting ready for bed. She has a very nice figure."

"I know, Connie. I've seen it. I'd very much like to see it again sometime soon. What did she say?"

"Well, she was surprised that you had phoned me and not her. I said you were afraid her phone line was tapped."

"Good thinking. What did she say about writing the check?"

"Well, she didn't say no. But there's a slight hitch."

"What?"

"Before she forks over the cash she wants to talk to you."

"Damn. No way can I call her. She'd recognize my new voice."

"Very true, Rick. You have quite a distinctive voice. Very masculine too for a kid with your build. Dr. Rudolpho is such a genius."

We looked up in surprise as the door opened. My Love glanced in and immediately reddened.

"Oh, uh, sorry," stammered Sheeni. "I was just looking for a place to lie down."

1:20 p.m. After lunch Sheeni spent a half-hour in the forward bathroom retching her guts out. Speculating that she had picked up a foreign microbe, Mrs. K dosed her from the Plock's extensive medical stores, told her to lie down in her parents' stateroom, and sent the cabin boy in with a cup of weak tea.

"How do you feel?" I asked.

"Rotten," she replied, holding an arm over her eyes.

My heart went out to My Love, though I kept my distance. In times of emotional distress I'm quick to offer a comforting shoulder, but for afflictions of the flesh I'm predictably useless.

"We're bypassing Mexicali," I pointed out.

"That is extraordinarily good news."

I gazed silently at my suffering darling and heard her stomach gurgle unappealingly.

"I wasn't doing anything with Connie this morning."

"I didn't imagine you were. Nor do I care if you do."

I sighed. My Love peered at me from under her arm.

"Is there something else?" she asked.

"No, I'm leaving. I hope you feel better. Let me know if you need anything."

"Thanks. You'll be among the very first to know."

3:42 p.m. My Love is still napping; Third World scenery continues to whiz past the windows. This part of Mexico is nice if you like barren brown hills, endless desert vistas, and giant trucks driven by machismo-steeped maniacs.

To help relieve the tedium, Mrs. K has been teaching her daughter and the Saunders to play bridge. None is proving a quick study, especially Sheeni's mother, who keeps interrupting the bidding to bad-mouth Nick Twisp and divulge facts of intense interest to the eavesdropping cabin boy. It seems Mr. Mince of my bank read news reports on the Twisp manhunt and ratted to the cops about my account. They traced the transactions back to Mario and Kimberly, and also to Sheeni, to whom my business partners had been mailing my checks.

"He created some sort of satanic timepiece," Mrs. Saunders explained. "A horrid thing intended to appeal to the most degenerate elements. The police at first thought my daughter was mixed up in it too. But she was merely forwarding the payments. Of course, we've punished her for that. Our lives have been a nightmare ever since she met that depraved criminal. And now he's spread his evil corruption to our son as well. Tojo, we're out of mixed nuts here."

"Right away, Mrs. Saunders," I replied, stifling François's forty-seventh homicidal impulse of the day.

"And did the police seize all of his assets?" inquired Mrs. K.

"Unfortunately not," replied Sheeni's father. "He moved everything offshore to an anonymous account quite beyond the reach of the FBI."

"They must at least know the name on the account," insisted Mrs. K.

"It's under the name Emma Bovary," he replied. "They have reason to believe that may be a pseudonym."

9:37 p.m. We're camped beside the Sea of Cortez on the outskirts of Puerto Peñasco. If I ever decide to have a down-and-out episode in a tawdry Mexican town, Puerto Peñasco is where I'll be making reservations. Presently jamming its dusty streets and rowdy mariachi bars are hordes of carousing youths (on spring break from Arizona colleges) and Connie Krusinowski. Dogo has accompanied her into town as designated driver, bodyguard, and deviate on the make.

Sheeni and I wanted to go too, but Mr. Saunders reminded his daughter that she was grounded, and Mrs. K reminded Bondo of his scullery duties. After hastily cleaning up the galley, I invited My Love for a dog walk along the beach in the deepening purple twilight. It's occurred to me that I should be taking advantage of these exotic foreign venues to commence Rick S. Hunter's dogged wooing of his future Trophy Wife.

"Sheeni, I don't see how you can be grounded 800 miles from home," I pointed out.

"My father is an idiot."

"How are you feeling?"

"Rick, you ask me that every two minutes. I feel OK."

"Sorry. Uh, what's that book you've been reading?"

"À l'ombre des jeunes filles en fleurs. It's by Proust."

"Marcel Proust?"

"Uh-huh. Have you read him?"

No way was I going to fall into the trap of revealing Nick Twisp's all-too-familiar (and pedestrian) literary tastes.

"Not me, Sheeni. I don't read, I live."

"I wasn't aware those activities were mutually exclusive. What sort of living do you do?"

"I live a life of action!"

"I see. You mean like vacuuming, cocktail-stirring, dog-walking—that sort of thing?"

"These domestic duties are just temporary. I'm experiencing life for my art."

Sheeni glanced skeptically at me.

"And what sort of art is that?"

"I intend to be an actor," I lied, "like my father."

My Love gazed intently into Rick S. Hunter's dingy brown eyes.

"Who was your father?" she asked urgently.

"Well, I'm not exactly positive. You see I was adopted—from an orphanage in France. My adoptive parents, the Hunters, died recently in a tragic car wreck before I could find out any details of my birth. I'm on my own now. But I do have this sense of a profound connection to . . . well, you probably know who I mean."

"That's incredible, Rick. Have you tried contacting him?"

"Why no," I replied, tugging sensually on my lower lip. "I'm sure I'm just an indiscretion he'd rather forget." My lip remained stuck far out from my face; I hastily shoved it back in place. "Mom and Dad were very strict. They never let me see any of his movies or learn a word of French."

"Rick, that's amazing. You really should go to France."

"I don't know, Sheeni. I'd rather make it on my own."

A stone struck me in the back of my head. A ragtag band of local youths on a nearby rock began gesturing obscenely to Sheeni and tossing pebbles at me. Although they risked a thrashing by the virile son of you-know-who, we grabbed our Chihuahuas and beat a hasty retreat.

Later I considered kissing My Love in the warm moonlight, but I decided to wait until I was sure her microbe had been subdued.

APRIL

THURSDAY, April 1 (April Fools' Day) — I spent an uncomfortable night in the back seat of the Plock II. Dogo got lucky and returned with a fortyish brunette with heavy thighs and a nervous giggle. I found out later from Connie that she was the chaperon for a sorority visiting from Tempe. I dragged my pillow and blanket back to the Plock II and tried not to think about what was happening in the luggage basement. No screaming at least. Oh well, it probably qualifies as safe sex—as long as he washes well beforehand. She was gone before I woke up. In the campground restroom Dogo looked well-rested and pleased with himself.

Every morning to keep in shape Dogo does 50 one-arm push-ups. He's promised to show me some exercises to beef up my physique. I realize I have to alter Rick S. Hunter's body in some basic way before I dare risk seducing My Love. Since I can't get any skinnier, my only recourse is to bulk up. The winkie is more problematic. No way I can subject that sensitive part to what my face just went through, even if such operations are a specialty of Dr. Rudolpho and might entail Angel changing my bandages and result in Breathtaking Size. I suppose I'll have to borrow a page from my old pal Lefty and insist that we keep the lights out.

9:15 a.m. Despite her hangover Connie was bubbling with excitement at breakfast. After I finished the washing up, she dragged me outside for a private conference on the beer can–littered beach.

"Rick, I spoke to our housekeeper Benecia this morning. She says Daddy spent last night in the pool cabana!"

"Don't get your hopes up, Connie. It could be an April Fools' Day prank."

"I've been bribing Benecia for years, Rick. She's completely trustworthy. Besides, she knows better than to cross me. She's in America illegally."

"Are you going to tell Paul?"

"Of course not. I can't risk Lacey becoming what Paulo cannot have. He'll find out when the time is right. How's it going with you and Sheeni?"

"Not bad. She thinks I'm the son of Jean-Paul Belmondo."

"I hope you know what you're doing. Rick, you've got to be a little more aloof. No offense, but whenever you're around Sheeni your body language screams availability. You've got to play it cool and let her come to you."

"But what if she doesn't?"

"She will. You're the only available male we've got—except for Dogo."

"That reminds me, Connie. What do you think of Dogo . . . as a man?"

"Do you mean would I like to do the ugly on his you know what?"

"Uh, well, yeah."

"Rick, it's pretty obvious what guys are all about. Your job is to put it there on the money. But a woman's sexuality is much more diffused. It's much more complex."

"My God, you've done it with him."

"Not me, Rick. Dogo's like a second daddy to me. But a couple of my girlfriends had a three-way with him once. They really dug his tattoos. Apparently one part of his anatomy has been decorated to look like a U-boat periscope—complete with simulated rivets." She glanced at her watch. "Oops, time for you to phone your sister in Oakland. According to Benecia, she's been calling Lacey every hour on the hour trying to find you."

9:45 a.m. Good thing I delayed making my amorous moves. Sheeni's microbe flared up, knocking My Love flat on her lovely back again in her parents' cabin. Mrs. Saunders wanted to send for a doctor, but My Love insisted she just needed to rest. Mrs. K has administered more antibiotics. Meanwhile, I borrowed Connie's cellular phone and dialed my familiar old number in Oakland. I wasn't sure what my sister was doing there, but I prayed my mother was away at work. Joanie answered on the second ring. Only by alluding to her long-ago teen fling with future radiator brazer Phil Polseta was I able to convince my skeptical sister that the strange man on the phone was indeed her fugitive brother.

"Nick, I want you to know I never made it with Phil Polseta."

"Then how come you had all those birth control pills hidden in your top dresser drawer?"

"Nick, you're such a sneak. You've got to come home at once. Mom's in jail. She shot Lance."

"Our mother shot Lance Wescott, her cop husband!" I exclaimed. "Did she kill him?"

"No, but he's in the hospital. He lost a lot of blood. She shot him in the groin."

"Our mother shot Lance in the groin!"

My surprise was misplaced. Knowing my mother, where else would she shoot someone?

"She was upset, Nick. Apparently, Lance was abusive and had other women too. And you know he's never accepted little Noel."

Noel Lance Wescott is my embarrassing infant half-brother whom I've never seen.

Joanie continued, "Lance was threatening to walk out. Mother put all your money from Miss Ulansky in his name. He was threatening to leave Mom without a cent! Somehow his gun got out of its holster and he wound up shot. Mom's in jail, Nick. I'm taking care of Noel. We need $25,000 for her bail, but Lance won't pay it."

"Joanie, is this some kind of sick April Fools' Day joke?"

"It's no joke, Nick. You've got to send us the money."

"I don't have it, Joanie. Sheeni has all my money."

"Then get it from her, Nick. I'm desperate."

"I can't talk to her, Joanie. It's kind of complicated. You'll have to call her yourself. I'll give you a number where you can reach her. But don't ask her for $25,000. She'd never agree to that much. Ask her for, uh, $6,000."

"But I need 25 grand, Nick."

"Trust me, Joanie. You'll get it. Ask Sheeni to make out the check to cash. And any extra you receive you have to promise you'll hold for me."

"OK, Nick. Are you coming home?"

"I can't, Joanie."

"Mom needs you, Nick. And don't you want to see little Noel?"

"He's just a baby, Joanie. He won't know me from Adam. Tell Mom I'll, I'll write her a letter."

"OK, Nick. But say hi to Noel before you hang up."

I said hello to my gurgling half-brother and advised him to watch his back at all times. Now I see where François gets his homicidal urges. Well, any fool who gives my mother access to a loaded gun deserves to get his pendulous nuts shot off. Boy, what a genetic heritage. It's no wonder honor-student Nick Twisp went bad. At least I can take satisfaction in having warned her (in lipstick on her dresser mirror) that her marriage was doomed. The good news, besides Lance getting shot, is that this incident is likely to cause a further diminishing of Sheeni's waning regard for Nick Twisp. All of which should make My Love even more susceptible to the reserved Gallic magnetism of Rick S. Hunter.

10:35 a.m. Five minutes after I hung up, Connie's cellular phone rang. She answered it, then took the phone in to Sheeni. A few minutes later I was thrilled to observe her retrieve Sheeni's purse from under a settee in the salon and carry it back to My Love's cabin. After what seemed like an eternity, Connie emerged carrying a stamped white envelope, which the cabin boy promptly intercepted.

"I promised Sheeni I'd take this straight into town to the post office," whispered Connie.

"And so you will," I whispered, "right after I amend it."

I pried open the still-damp envelope flap and removed the check, signed "Emma Bovary" in a looping 19th-century hand. The distinctive sea-green ink I knew to be a characteristic of the numerous engraved Krusinowski Metal Products Co. ballpoint pens scattered about as advertising keepsakes. Employing another such pen, I quickly added a fourth zero to the dollar amount. On the line with the written amount there was just enough space between the "six" and "thousand" to loop a "ty" onto the "six." (Too bad I couldn't squeeze in "hundred" instead.)

"Sorry about your mother, Rick," whispered Connie, watching my operation with interest.

"She should be OK," I replied. "If they put Lance on the stand, no jury in the world would convict her—even if he is a cop."

I then replaced the check, resealed the envelope, and handed it back to my accomplice in crime. Sneaky, I admit, but let us not forget whose money I was embezzling.

Five minutes later. Another bad shock. It just occurred to me that the moisture on the envelope flap I licked was Sheeni's own microbe-laden saliva!

1:22 p.m. No ill-effects as of yet. We are once again hurtling south into deepest, darkest Mexico on a broad four-lane highway. Small sun-baked villages every now and then. A few moments ago Mrs. K ordered Dogo to bring our massive rig to an emergency halt so we could all troop out to view a tall roadside cactus in bloom. Miraculously, it had gathered enough sustenance from its arid surroundings to produce a credible simulation of a made-in-China red plastic flower. To help the cause, Vronski and Anna peed on its trunk.

2:50 p.m. I just took the invalid her afternoon tea. My Love was sitting up in the berth and listening to her Walkman. Projecting as much indifference as Rick S. Hunter could muster, I dumped her teacup on the table, sneered, and turned to leave. My Love stopped the tape and removed her headphones.

"Rick, don't you love the Borodin string quartets?"

I paused with my hand on the door handle. Given Nick Twisp's uniquely retro musical tastes, I knew I would have to trod carefully around this topic.

"I prefer the Young Dickheads," I lied.

My Love moved aside on the berth in a gesture clearly inviting me to take a seat next to her. I did so warily while maintaining as aloof a posture as possible.

"Really, Rick? What songs by them do you like?"

Land-mine dead ahead.

"Oh, I like them all. What was that phone call you got this morning?"

"Alarming news, Rick. My friend Nick's mother has shot her husband. His sister called me in a state. He's the boy who's running from the police."

"Sounds like a pretty crazy family."

"I'm afraid they could all benefit from psychological intervention—especially Nick."

I didn't point out that lately her family had been running up nearly as impressive an arrest record as mine.

148

"Yeah," I grunted. "Sounds like you're well rid of that guy."

"I think so sometimes."

"Only sometimes, Sheeni?"

"It's complicated, Rick. Do you have a girlfriend?"

"I get my quota."

Sheeni was close and getting closer. I recognized that subtle tensing of her disarming lips. If she imagined I was going to subject Rick S. Hunter's immune system to any more of her microbes, she was out of her . . .

We kissed, but only for ten minutes or so. I then ripped my lips from hers, twisted them into a sneer, and lurched for the door.

9:12 p.m. All the way south through the sprawling state capital of Hermosillo and beyond I struggled to compose a letter to my mother. I wonder how many cases of paralyzing writer's block are attributable to parents? What does one say to a close maternal relative who is facing prosecution for shooting a despised stepfather? Sorry your aim was off? Too bad you didn't get a chance for a second shot? Better luck next time? All I could think to write was I hoped she was feeling OK about the attempted homicide and wasn't looking to go into marriage counseling later with her intended victim. I put in a few good words for her previous boyfriend, tall Wally Rumpkin, and said I hoped this episode had given her a new appreciation for the kinds of extreme steps people like her and her elder son were sometimes forced to take in desperate circumstances. I closed by saying I hoped little Noel would be able to visit her often in prison, even if her other son couldn't make it. All in all, a fairly inspiring missive that someday may prove a controversial highlight of the Collected Letters of Rick S. Hunter. I addressed the envelope to Mom's house, and to throw off the cops I wrote as return address the Chihuahua Lovers of Mexico, Sonora State Branch.

We reached Guaymas on the coast by late afternoon. Lots of high-rise hotels amid verdant tropical gardens, but none of the area campgrounds met Mrs. K's demanding standards. So we camped right on the beach in a blue-water cove a few miles south of town in the shadow of jagged Mt. Teta Kawi. No hookups, but we're making do with the Plock's marine batteries, propane supplies, diesel generator (to power the vital air conditioning), and 300-gallon fresh water tank. The satellite TV reception is flawless, but Mrs. K's and Connie's cellular phones are now beyond the range of civilization. Looks like we'll be roughing it.

Dogo had a few stiff margaritas to relax from the road grind, then grilled a freshly purchased swordfish over a pit Bondo dug in the beach. We sat on the warm sand and stuffed ourselves as an orange and pink sun settled gingerly into the cobalt waters of the Sea of Cortez. Sheeni's mother smacked her lips and said my virgin mai-tais were by far the best she'd ever had. Despite my standoffish vibes, My Love parked herself right next to me. I ignored her as much as was humanly possible.

FRIDAY, April 2 — Another killer hot day. Somehow Guaymas contrives to be both desert-like and humid. It was already warm when Dogo and I rolled out of our adjoining berths in the luggage basement. He set up the curtain around the Plock's outdoor shower, then stripped down to his well-ornamented buff for bathing. Sneaking a peek, I spotted an eagle, a wigwam, and what looked like a 1932 Ford coupe, but nothing resembling a riveted U-boat periscope. Drying off after my shower, I had to clutch my admiral's uniform to my still-moist torso when My Love suddenly bounded out the door in the same purple bikini that had proved so wrenching to my nervous system last summer at Clear Lake.

"Come on, Rick," she called, "let's go for a swim."

"Already took one," I lied. "Have to squeeze Mrs. K's orange juice."

I wanted to squeeze something, but it wasn't a member of the citrus family.

The main topic of conversation at breakfast was Nick Twisp's homicidal mother. Looks like My Love spilled the beans. Few particulars of the case were known, but that didn't stop Sheeni's mother from launching another vituperative obloquy on The Menace of the Twisps. It was all I could do to restrain François from pissing in her oatmeal. It didn't help that whenever Dogo joined in the discussion he referred to my erstwhile family as "them Twirps."

In the middle of the meal someone knocked on the door, triggering a frenzy of high-pitched dog yapping. I opened the door. An exasperated backpacker from down the beach asked if we could please switch off our "noisy generator."

"I wish I could, honey," replied Mrs. K, "but I have to keep my little dogs cool."

"There's nothing worse than a hot Chihuahua," I told the red-faced man. "Care for a cappuccino? I've got the steam up in the espresso maker."

He muttered something about "damn despoilers of the planet" and stomped off.

12:20 p.m. After Bondo finished his scullery chores, My Love threw an extra-large Chihuahua T-shirt over her now-dry bikini, and we sneaked away from the campsite. To avoid issues of grounding, she wisely avoided seeking her parents' permission for our excursion. Despite my eremitical vibes, Sheeni entwined her familiar warm digits in mine. We made our way to the highway and caught the rickety local bus into town. In the midmorning heat Guaymas smelled strongly of rotting fish. In case its involvement in that industry wasn't apparent enough, the city fathers had seen fit to erect something called "Monumento al Pescador," an enormous statue of a heroic peasant wrestling a giant fish.

We strolled along the harbor, then My Love asked to be excused and ducked into a farmacia. I watched from the busy entrance as she made an alarming purchase from the anticoncepcionismo aisle. Did she imagine we were going to rent a cheap hotel room for the afternoon? A marvelous idea, but only if they offer total blackout conditions in their rooms.

Sure enough, halfway down the next block, she steered me into a hotel. We strolled across the dim cool lobby and toward an adjoining cantina.

"Shall we have a soda, Rick?" proposed My Love. "You look like you're about to faint in that heavy coat."

"OK," I grunted.

We ordered tall mango concoctions from the attractive waitress, then Sheeni excused herself to go the restroom. A few minutes later she returned—a dazzling smile illuminating her face.

"You look pleased with yourself," I growled.

"I am, Rick. Very pleased indeed. Look!"

She handed me a small rectangle of plastic-encased cardboard.

"What's this?" I asked.

"It's a pregnancy test, Rick. See, I passed."

"You mean you're pregnant!" I exclaimed.

"No, silly. It means I'm not. See, the little window didn't turn pink."

"You thought you were expecting a baby?" I asked, still dazed.

"Much worse than that, Rick," she replied. "I feared I was expecting a Twisp. My friend Nick took advantage of me last month in a moment of emotional vulnerability. I'm underage, so it's technically statutory rape."

I gulped. "But you're OK, right?"

"Uh-huh. I was a few days late and feeling pretty strange. The vomiting worried me too. But my periods can be somewhat irregular. I've skipped whole months before."

"Sheeni, you've got to be careful about these things. Guys aren't programmed to act responsibly. They'll always take advantage of you if they can."

"Rick, you sound just like my mother. And besides, Nick never impressed me as a likely candidate for reproductive success."

Mildly offended, I reached for the check and my arm knocked the cardboard rectangle off the table. I bent over to pick it up and experienced a massive scrotal spasm.

THE DAMN WINDOW HAD TURNED PINK!

If my genes were thrilled, they were keeping it to themselves. The rest of me felt violently ill. Fighting panic, I eased the telltale test into a pocket of my coat.

"Rick, you're white as a sheet."

"Excuse me . . . got to . . ."

I fled to the restroom and expelled my breakfast in fiery waves. After the final harrowing heave, I ripped the test cardboard into a hundred pieces and flushed the whole disgusting mess of my life down the toilet.

When I returned to our table, Sheeni was looking for something.

"Nickie, I've lost my test."

Another jolt.

"What did you call me?" I demanded.

"Rick, of course. Have you seen my test?"

"Uh, the waitress must have taken it when she cleared the table. Let's go."

As we were exiting the hotel, My Love suddenly gripped my arm and pulled me back under the portico. Across the broad avenida Sheeni's father was walking arm-in-arm with Mrs. K.

"Maybe they're just being politely friendly," I gasped.

We watched dumbfounded as the chummy couple disappeared into the hotel across the street.

"Hypocrisy, Rick," announced Sheeni. "It's rearing its very ugly head."

3:20 p.m. After a downsized lunch (the two absentees were "shopping in town," blithely explained Sheeni's jilted mother),

I took the dogs for an abbreviated walk to save them from heat-stroke, then sought the younger Krusinowski's counsel under a swaying palm tree. I slathered suntan lotion on Connie's bare back as My Love frolicked in the waves across the cove with Dogo. No T.E. from this sensual operation; today's events may have rendered me impotent for life.

"I thought I saw those two making eyes over the bridge table," Connie commented after I had related the shocking events of the morning. "Not someone I would have chosen, but I've noticed that women seem much less discriminating after age fifty. Menopause must be even more depressing than I thought. There was a time my mother would have laughed in that priggish windbag's face. Mr. Saunders's attraction to Rita is more understandable. How would you like to face his bedmate every night?"

I shuddered. Could darling Sheeni ever get that old and repulsive?

"What am I going to do about Sheeni?" I wailed.

"Fifteen and expecting," sighed Connie. "I'm sure that wasn't in her plans."

"She thinks she's not pregnant," I pointed out.

"Well, that can't last, Rick. From what my girlfriends tell me, pregnancy has a way of making itself known to the victim. When she finds out, I imagine her first impulse will be to lash out at the guy responsible."

"What if I offered to marry her?"

"I can't begin to tell you how fast you'd be behind bars."

More emotional turmoil; I felt my wizened tool wither even further in my pants.

"Then what should I do?"

"Absolutely nothing, Rick. Just go on playing it cool. I like the way your body language has improved."

"But what about poor Sheeni?"

"She should be fine, assuming she keeps her parents in the

dark. Thanks to you, Rick, she can afford the best abortion money can buy."

"But I thought we could get married. Sheeni could have our baby. We could keep it around for a few months to get emotionally bonded, then send it to boarding school. It wouldn't be that inconvenient."

"Bad idea, Rick. You're not ready for parenthood."

"Who is, Connie?"

"Hardly anyone, Rick, though I hope to nail handsome Paulo very soon."

I looked up and gazed longingly at My Love. I didn't like the boisterous way our tattooed chauffeur was flinging her across the waves in her condition.

"Connie, I saw no evidence of a submarine periscope or simulated rivets on Dogo's repulsive body."

"I suppose not, Rick. But then you can't believe everything people tell you on April Fools' Day."

7:05 p.m. In the late afternoon the lovebirds returned from town lugging groceries and acting as if nothing had happened. I find it interesting that it's not just teenagers who have to sneak around and pretend to be indifferent to sex. After an extended cocktail hour, Dogo prepared another fabulous barbecue on the beach. My Love made a face as I served her a genuinely virginal mai-tai. I figured I should give the kid a break, since it was probably still hung over from the benders of the previous days.

As I sat on the sand and ate my spit-roasted chicken I glanced over at My Love's slender abdomen. Somewhere in there a tiny zygote was struggling into existence. It was facing some tough odds, what with having a load of Twisp chromosomes in its DNA and a host who would not be pleased to learn of its presence. I wondered if I should be rooting for it. Did this overcrowded planet really need one more human being? And what kind of inhospitable world would it face if it did make it to birth? Ultimately, I knew, its fate was up to Sheeni to decide, but I couldn't help feeling sad.

10:45 p.m. The moon was almost full. I was sitting under a palm tree and thinking morose thoughts to the drone of the generator when My Love sauntered over and kicked off her sandals.

"Mind if I join you, Rick?"

"It's a public beach," I grunted.

Sheeni sat down, leaned back against the tree, and languidly adjusted her bikini top. She reached over and sprinkled a handful of white sand on my uniform trousers.

"Warm night," she said. "How can you stand being in that coat?"

"Moon rays. Bad for you."

"Phhhh. I've decided you're ashamed of your body."

"Could be. My motorcycle crash was pretty bad."

"What happened, Rick?"

"I blew a head gasket at 110 miles per hour. The bike wiped out. The doctors said I would never walk again. Showed those suckers."

"Do you have terrible scars?"

"Maybe."

"I wouldn't mind, Rick."

"So you say. Mind if I ask you a question? What would you have done if your test today had turned out the other way?"

"Oh, God, Rick. I don't know. It's too frightening to think about."

"Would you have married the guy?"

"I don't even know where he is."

"Do you . . . love him?"

"What does love mean, Rick? That word is so overused it's lost all meaning. Nick was always telling me he loved me. OK, fine.

How did that make me feel? Like a very clinging boy was trying to adhere himself to me—like lichen to a tree."

"You didn't like him at all?" I asked, alarmed.

"I'm not saying that. He had a way of growing on a person. But I slept with him mostly to sleep with him."

"I don't get it."

"I mean I had sex with him to spend the night with him. I don't think people are made to sleep alone. If I had a daughter, I'd say no sex until you're 16, but you can sleep with your boyfriend every night."

"That might be pleasant for her, Sheeni, but I don't think the guy would be getting much rest."

"It must be weird being a boy, Rick. Having this appendage that you feel compelled to stick in other people."

"It keeps the species going."

"I suppose. Do you like me, Rick?"

"You're OK, I guess."

"I could sneak out tonight. We could meet in the little boat car."

"Maybe," I yawned. "I'll see if I feel like it."

SATURDAY, April 3 — Needless to say, I felt like it. Sheeni, still garbed in her purple bikini, was waiting in the back seat when I arrived in full uniform. We lay back together in the cramped seat; moonlight streaming in through the portholes bathed her enticing curves in a silvery aura. Freed from microbial fears, my massive lips went immediately to work. My Love placed my hand on her yielding breasts, then brushed her fingers along the bulge in my trousers. My interval of impotence had abruptly terminated. I pushed up her bikini top and fondled a familiar nipple, taking care not to dip too deeply into Nick Twisp's repertoire of exclusive love caresses. Eventually, our lips parted.

"Are you going to take off that coat, Rick?" she asked. "I feel like I'm kissing a majorette."

Just my luck. Why couldn't it have been a cloudy, moonless night?

"I, I better not, Sheeni. I don't have any condoms."

"I brought some, Rick. They're top-rated by Consumer Reports."

"I thought you didn't believe in sex until age 16?"

"I come from a long line of hypocrites, Rick," she whispered, slipping off her bikini bottoms. "Let's do it."

Against my better judgment, I slid a finger into the steamy recesses of her chestnut tangle. She moaned and struggled with my zipper. I pondered my dilemma. Even putting aside the T.E.-in-the-moonlight identification issue, I wasn't sure it was medically safe for her to be doing this sort of thing in her present condition. Reluctantly, I pushed her hand away from my trousers.

"We better not, Sheeni."

"Why not, Rick?"

"Uh, the doctors say I shouldn't use it for a while. It got pretty tore up when I hit the handlebars. They only removed the splint last week."

"Really? It feels OK to me."

"Better not chance it. Here, I'll do you."

From long experience I knew exactly what was required. I did the deed; she convulsed in my arms, then lay back spent.

"That was wonderful. What about you, Rick? Would it be jeopardizing your recovery if I stroked it lightly through your pants?"

"Uhmm, I suppose that would be permissible. If you don't mind."

"Not at all. Tell me if I'm hurting anything. I don't want to apply too much pressure."

Her gentle touch was unimaginably exquisite; all too soon I

pitched headfirst into that vaporous realm beyond reason, then reluctantly drifted back to earth. We entangled our limbs to the fullest extent possible and listened to the pulse of our hearts and the slow rhythm of our breathing. Her soft hair smelled of the sea. I buried my face in its cascading folds and kissed her neck. I wanted the night never to end.

"This is awful, Rick," she said, fondling one of my brass buttons. "I'm not going to see you after Sunday."

"That's life, kid," I growled.

"Rick, do you care anything for me?"

"Sure, I like you all right. Let's go to sleep."

"I wish we weren't so young."

"Go to sleep, Sheeni. Take each day as it comes. That's my motto."

I wish!

11:09 a.m. We've pulled up stakes and are heading back north. Mrs. K had hoped to get to the historic old mining town of Alamos (160 miles farther south), but she got Sheeni's father instead. This morning her clandestine lover made a great show of cooing over Vronski, which I interpreted as signaling a desire to caress their mutual mistress, though I think petting Anna would have sent a less ambiguous message. Too bad for those two that privacy is in such short supply aboard the Plock. Sheeni and I could use a little of it ourselves. Fortunately, no one seemed to notice that My Love and I were yawning all through breakfast. I got about two hours sleep, and begrudge even those few minutes of unconsciousness as precious time I could have been experiencing my darling's sweet arms. As Rick S. Hunter says, I'll have enough time for sleep when I'm dead or incarcerated.

My Love threw up again after breakfast, touching off another tirade by Sheeni's mother against lax Mexican sanitation standards. Personally, I don't see why our parasitic zygote should be expelling all that potential nourishment. Soon they were both resting peacefully in the Saunders' cabin, allowing the cabin boy to rendezvous with Connie in her mother's stateroom for a private chat.

"I take it you passed a pleasant night with your friend," said Connie.

"Extremely. It's uncanny, Connie. The more indifference I display toward Sheeni, the more loving she becomes."

"Congratulations, Rick. You have discovered the fundamental flaw in the human brain. Somehow our wires for pleasure and pain got crossed. Paulo's never even kissed me, I'm totally miserable, and I can't get enough of the guy. Of course, Sheeni's hormones are in an uproar now. You may be benefiting from that as well."

"She's amazingly loving. I'm almost jealous that Rick S. Hunter is having such an easy time with her."

"You're marvelously neurotic, Rick. I'm impressed that you can be jealous of yourself. So did you make it with her?"

"Everything but that. I wasn't sure it was safe to do it—you know, considering her condition."

"It's totally safe, Rick. People practically do it right in the hospital delivery room. Didn't they cover that in your health class?"

"They may have, Connie, but I wasn't paying attention. I never thought it would apply to me."

"Well, wake up and smell the baby powder, guy. Or should I call you Dad?"

3:45 p.m. We stopped for a quick roadside lunch in the little town of Imuris, about 20 miles south of the border. By the time I was clearing away the dishes, the entire population had gathered round to ogle the wondrous gringo RV. Dogo didn't appreciate the fingerprints on his wax job, and blasted his diesel horn to scare off the kids as we pulled away. The plan was to cross into Arizona at Nogales. Connie could see I was getting nervous and took me aside to tell me not to worry. Easy for her to say! She wasn't the alleged Rick S. Hunter bearing a forged birth certificate identifying him as Nick S. Dillinger.

There was a half-mile backup of cars at the border, which afforded plenty of time for my anxiety to reach life-threatening levels as we crept along toward the crossing checkpoint. I sat on a settee next to My Love and felt my racing heart approach its RPM red-line as sweat oozed from my forehead like slime from a slug.

"Rick, is something the matter?" inquired My Love, squeezing my hand.

"Just a flashback to my accident," I rumbled.

And then the truck ahead of us pulled through the gate and it was our turn to be inspected. Dogo pressed a button to extend the front steps and opened the door. A smiling female border agent stepped aboard. I ceased breathing. Anna and Vronski barked fiercely from Connie's lap.

"Any fruits or vegetables?" she asked.

"We finished the last of them for lunch," Mrs. K lied.

"All U.S. citizens?" the agent asked, glancing around at the passengers, one of whom I knew looked suspicious as hell.

"Sure thing, honey," Mrs. K replied.

"Very nice rig!" the agent exclaimed. "OK, folks, have a nice day."

She stepped off, Dogo withdrew the steps and closed the door, he accelerated, and miraculously my breathing resumed. I was back in the United States and I hadn't even been strip-searched. Boy, no wonder this country is awash in drugs. We should have loaded up the luggage basement with cocaine before crossing over.

7:05 p.m. We're camping outside Tucson in a ritzy RV park that has its own swimming pool, tennis club, and golf course. After you spend time in the Third World, this country seems affluent beyond belief—as if dollars were raining perpetually from the skies. After Dogo (with my help) hooked up the hoses and cables (and flushed the brimming holding tanks), Connie decided there was still enough daylight to get in nine holes of golf. As a child of wealth and privilege she plays that dumb game. Surprisingly, so does Dogo, although he has a bigger handicap than most golfers. Perhaps he swings the club with his feet.

Sheeni's mother went with them because she needed some air after the long journey and she enjoys driving the little carts. As a high-priced lawyer Mr. Saunders is also a golf nut, but he volunteered to stay behind and "keep our hostess company." Sheeni was all for sticking to those two like leeches, but Mrs. K suggested "you young people" go explore the campground. As we exited the Plock, I heard the door click locked behind us.

"If they weren't such hypocrites," observed My Love, taking my hand, "they could have gone in one bedroom and we could have gone in the other."

We explored the RV park, set in a desert landscape that looked like the surface of the moon with cactuses. This campground was much fancier than the modest church trailer park in Clearlake where I had met The Love of My Life. We walked through the recreation hall with its pool tables, video games, and giant-screen TV. We checked out the swimming pool and adjoining hot tub, aboil with silver-haired retirees. (I refused to get within 50 feet of it.) We watched colorful leisure-wear spin in the fully equipped laundromat. We bought sodas in the park store and speculated on the lifestyles of the occupants of each RV as we strolled up and down the rows in the fading light. Every convenience was offered except a place where young people of the opposite sex could go and be alone together. Worse, the park was too public and too well-lit to make the Plock II a credible venue for such intimacies. Sheeni expressed frustration over this, but Rick S. Hunter had to pretend he didn't care.

"This is our last night together, you know," she pointed out.

"Yeah, I guess so," I replied. "I wish those golfers would get back. I'm starved."

9:45 p.m. Mr. Saunders splurged and took everyone out to dinner at a fancy steakhouse, not excluding the cabin boy and Dogo. (We followed in the Plock II as the main party traveled by cab.) Connie and I ordered the most expensive item on the menu—the filet mignon and jumbo prawn combo—earning dirty looks from our future father-in-law. Sheeni only picked at her petit filet, causing me to feel a fresh pang of sympathy for our beleaguered zygote. Our host sat between his wife and Mrs. K, and for all I know may have played footsie with both of them. Complaining it was "too watery," Mrs. Saunders angrily sent back her virgin mai-tai; I fear I may have spoiled that cocktail for her for all time.

So now we're back and everyone's upstairs having nightcaps and watching satellite TV. Dogo has not yet emerged to join me in the luggage basement. The plan is for Sheeni to sneak out after lights-out and link up with Rick S. Hunter. Perhaps we can do it in the pitch-black laundry room atop a vibrating clothes dryer. I have a pocketful of quarters just in case. Wish me luck!

SUNDAY, April 5 — 1:15 a.m. A DISASTER! Sheeni's in the hospital! I'm a nervous wreck. Finding the laundry door locked (were they worried someone was going to steal the dryer lint?), My Love suggested we stroll over in the warm moonlight to the pleasantly deserted golf course. We kissed in the shadows of a clump of trees beside a sinuous pond, and as we lowered ourselves onto the invitingly lush grass My Love suddenly cried out in pain. Something had bitten her leg! I spotted a small lobster-like creature scuttling away and stomped on it. My Love was nearly hysterical from pain and shock, but somehow I managed to get her back to the Plock, where her pajamas-clad parents pitched a major abusive fit, while Mrs. K calmly dialed 911 on her cellular phone. By then My Love's face had begun to swell alarmingly and she was having difficulty breathing. While waiting for the ambulance, Connie put ice on the bite and Mrs. K sent Dogo and me out with flashlights to retrieve the dead creature, which somehow we found and which Dogo said was a scorpion—a "big one."

I got in the ambulance with My Love, but her father dragged me out bodily. The Saunders went in the ambulance, and Connie and her mother followed in the Plock II. Mrs. K told me I had to stay behind because I would just be in the way and "had caused enough trouble already." Connie told me not to worry, slipped me one of her cellular phones, and said she would call as soon as she heard any news. Dogo has been refilling my glass with brandy. If the phone doesn't ring in the next two minutes, I'm going to lose my mind.

2:10 a.m. Connie just called. My Love is OK. They've given her anti-venom serum and she's resting peacefully. The doctor said it was good they got her to the hospital right away, because it was a bark scorpion, one of the most dangerous kinds, whose bite can be fatal. He also assured Mr. and Mrs. Saunders that neither the venom nor the treatment should affect the baby, which is when the parental shit really impacted the fan.

Too exhausted (and plastered?) to worry about that. I'm going to bed.

11:45 a.m. On the road (Interstate 10) heading west toward California border. Have terrible hangover. Feel rotten. Very surly to employer at breakfast. The Saunders are no longer with us. Sheeni's father came back while I was asleep and cleared out their stuff. My Love was discharged early this morning, and the three of them caught a plane to San Francisco. We didn't even get a chance to say good-bye!

Connie just divulged shocking news. When pressed by irate parents, Sheeni named as father of surprise zygote despised affected twit Trent Preston. Could it be true? Doesn't seem possible. Connie agrees. She deems it sinister ploy by Sheeni to wreck former boyfriend's new marriage. Is my Sweet Darling capable of such treachery? Prefer to believe her mind still muddled by scorpion venom. Thankful, at least, she didn't name Nick Twisp or Rick S. Hunter, though Connie revealed that parents blame Sheeni's brush with death on my fiendish attempt to seduce their once-virginal daughter. I'm now object of their unbridled hatred—so what else is new? Wonder if they despise me more than Nick Twisp? Or Trent? Though my racial purity may be suspect, at least I'm not a married man.

9:20 p.m. Spring Break is over. When we got back to Bel Air, Mrs. K paid me $700 in cash and added a $50 bonus for "disappointments in love." She said she would hire me for future trips as long as I didn't outgrow my uniform or change my face to "some unacceptable film star." I thanked her and assured her that this would be my look from now on.

Lacey says Rick S. Hunter is "much cuter" than the old Nick. She likes my new voice too. I value her opinion on these matters because she's a professional devoting her life to superficial appearances. Tonight I may realize a longtime ambition to spend the night with her alone. No sign of Mr. K, who I presume is having a loving reunion with his wife and daughter. My hostess just closed the cave walls and is making some popcorn in the microwave. Rick S. Hunter is stretched out on the daybed with his laptop. I'm hoping faux leopard skin proves a flattering complement to my virile new lips.

MONDAY, April 5 — Lacey's a mess. She bared her soul to me last night while we cuddled on the daybed, I sipped white wine, and François schemed to bare the rest of her. At one point she asked me whether I thought it was better to be in love "with a poor musician or a rich married man?" Out of loyalty to Connie, I replied that a woman's first concern always must be the economic well-being of her unborn children.

"But I don't have any unborn children," she objected.

"Of course you do," I assured her. "It's just that they're, well, unborn."

"Oh, I see . . . I guess."

"Lacey, I know you love Paul, but let's face it, the only thing he'll ever have in common with Charlie Parker and Stan Getz is a prison record for drugs. The guy's not destined for jazz superstardom. Do you want to raise your children in rented pool cabanas?"

"No, but I don't want to break up Bernie's marriage either."

After swearing Lacey to absolute secrecy, I divulged the shocking details of Mrs. K's Mexican liaison with Paul's father.

"That's amazing!" she exclaimed. "I dig older men, but Mr. Saunders makes my skin crawl. I'd dump Paul in a minute if he ever got to look like his father."

"I feel the same way about Sheeni," I confessed.

"Bernie did say his marriage has been on the rocks for years," she admitted.

"What more proof do you need?"

Lacey nibbled her popcorn and mulled it over.

"Bernie's a very sweet guy, Nick, I mean, Rick, but I wasn't born yesterday. I could just be a spring fling to him."

"You can land him if you put your mind to it, Lacey. I'm talking multi-carat diamond ring, trousseau shopping on Rodeo Drive, the whole nine yards. Men Bernie's age are always looking to settle down with that second trophy wife."

"It'd be awful to dump Paulie while he's in jail, Rick."

"A guy can do a lot of emotional healing while meditating in a cell. And don't forget, he said the thought of marrying you made him barf."

"Paulie did say that," she conceded, "the rat."

François suggested it might be helpful in making Bernie jealous if I were to spend the night with her on the daybed. She gave me a playful tap and said having a "cute guy like you" in the pool utility room would be enough "to get Bernie plenty steamed"—even if I was supposed to be her brother.

At least I persuaded her to try out François's new lips. She liked them too.

9:50 a.m. When I crawled out of my cave this morning to cough out eight hours of accumulated chlorine fumes, Bernie Krusinowski was soaking his corned-beef body in the hot tub. He waved me over, but I approached cautiously and kept a safe distance.

"So, you didn't listen when I warned you to stay away from my daughter. Now look at you. Do you have to iron those lips or are they permanent press?"

"They're still a little swollen from my surgery."

"How much did that quack soak you for?"

"$11,400, but I'm not complaining. Everyone missed you on the trip."

"Mexico's a nice enough place—if you're a Mexican. I had more important matters to attend to here."

"I hope, Bernie, your intentions toward my sister are honorable."

"Hold it down, bub," he cautioned, glancing about. "What did Lacey tell you?"

"We have no secrets in our family. I've advised her to look for a younger man who can satisfy her every need."

"I can satisfy everything she needs satisfied, bub. Don't you worry about that."

"She wants children and a home, Bernie. If she doesn't get a ring, she'll walk."

"She never told me that."

"Don't let her know I mentioned this, but the same sad story played out last year in Ukiah. The guy's name was George W. Twisp—very big in concrete and lumber up there. He's still a basket case."

"Really?"

"She leaves a very big void, Bernie. And when she walks, she's gone. My sister never turns back."

"She's got her pride, I suppose."

"Why shouldn't she? She's one in a million."

"Better than that, bub. Our Lacey's one in a billion!"

OK, I'm trying to figure this out. Let's assume I marry Sheeni. If Paul marries Connie, she becomes my sister-in-law. If Lacey weds Mr. K, she becomes Paul's stepmother-in-law and Connie's stepmother. Also my stepmother-in-law, though I doubt that would restrain François. If Mrs. K marries Sheeni's father, she becomes her daughter's stepmother-in-law, my stepmother-in-law as well (achieving parity with Lacey), and some sort of weird in-law to her first husband. Any way you look at it, I end up surrounded by millionaire relatives. And blissfully united to the ultimate Trophy Wife, who comes to the marriage bed already loaded with my money.

2:24 p.m. Connie was so pleased by my conjugal machinations, she took me out to breakfast again in West Hollywood. I ordered a full-stack of blueberry Bette Midlers; Connie tried the John Travolta waffles with pork sausage sideburns. Almost too realistic to eat. Afterwards, she drove me all the way out to East L.A. to pick up Rick S. Hunter's new identity cards. Mr. Castillo marveled at my latest transformation.

"A very professional job, Mr. Hunter," he said, admiring my face. "Very nice work. Most people play with the cards life deals them, but you're a man who makes up his own rules."

"I'm hoping to hold on to these cards for a while though," I admitted, counting out three more $100 bills from my meager stash.

Not only did Mr. Castillo provide my latest set of documents (complete with forged high-school transcript) for half price, he said that when I'm ready to apply for college he can supply me with perfect SAT test scores—double 800s on my verbal and math. Although I'd like to think Rick S. Hunter could score that well on his own, it's nice to have insurance just to be assured of attending the same rigorously elite college as My Love.

It occurred to me as I was admiring my latest driver's license that all my life Nick Twisp has been receiving "don't exist" messages. And now, through the miracle of modern surgical and counterfeiting techniques, he no longer exists. Yet I have achieved a successful integration of these messages without resorting to the conventional recourse of suicide. You might say I've disappeared, but still I live. Even better, the waitress at the restaurant this morning actually flirted with me. What a revelation: Rick S. Hunter is attractive to women. Eat your heart out Trent Preston!

6:05 p.m. I desperately wanted to call Sheeni, but Connie advised me to play it cool. Instead, she suggested we visit the other Saunders sibling. The county jail facility sprawled across a treeless suburban tract like everyone's worst nightmare of junior high school—enlarged about ten times and surrounded by parallel rows of razor wire. It even smelled like junior high. I was pretty nervous about subjecting myself to such a concentration of law enforcement, but Connie thought it would be a good test of my new IDs. My faith in Mr. Castillo's art was vindicated. Rick S. Hunter's driver's license was examined at least a half dozen times and no one batted an eyelash. As we trooped down grim corridors and waited in line at metal detectors, I prayed to whichever indifferent gods watch over me to let me stay out of places like this.

I felt I blended in well with the other visitors, but my exotically garbed companion attracted many curious stares. Her hair had been styled in improbable upsweeps and she had removed her contacts (Paul prefers her eyes in their natural Polish state).

The visiting room was something of a disappointment. No dividing wall of bulletproof glass with greasy handsets dangling on short armored cords. No forbidding iron bars. Not even a steel mesh barrier to keep the lawbreakers separated from the law-abiding. It was just a large cheerless room furnished with banged-up tables and metal folding chairs. Lots of screaming kids chasing around and not paying much attention to Dad. The nervous atmosphere of forced sociability reminded me of hospital or funeral-parlor visiting hours—except the bored attendants here were heavily armed.

Paul looked sharp in his crisp orange jumpsuit. He gave Connie a friendly kiss on the lips and shook my hand. All through the visit he held Connie's hand, which could have been just a show of good fellowship, except (as Connie pointed out during an exhaustive deconstruction of the visit on the drive back to Bel Air) he only held her hand and not mine. And when we were leaving, he kissed her good-bye and not me. Thank goodness for that.

Introductions were not required. Paul winked and said it was a pleasure to meet Rick S. Hunter. He said he thought Jean-Paul Belmondo was a good choice to impress diehard Francophiles.

"Well, he's doing fairly well so far," I admitted.

I asked Paul how a fellow with his street smarts and foresight could get nailed by the police. He shrugged and said these things happen. He said he was meeting some interesting guys in jail and had been invited to join a small R&B group. Real instruments weren't allowed in prison, so they improvised. Paul was learning to play the tissue paper and comb.

Connie told him he might be getting a niece or nephew for Christmas this year, but probably not to count on it. Paul smiled and asked Rick S. Hunter what he thought of that development. I said I thought it was extremely dire, but I was more than willing to do the honorable thing.

"That might have to take place over my mother's dead body," he pointed out.

"Yeah, probably your father's too," I conceded. "And maybe even your sister's."

"I can tell you what my mother wants," said Paul. "She called me yesterday. She wants me to undergo a religious conversion, get married to someone other than Lacey, find a high-paying job, and adopt Sheeni's baby. What do you think of that?"

"No problem, honey," replied Connie, squeezing his hand. "Except we might have to fake the religious stuff."

I only smiled. Sure I like Connie and Paul, but they may not be first on my list of potential foster parents. Kids only get one shot at childhood. If it's not too much to ask, I think the next generation of Twisps should be raised by normal parents for a change.

TUESDAY, April 6 — On the bus to Oakland. Although adapting well to the challenging Bel Air lifestyle, I decided Rick S. Hunter should be getting on with his life. After a libido-inflaming farewell hug from Lacey, I went out to breakfast with Connie, who then dropped me off at the bus station. I said good-bye to my ally in amours at the curb, greatly impressing the assembled panhandlers. Connie gave me my second electrifying hug of the day, a semi-smoldering kiss on the lips, and the number of her most private cellular phone (she has three of varying exclusiveness). We have promised to keep each other fully informed on all developments.

I just counted my anorexic wad: fifty-nine $100 bills in my money belt, plus $42 in my wallet. And no more Connie to chauffeur me around for free and pick up the tab for my meals. Back to life at the margins. Good for my art, I suppose, assuming

Rick S. Hunter opts to specialize in gritty novels of working-class privation, relieved only by spectacular sex.

8:45 p.m. I slept most of the way up through the Central Valley. I can't believe people actually live there. Aren't they bored silly by pool-table-flat terrain sectioned into endless fields of anonymous plant life? I prefer vibrant, urban Oakland, even if it does have a high crime rate. Another expensive cab ride up to Oakland's exclusive hill district brought me to my mother's new home: a two-story Brown Shingle purchased with my inheritance from the late Bertha Ulansky. Not in the same league as the Krusinowskis' imposing mansion, but it was a big step up from Nick Twisp's humble origins down in the flats.

Fortunately, the lady of the house was still behind bars. When my sister opened the big oak door, I sucked in my lips, smiled, and said, "Hi, Joanie. Guess who had expensive Mexican plastic surgery?" She stared open-mouthed at my retooled visage. Yes, the handsome stranger on the porch was her long-lost brother.

"Well, it's an improvement," she said at last, "I guess."

Good thing the Twisps are so undemonstrative. Had I been tempted to hug my sister, I would have been blocked several feet from my target by her grossly distended abdomen. We shook hands instead.

"Yeah, I'm pregnant," she admitted, showing me into the living room—a gracefully proportioned room savaged by Mom's shabby old flatlands furniture. And where was Jerry's dead Chevy?

"What are you in your 13th month?" I asked.

"I was fine until I came up here, Nick. Being around little Noel has made Tyler balloon in size. I feel like a blimp."

Could it be that My Love's lithe form will be so misshapen in a few months? The thought made me shudder.

"You've named it Tyler?"

"Uh-huh. We know it's going to be a boy. He's due at the end of May. Nick, want to see your brother?"

"Is it compulsory? And please call me Rick."

It was. Joanie took me upstairs to the lavishly furnished nursery. Noel Lance Wescott was lying in his crib and picking his nose. He took one look at me and started to howl. Joanie picked him up and he copped a nice feel. He was a Twisp all right. He even looked like Dad. I pointed this out to my sister when Noel's 200-decibel screeching at last subsided.

"I finally got the whole story from Mom in jail," Joanie replied. "When Dad was still living in Marin, she went over one weekend to hound him for your child-support payment. He opened a bottle of wine, they wound up in bed, and she never even got the check."

"But they've hated each other for years."

"I thought so too, Rick, but I guess there was some kind of spark left."

Little Noel is a real Twisp. That is such a shock. And so gross.

WEDNESDAY, April 7 — I spent the night in the guest room, grabbing a few snatches of sleep here and there in between violent Noel outbursts. I can't believe someone hasn't made a fortune building soundproof isolation chambers for screaming infants. Just how is a person supposed to cope? Joanie thinks Noel has regressed because he misses his mom. That hardly seems possible, but I suppose he hasn't known the woman for long.

Speaking of Mom's male offspring, I've search all through the house without discovering a single Nick Twisp item. Not even a spare sock to add to my skimpy pack. I've been completely expunged from my maternal home. Good thing Nick is no longer with us to receive these gratuitous "don't exist" messages.

Joanie stuck a bottle in Noel's face so we could converse over breakfast. Sheeni's check arrived on Monday. Joanie immediately deposited it in a laid-back bank in Berkeley in a new account she opened under an assumed name. The bad news is it might take a week or more to clear. Meanwhile, Mom continues to chill in the slammer. The worse news is they want to use another big chunk of my $60,000 to hire a lawyer. I suggested Joanie find someone offering budget rates. Perhaps a student attorney whose legal training is still fresh in their mind. Besides, those kids have to start their careers somewhere.

Lance remains in the hospital, but is now out of intensive care. No, Joanie hasn't visited him, but she did send him a card. Reconstruction surgery starts this week. I say why bother? Better yet, perhaps they could minimize costs and fuss by altering him into a Lancette.

Joanie gave me Noel to hold while she ate her eggs. What an ungainly package: incessant squirming, foul discharges from every orifice, and you have to hold up his drooping head or it will fall right off. They should pass these things around in high-school health class, if they really want to scare kids into using protection.

Joanie is worried who'll take the kid if Mom gets sent to prison.

"Can't you just toss him in the crib with Tyler?" I asked.

"It's a big responsibility, Nick. I don't know how I'll manage as it is as a single mother."

"What about Dr. Dingy? And please call me Rick."

"It's Dindy, Rick. I'm afraid Philip was a mistake—a bad one. Being away from him this week has helped me see that. He conducts life like a scientific experiment—with every aspect under his personal control. I practically have to ask permission to blow my nose."

"You're going to break up with the creep?"

"I think so. I might as well for all the help he'll be. His wife got a very good lawyer. All he has left out of his university salary is a little pocket money. I've been supporting the guy!"

My sister was now batting zero for 312 in boyfriends. She sighed, nibbled her bacon, and studied me. Uh-oh, I could feel her sensitive antennas probing into my psyche. I strove for obtuseness in thought and demeanor.

"That girlfriend of yours is pregnant," she announced at last.

"Er, what makes you say that?" I demanded.

"Oh God, Nick! That is all we need!"

"It's all under control," I lied, "and please call me Rick."

6:30 p.m. On the bus to Ukiah. I had to get out of Oakland fast. There was a disastrous incident involving my brother. Joanie invited me to go with her to visit Mom, but I opted to remain behind and provide vital childcare. Big mistake. All was fine until little Noel woke up from his nap and starting wailing. You didn't have to be a bloodhound to detect the aroma emanating from his pants. I was all for letting him marinate, but Twisps are nothing if not persistent.

So I found the jumbo box of diapers and read the instructions on the back. It sounded fairly basic. I grabbed the kid, placed him on the changing table, and removed his soiled nappy. Too gross for words. I reeled from the noxious olfactory assault, greatly amusing its creator. I wiped off his messy bum and privates as best I could. You definitely could tell the kid was a Twisp. I wondered if it was supposed to be that small or if something had gone awry during the circumcision. I was maneuvering the fresh diaper under him when, boom, he wiggled away from me. I DROPPED MY BABY BROTHER ON THE FLOOR!

He landed with a sickening thud. Nightmarish infant scream-ing, so at least the impact wasn't fatal. Somehow I got his cat-erwauling, flailing little body back on the table and checked for broken bones. No obvious breaks, but the back of his skull felt a little squishy. Part of his brain may have turned to mush! Eventually, I got him quieted down and re-diapered. In my panic

I wondered if there were any quick home intelligence tests for infants. I switched on the TV and put his face right up to the screen. He didn't seem that interested, even when I changed the channel to a kiddies show—a bad sign, I think. More guilt for Rick. My only brother may grow up retarded because of me. He may have to look to sheltered workshops for career opportunities. Thank goodness it wasn't my own gifted child I fumbled. I don't care how committed Sheeni is to equal rights. She's doing all the diaper-changing in our household!

THURSDAY, April 8 — I hope my brother lived through the night. I wish I were a sociopath like François. Having a conscience really puts a dent in one's enjoyment of life. I spent the night in a "budget" motel on Ukiah's main drag that was no nicer than the Christina Hotel and about five times pricier. So the first order of the day is to find someplace cheap to live. I'm willing to consider anything that's not an actual drainage culvert.

I had breakfast at my favorite donut shop downtown in hopes that Sheeni might drop by on her way to school. No such luck. I did see fat Dwayne Crampton ride by on my Italian mountain bike. His mother must have grabbed it in lieu of that last paycheck I owed her for slave maid service. I ate my usual assortment and read the local paper, which was nicely devoid of Nick Twisp manhunt news. I checked the classified ads. The least expensive apartment, listed at $575 per month, was available only to "employed adults with references." That leaves me out in the cold.

7:15 p.m. I'm writing this in my new apartment. A real-estate agent might even call it a penthouse, since it's situated on the uppermost floor of the two-story commercial block that houses the donut shop. Believe it or not, my window opens directly on the exhaust vent above the donut fryer—suffusing my abode with wonderful sugary smells and a fair amount of grease.

As I was leaving the donut shop this morning, I spotted a

faded "rooms for rent" sign in the window of the jewelry store next door. Old Mr. Szwejk, the jeweler and building owner, was skeptical of Rick S. Hunter's fitness as a tenant, but he found my cash persuasive. The rent is $108 per week; I paid for four weeks in advance.

I have two small rooms and a tiny half bath in what were once commercial offices. The businessmen all moved on to greener pastures long ago, making way for the retired, the deranged, and the generally down and out. Half-wall partitions of varnished blond oak are topped by large fixed panels of a ribbed smoked glass. All the office glass along the corridors has been painted over on the inside with a yellowing paint, rendering it opaque and blocking light to the murky hallways. Neatly painted on my door, made of the same pale wood and ribbed glass, is the name: "Julius T. Marvin, Insurance Broker."

My "furnished" rooms are eclectically decorated with what appear to be discards swiped from the curb on neighborhood cleanup days. No bed either. The purple vinyl sofa, scarred by numerous cigarettes and something with sharp claws, opens up to make a lumpy bed. I have dragged it from the room facing the back alley to the cave-like interior room. I also have a small metal table, some mismatched chairs, a dark oak dresser with scaly mirror, two battered lamps, a wardrobe closet with peeling veneer, and a circa-1950s enameled metal cabinet kitchenette, complete with sink, two-burner range, compact refrigerator, cupboard, and two musty drawers.

The rusty claw-foot bathtub (no shower) is down the hall in its own dank closet. Some of my fellow tenants have not been good citizens about cleaning up after their baths, but Mr. Szwejk said at these rates "maid service" was "out of the question." Even if they hadn't been such slobs, I wouldn't have stepped in that tub on a bet.

All in all, my new home is a big comedown from Granny De-

Falco's snug bungalow, but it's better than nothing and you can't beat the convenient central location. Maybe I can find something nicer if Joanie comes through with some cash or I pry my Wart Watch windfall loose from My Love.

After moving in, I rented a post office box for mail deliveries, called up to arrange for phone service, secured a new library card, and dropped over $80 at a nearby thrift shop loading up on sheets, blankets, towels, kitchen stuff, and Rick S. Hunter's none-too-fashionable school wardrobe. It was a pain being Carlotta, but at least she was equipped with every garment a chick could want. And sliding off her pantyhose was always good for a cheap thrill. Not to mention her bra.

FRIDAY, April 9 — I enrolled again today at Redwood High. This was my first matriculation as a junior, my second as a male, and my third as an entirely different person. That must be some sort of California high-school record. No sign of Miss Pomdreck, my aged guidance counselor. Today's enrollment was processed by Miss Drelfleur, a severe-looking older woman with blotchy skin and ratty hair teased into a gray tumbleweed.

"I thought Miss Pomdreck was in charge of new students," I said.

Miss Drelfleur studied my application form and forged transcript. "Miss Pomdreck is no longer employed by this district."

"Oh," I said with a sinking feeling. "Did she retire?"

"You might call it that. So you were a student at John Wayne High School. Where's that?"

"In Orange County, down south. We were the Fighting Green Berets."

"Well, now you're a Marauding Beaver. I hope you can make the transition. Why is it you're 18, but only a junior?"

"Uh, I was sick when I was 10 and missed a year of school.

178

They thought it was Lou Gehrig's disease, but it turned out to be Babe Ruth's disease. That's why I'm kind of short for my age."

"I see. Well, Rick, you have good grades, but I have to tell you most of our tracked classes are full now."

"I understand, Miss Drelfleur. I'll take what's available."

She gave me a printout of my schedule (wood technology II, boys' gym, California problems, computer lab, lunch, study hall, life skills, and driver's education), and assigned me locker 859, recently evacuated by problem student Carlotta Ulansky. The interior of my former locker revealed traces of a suspicious white powder. The cops must have been dusting it for my prints!

By then first period was over, so I went straight to gym class, where most of my fellow juniors were 17 and outweighed me by at least 30 pounds. Today's activity was basketball for aggressors, and I almost got the ball once. Lots of nude towel-snapping afterwards in the locker room by hairy-chested guys with large flopping penises. I hope Rick S. Hunter looks like that in a few years. As you might expect, most of the horseplay was directed at the new guy. All in all, I think I prefer girls' gym.

Needless to say, I kept my eyes peeled in the hallways for Sheeni, but I saw no sign of her. And vile Vijay dined alone at lunch, which led me to conclude My Love was absent today from school. I hope she hasn't had a scorpion venom relapse. I'm dying to phone her, but I know what Connie would say to that idea.

Trent, I noted with interest, no longer eats lunch with his swim-team buddies. Instead, he and Apurva occupy prestigious seats at a table reserved for Redwood High's Cutest Couples. Speaking of which, Candy Pringle once again may have severed relations with Bruno Modjaleski. I spotted her snacking lightly with her fellow cheerleaders, while the disgraced quarterback kept a low profile at the same socially second-string table as Fuzzy DeFalco, believe it or not.

I've decided it's too risky to reveal Rick S. Hunter's former identity to my best pal. Fuzzy's pretty dependable, but few kids can stand up indefinitely to brutal police interrogation. Besides, he now may be under the impression I owe him some money. On my way to life skills class, I spotted him nuzzling Lana at her locker. She was wearing a new outfit and looking not unfetching. I'd pay somewhere in the low one figure to know what base my pal has landed on with her.

Despite my having rocketed ahead two academic years, school was predictably tedious until last period, when I piled into a big Chevy sedan with Mr. Nurlpradt and three other juniors, one of whom was studious newlywed Apurva Preston. Since I was the newest and greenest driver's ed student (despite my forged license), I got to go first. We cruised around quiet residential streets (past My Love's own house!), and I made all my turns, dodged all oncoming cars, and ran over zero pedestrians. Those sexy automobile commercials don't lie. What a sense of power and freedom—even with Mr. Nurlpradt's cautious foot ever poised over the auxiliary brake pedal.

I managed to exchange a few pleasant words with Apurva. She was looking very fine, but perhaps a trifle troubled? I must get to the bottom of things. Not easy, since I am once again a total stranger in school, a dreary role that still rates just slightly worse than terrorist hostage.

SATURDAY, April 10 — My second night in my new home. Good thing I'm a sound sleeper. Some of our hard-of-hearing tenants like to turn their TVs up LOUD. And bikers on high-revving Harleys enjoy roaring up and down our alley at two in the morning. I think that may be when the bars close.

I met my neighbor across the corridor, who turned out to be Ida, the elderly lunch-counter waitress at Flampert's Variety Store.

Considering the tips Carlotta used to leave her, I can see why she has to live here. She said hello while strolling back from the bathtub in a plaid robe I recognized as a $12.95 Flampert's Original. She addressed me as "Mr. Marvin," and said she hoped I would prove a better neighbor than the previous Mr. Marvin, who was always going off her medication with disruptive results.

Apparently there is a tradition among the tenants of referring to each other by the names on their doors. Ida herself is identified on her door as "Walter M. Whatley, Certified Public Account," so she is addressed as Mr. Whatley, though some long-term tenants call her Walt. Me, I'm happy I didn't wind up in the office of "Evelyn O. Selzer, Stenographer and Typist." Those rooms are currently occupied by a retired sawmill hand and his illegal cat.

4:40 p.m. Back from Radio Shack, where I purchased their cheapest combined telephone/answering machine. I plugged it in, discovered my phone jack was now working, and made my inaugural call to Connie Krusinowski, who was lounging in the hot tub with Lacey.

"Is she wearing a bathing suit?" I asked.

"Yeah, not that I noticed."

"Are you?"

"Of course not."

"Can you talk freely?"

"I hardly think so, Roger."

"Have there been any developments, Connie?"

"Yes, a promising one."

"Does it concern your father?"

"Mostly the other one."

"Lacey?"

"No, the other one."

"Your mother?"

"Yes, Roger, Mother's gone to our house in Palm Springs."

"She moved out?"

"Yes, took the dogs with her. And Dogo too. I think she may be staying there for some time."

"She found out about Lacey?"

"Yes, Roger, Benecia's a gem."

"Your housekeeper spilled the beans?"

"Uh-huh, good help can be expensive."

"Oh, your mother bribed her. So how's your father taking it?"

"Lovely, just lovely. And there's so much to do, day and night."

"He and Lacey are constantly going at it?"

"That's so true, Roger. And how are things with you?"

I filled her in on the events of the past few days, including the muffed diaper disaster.

"Dropped the ball on that one, did you, Roger?"

"Connie, I'm worried sick my brother may grow up mentally impaired!"

"Not to worry, Roger. People drop them all the time. Mom was always firing housekeepers for dropping me. And we have expensive terrazzo floors. So unyielding to the flesh. By the way, how's your lovely fiancée?"

"I haven't seen Sheeni yet, Connie. She wasn't at school yesterday. I'm thinking of calling her."

"Of course not, Roger. Remember what I said. She's exactly where you want her."

"Connie, she's pregnant and miserable. And so am I—miserable, I mean."

"Your patience will be rewarded, Roger. I'm offering a woman's perspective on this issue."

"So you say, Connie. Well, good luck on your end."

"And good luck to you too, Roger."

9:35 p.m. I had a lonely dinner for one at the Golden Carp,

Ukiah's budget-conscious Chinese restaurant. Steve the waiter served me attentively for a change as he had not yet experienced grave gratuity disappointment from my latest personality.

After dinner I took a walk and found myself strolling past Sheeni's stately Victorian home. No sign of My Love or her wearisome parents. Alarmingly, one of the cars in the driveway was a late-model Acura the same color as Trent's. I kept on walking and came to Carlotta's former house, where Apurva was pushing Granny DeFalco's rusty reel-mower across the lawn in the ebbing light. She was looking most alluring in jeans and one of Trent's white dress shirts with the sleeves rolled up. I stopped to say hello, and tried to ignore loathsome Albert and Jean-Paul barking at me from behind the screen door.

"Shouldn't your husband be doing that?" I asked.

Apurva called for the dogs to hush; they ignored her. "Oh, I do not mind, Rick. I need the exercise. I haven't been sleeping well."

"Is it tension from starting a new school? I feel that too."

"Perhaps partially," she replied, smiling weakly.

"I'll have to meet your husband sometime, Apurva. He seems to be quite a popular student. Is he home now?"

"Uh, no," she replied, contemplating the handle of her mower. "He is not home—at the moment, no."

"Oh. Well, maybe some other time then. Uh, see you in driver's ed."

"Yes, Rick. That will be nice. I was quite impressed with your driving skills."

"You did very well too, Apurva. Well, good night."

"Good night, Rick."

Something was clearly amiss. Apurva looked almost as miserable as I feel. Too bad Carlotta wasn't available for an intimate girl-to-girl chat. Chicks are so much less forthcoming with guys. I've got to find out what the hell is going on!

. . .

SUNDAY, April 11 — Another no-show by Sheeni at the donut shop. Doesn't our zygote have to eat? Or is it an embryo by now? Guess I spent too many hours in health class pondering the erotic diagrams and not enough time studying the medical terminology.

After breakfast I reached deep within the bowels of my sofa, extracted my concealed money belt, and sucked out another $100. Thus, my banking technology has regressed about 500 years from Carlotta's ATM card. I hit the neighborhood garage sales and managed to score an old French-made ten-speed for a mere $20. For another fiver, the guy threw in a lock, chain, and brain bucket. Once again I have wheels, though what François really desires is a car.

Even if I could find a decent cheap car, I remind him, the compulsory insurance would be financially mutilating. Plus, if I ever got pulled over by the cops, they might wonder why my driver's license number wasn't in their computer. I could use my fake birth certificate to apply for a real license, except I'd have to give the DMV an incriminating thumbprint. So it looks like I bike it for now. What a waste of taxpayer-funded driver's education.

5:08 p.m. I just had an unnerving conversation in Flampert's Variety Store with Sonya Klummplatz and Lana Baldwin. I was jawing my way through a piece of stale pecan pie at the lunch counter (it was Ida's day off), when Sonya seated her bulky frame on the adjoining stool—greatly crowding me and my plate even though many other empty stools were available. Her friend squeezed in on the other side of her. Interpreting this unexpected proximity as an invitation to get acquainted, I remarked that I had just transferred to Redwood High and asked if they were fellow students. They conceded they were, we introduced ourselves, and chatted amiably about my new town and school. Eventually,

I steered the conversation around to the latest gossip sweeping the campus.

"Yeah, the guy's name was Nick Twisp," Sonya explained. "The whole school was crawling with cops looking for him. The FBI too. We even had TV reporters up from San Francisco. The cops dusted his locker for fingerprints, but we wiped it all down before they got there."

Sonya I could (almost but not quite) kiss you!

"But how did you know Nick's locker combination?" I asked.

"Easy, Rick," replied Lana in her West Virginia drawl. "I work in the office and snuck the number out of the locked file. 'Tain't no big secret where they hide that key."

"I hear the cops questioned a girl named Sheeni Saunders," I said.

"Stuck-up bitch," sniffed Sonya. "She's knocked up, you know."

"Really?"

"The joke's on her though, Rick," she continued. "The father is this cute guy Trent Preston. Only he's married—to this gorgeous Indian girl, you know, from India."

"I think Apurva's real sweet," commented Lana.

"Maybe," said Sonya, "but I'd like to murder her anyway."

"What makes you think Trent is the father?" I asked.

"Sheeni's parents flipped out, Rick," replied Sonya. "I hear they're very conservative. They called up Trent's parents and demanded he divorce Apurva and marry Sheeni. Everything's in a big uproar."

"The rumor is Apurva could be expectin' too," Lana added.

"But surely Trent has denied any involvement with Sheeni," I said.

Sonya slurped her soda. "You're out of the loop, Rick. Trent admitted it's his kid. Apurva's standing by him though. I'd do the same, I guess, though I'd prefer to be lying under him. Oops, me and my dirty mind. Do you have a date for the spring dance, Rick?"

"Uh, what? No, I don't think so."

"Well, you do now, Rick. It's girls ask boys. You're my witness, Lana."

"That's right, Rick," confirmed Lana. "I'm kinda amazed, but she nailed you fair and square. That's just what she said she was gonna do over at the cosmetics counter."

"Lana dear, let's not give away all of our little secrets," admonished her friend.

Another unmitigated disaster. My genes are in an uproar over Trent's embryonic usurpation. And how is it possible I have a dance engagement with Sonya?

MONDAY, April 12 – I was on my way to computer lab and trying to dodge Sonya Klummplatz, when I heard someone call my name. I turned around and my heart somersaulted in my chest. It was My Love, looking impossibly beautiful and very surprised to see me. I seized conscious control of Rick S. Hunter's body language.

"Oh, hi, Sheeni," I replied with feigned nonchalance.

"Rick! What are you doing here?"

"Going to school. What are you doing here, Sheeni? I thought you lived in Redding."

"No, I told you I was from Ukiah. But, but, why are you here?"

"My physical therapist recommended it. She said the climate up here was ideal for recovering from life-threatening injuries."

I never made it to computer lab. At Sheeni's suggestion, we cut class and sneaked across the street to the Beaver Lodge cafe, Redwood High's off-campus teen hangout. We ordered tall lattes (as she can only tolerate the blandest of foods, Sheeni specified no coffee in hers) and ducked into a private booth, where My Love gave Rick S. Hunter an impassioned kiss.

"How's the scorpion bite?" I asked, when we came up for air.

"God, that was awful, Rick. I'm OK now. But why didn't you come to the hospital?"

"I'm allergic to hospitals. They remind me of my accident."

"I thought I was never going to see you again, Rick. You didn't write or anything."

"I'm not much of a writer, Sheeni," I lied. "How have you been?"

"Terrible, Rick. It's been a hellish week. That test was a joke. It turns out I am pregnant. The doctor in Tucson told my parents!"

"They didn't take it well?"

"Hardly. And they're insisting I have the kid. Most so-called pro-life fascists at least sensibly make exceptions for their immediate family, but not my parents. Not those hypocrites. They insist on standing firm on their principles—by holding me and my body prisoner."

"They won't let you out of the house?"

"Only to go to school, Rick. My mother drops me off and picks me up. Can you believe that? So I've been cutting classes left and right. My friend Vijay is appalled. He thinks my grades will suffer—as if I could care about that now."

"What's this I hear about Trent Preston being the father?"

"I suppose everyone in school is gossiping about that. What does it matter who the father is? I'm not going to have it anyway, Rick."

"Trent's wife is in my driver's ed class, Sheeni. She seems a bit upset."

"She should have my problems."

"So Trent is the father, Sheeni?" I was nothing if not persistent.

"I said it to shock my parents, Rick. I was sick of their high opinion of Trent. So, of course, he turns out to be too much of a gentleman to deny it."

"And now your parents want him to marry you?"

"Do they ever. I think they'd even consider bigamy, if it were legal. I could be esteemed Wife Number Two and sleep with him on Tuesdays, Thursdays, and Saturdays. On Sundays we could flip a coin. I don't know why they don't hate Trent. They certainly despise you, Rick."

"Most parents do," I admitted. "What do Trent's parents say?"

"Oh, they hate me. They've decided to make the best of Apurva and their Indo-American grandchild."

"Is that a rumor or a fact?"

"The latter, unfortunately. There was a big parents' conference at my house last night. Apurva and I appear to have conceived at approximately the same hour. We may have adjoining beds in the delivery room. Won't that be fun? Darling Trent can assist with both deliveries."

"So what does Trent say?"

"Well, last night he graciously volunteered to adopt my kid. I'm not certain he cleared that idea beforehand with Apurva. I suppose they'd be raised as twins—one of mixed race and one not. Quite the modern blended family. That's when I started screaming hysterically and locked myself in the bathroom."

At that moment a dark shadow fell across our table. I looked up into the violet-highlighted eyes of Sonya Klummplatz, who was smiling at me while pointedly ignoring my companion.

"Oh, there you are, Rick. I've been looking for you, honey. We need to discuss the colors I'll be wearing to the spring dance on Saturday."

My Love released my hand and gazed at me in stunned surprise. True to his Gallic roots, Rick S. Hunter could only shrug.

After Sheeni left in a huff, Sonya informed me that she would be wearing a lilac gown (no surprise there) to the dance, and that I should keep that in mind when selecting her corsage.

"Definitely no yellow mums, honey," she stressed. "I don't want to wind up looking like the Easter Bunny."

Since My Love opted to eat her bland bagged lunch with odious Vijay, rather than risk another Sonya encounter, I walked the few blocks to my apartment and fixed a sandwich. Lunch is always the most stressful part of the school day for friendless new students, and Rick S. Hunter is not the type of guy to linger on the fringes and be snubbed.

Later in driver's ed I drove all the way to Hopland on Route 101 at freeway speeds and had only one minor near-miss with a logging truck. On the return trip I sat next to Apurva in the back seat, and we had a hurried whispered conversation. I told her that I had met Sheeni recently in Mexico and she had assured me that the father of her kid was some guy named Nick Twisp. Apurva brushed back a tear and replied softly, "Yes, Rick, I know." I thought she would appreciate hearing her husband wasn't a two-timing louse, but it didn't seem to cheer her up.

8:15 p.m. Taking no chances, I just called Joanie in Oakland from the pay phone down the block. To my surprise and displeasure my mother answered. It was the news I wanted to hear, but not a person I wished to speak with.

"Miss Joan Twisp please," I said in Rick S. Hunter's most resonant voice.

"Who's calling?" she demanded suspiciously.

"Uh, Polonious DeFalco," I replied, saying the first name that popped into my head.

"Never heard of you. Joanie's out walking the baby."

Do infants have to be walked like dogs?

"Fine," I said, "I'll call back tomorrow." Click.

A brief but illuminating conversation. Sheeni's check must have gone through. I may be in the chips!

TUESDAY, April 13 — After my class in California problems (social studies floundering for relevance), I spotted My Love loitering beside Rick S. Hunter's locker. I shifted my body language into smoldering languor and sidled toward her.

"Hello, Sheeni."

"Hello, Rick. Where's your Miss Klummplatz?"

"I couldn't say."

"Isn't she your girlfriend?"

"I don't have a girlfriend," I lied.

"Want to cut class with me?"

"Sure, Sheeni."

"I haven't seen your new place, Rick."

"Let's go check it out."

We dumped our books in my locker and strode purposefully toward the nearest exit. Once off campus I wanted to take Sheeni's hand, but decided I'd better resist the urge.

"What class are you cutting now, Rick?" asked My Love, also keeping her hands to herself.

"Computer lab."

"Vijay says that class is a joke. He says everyone ignores Mr. Hiesgweem and just plays computer games or cruises the Internet for porno."

"Some do, but I'm working on my programming skills." I felt I could use a brush-up after that Geezer Virus fiasco.

Sheeni was appalled when I told her my class schedule. "They put you in life skills, Rick? I thought you had to be retarded to get in that class."

"Well, it's not a prerequisite, but it helps. Yesterday we studied how to create a shopping list for the grocery store. And here I'd just been grabbing things off the shelves."

"Rick, you could have the most scholastically unchallenging schedule in the history of secondary education."

I admitted that I tend to wash up in sixth-period study hall with no homework to occupy my atrophying brain.

My Love was full of superlatives today. She said my new digs smelled nice, but declared it was the "most depressing and squalid" apartment she had ever seen.

"You only say that because it's in Ukiah," I replied, putting my secondhand kettle on to boil. "If this place were in Greenwich Village or Clichy, tourists would be raving over its picturesque Bohemian charm."

Sheeni glanced into my bedroom cave. "Is this where you sleep? Sonya must have taken one look at that purple sofa and lost her last shred of inhibitions."

"Sonya's never been here. Tea or instant coffee?"

"Just hot water, Rick. I'm sick of throwing up. I suppose you don't find me attractive now because of my condition."

"I never said that." To prove it I kissed her lovely, sweet lips.

My Love never got her hot water. We wound up together on my lumpy bed. I blocked the last sliver of light from under the closed door with a strategically placed towel. We quickly shed our clothes and groped for each other in the all-encompassing darkness. I was thankful I had showered that morning in gym. So as not to smell like the old Nick, I have switched to a trendy new deodorant called Male Stench.

"Rick, have you always dreamed of making love in a coal mine?" inquired My Love.

"Sorry, Sheeni, but I vowed to my adoptive parents before they died that no one would see me naked until I was married."

"A curious promise. What about the 35 guys in your gym class?"

"They don't count."

I caressed her exquisite breasts.

"Gentle, Rick," she cautioned. "My nipples are very sensitive now."

My Love ran her fingers over my chest and shoulders (feeling for scars?).

"Rick, from what I can detect in the total absence of light you appear to have the same body-type as your father's—thin but muscular."

My morning Dogo exercises were working!

I kissed her lips and felt a warm hand grip my T.E. with the lightest possible touch.

"How's the wounded veteran?" she asked. "It feels OK to me."

"I guess we can chance it. Shall we bother with a condom, Sheeni? I haven't had sex with anyone since I got out of the hospital, where I passed every blood test known to man."

"I aced a battery of tests myself in Arizona," replied My Love. "And I couldn't get any more pregnant if I tried. Besides, you'd have to be a bat to locate a condom in this room."

And so while my computer lab classmates searched the Web for vicarious erotic thrills, we experienced the real thing—and on school time too. The darkness, unfettered flesh-to-flesh contact, and rich donut aromas combined for a profoundly soul-satisfying sensory experience. Afterwards, we rested in each other's arms and thought our private thoughts. I glided a hand over the tactilely inviting contours of her perfect ass and wished I could freeze that moment forever. I thought about our embryo and wondered how it was getting on.

"Do you know what sex it is, Sheeni?" I asked, caressing what I presumed was her abdomen.

"My mother took me to a doctor in Santa Rosa last Friday. She didn't dare involve our regular doctor because of the scandal. It's a girl, not that I care."

A daughter! How strange that a guy could engender a girl. Somehow I had assumed it would be a boy.

"Rick, do you have a passport?" inquired My Love.

"Sure."

"Would you like to go away with me?"

My heart seized.

"Where? When?" I asked.

"To Paris. I'm leaving when my passport arrives. I've requested it be processed with expedited service. I'm hoping it arrives by the end of the week. Don't worry, Rick, I've got plenty of money."

Right, Sheeni, and I know where you got it.

"Oh? Where did you get it?" I asked.

"From my old friend Nick. It comes to nearly $200,000."

A modest half-million dollar understatement. It appears Rick S. Hunter is not entirely to be trusted.

"Doesn't Nick want it back?" I asked.

"I suppose, but it's his kid that is obliging me to run away. So in a sense he is financially liable. We could get an apartment there and go to school. You could learn French and find your relatives."

"Your parents will track us down, Sheeni," I pointed out. "And they'll murder me."

"No, Rick, I'll leave clues that will make it appear that I went to Los Angeles. They'd have no reason to suspect I'd gone all the way to France. I have a secret post office box here in town. That's where I'm having my passport sent."

"I have a post office box too. What's your number?"

"312."

"Mine's 418. I don't know, Sheeni. I'll have to think about it. Who else knows about your plan?"

"Just Vijay. He wants to go, but he doesn't have the nerve to leave his parents."

"So I'm your second choice?"

"No, Rick, although I seem to be your second choice for going to dances."

"What can I say, Sheeni? Sonya asked me before you did. Besides, you're grounded and your parents hate me. They'd never let you go to that dance."

"I know, Rick. Vijay's devastated that I had to decline his invitation."

Poor Vijay! But I think François may have a plan for dealing with that despised interloper.

Since we had lingered in bed into the lunch hour, I fixed My Love her requested sandwich (plain lettuce on white bread, no mayo), then made something more calorie-laden for myself. After dining intimately at my rickety table, we strolled back to school in time for sixth period, which I spent in study hall musing on Sheeni's dramatic proposal. It's very good that Sheeni likes Rick S. Hunter enough to invite him to run away with her (not to mention have unprotected sex with him), but very bad that she wants to go to Paris on my money. I'm terrible at foreign languages, a fact I know would prove a hindrance in defending My Love against hordes of horny, avaricious, Sartre-quoting Frogs.

Securing a bathroom pass from the study-hall monitor, I slipped into Redwood High's most private student phone booth and dialed Sheeni's number. Her 5,000-year-old mother answered on the second ring.

"Hello, Mrs. Saunders," I said in my best Indian accent. "This is Vijay Joshi."

"Has your sister come to her senses about giving up Trent?"

"Not yet, Mrs. Saunders. And the child does complicate matters. Now I have something most shocking to relate that concerns your daughter." I told her about the planned escape, passport application, and secret post office box. Many expostulations of maternal rage and anguish followed. Eventually, she regained her capacity for coherent speech.

"My husband Elwyn knows the postmaster. We'll intercept that passport!"

"Very wise, Mrs. Saunders. But you mustn't tell your daughter that I informed on her. If she doesn't learn of my confidences to you, I can keep you further updated on her activities."

"Oh, Vijay, would you do that for us?" she blubbered.

"Gladly, Mrs. Saunders."

"Thank you, Vijay. I always liked you in spite of your family. You're a very nice young man for being a godless foreigner."

"Thank you, Mrs. Saunders. And good day to you."

That should keep My Love nicely confined within our territorial borders. And if Mrs. Saunders does spill the beans, it will be Vijay who takes the rap for back-stabbing treachery.

Emptying all my pocket change on the little shelf under the phone, I dialed Mom's number in Oakland and fed in the quarters. This time, fortunately, my sister answered.

"Nick, why didn't you talk to Mother when you phoned yesterday?"

"Call me Rick, Joanie. Did Sheeni's check go through?"

"It went through. We hired a very nice lawyer. She filed an injunction against Lance to prevent him from evicting us. Can you believe that jerk is trying to kick Mother out of her own house?"

Well, I could see how a bullet or two to the testicles might incline one toward revenge, but that could just be the male point of view.

"Joanie, I want you to mail me $30,000 in small bills to my post office box in Ukiah."

"Don't be silly, Rick. We can't send that much cash through the mail. Besides, we need money for Mother's expenses. She's been suspended from her job, you know."

"OK, mail me $25,000."

"We might be able to manage $10,000, Rick. But it's awfully risky."

We compromised on $15,000, which my sister promised to send tomorrow by Priority Mail. Talk about greed. Those chiselers are grabbing three-quarters of my $60,000.

Why is it that everyone treats my money like a public resource? Shouldn't people of means have some say in their personal philanthropy? Can't a guy decide he's maxed out on his charitable contributions for the year? How ironic that with capitalism triumphant across the globe, I may be bourgeois society's last Victim of Communism.

WEDNESDAY, April 14 — After Rick S. Hunter confided to My Love in the hallway before first period that he would love to run away to Paris with her, we took the rest of the morning off to celebrate. Not surprisingly, most of it was spent in my pitch-black bedroom exploring the limits of the Human Sexual Response—even venturing, much to my amazement, into the realm of female-to-male oral pleasuring. Doing it in the dark is fabulously erotic. I can only assume blind people have wonderful sex lives as partial compensation for their dearth of vision. Eventually, we got most of our clothes back on straight and sat down ravenous to another impromptu lunch.

"Any sign of your passport, Sheeni?" I asked.

"Not yet, Rick. Every day I cut the last period to check at the post office. Yesterday I was late getting back to school and kept my mother waiting nearly five minutes. She was pretty hostile. I hope she doesn't suspect anything."

"Sooner or later she'll find out you're cutting class."

"I suppose—not that my teachers lament my absence. I have a tendency to point out their more egregious errors."

I picked up my ringing telephone. It was Sonya Klummplatz tracking down an expectant but elusive lunch partner.

"Oh, hi, Sonya."

My Love made a face, grabbed her purse, and quickly departed.

"Rick, honey, are you sick?"

"No, Sonya, I took the morning off for independent study. What's up?"

"Rick, I was wondering if you'd like to invite any of your upperclassmen buddies to double-date with us on Saturday?"

"Sonya, I only transferred to your school on Friday. I don't have any friends yet."

"Well, you seemed pretty chummy with Sheeni Saunders. No matter. I thought perhaps we could go with my friend Lana and her boyfriend Fuzzy DeFalco. He's not much to write home about, but his parents are loaded."

"OK," I sighed.

"Good, Rick. You can drive Fuzzy's car. He's only 14 and doesn't have his license yet. What color is my dress?"

"Army fatigue green?"

"No, silly, it's lilac. Now don't forget!"

Wow, I get to drive Fuzzy's vintage Falcon after just one week of driver's ed. A scary prospect, but at least François is thrilled.

6:45 p.m. After wasting an entire period of driver's ed practicing parallel parking (François needs road miles!), I discreetly followed Apurva to the public library, where she was soon immersed in a thick book from the "Motherhood and Child Care" shelf. I dropped my life skills textbook, stooped to pick it up, and pretended to be surprised to see her.

"Oh, hi, Apurva."

"Hello, Rick," she replied, hiding the motherhood book under her notebook. "I'm sorry you had so much trouble parking today."

"Yeah, I guess it's good we live in a rural area. I don't know why Mr. Nurlpradt is so obsessed with parking. I mean, it's not like we're all planning to move to San Francisco tomorrow. Say, I hope you don't think I was butting my nose in your business the other day."

She reddened. "No, of course not."

"I just know that sometimes it's nice to have someone to talk to—especially since we're both the new kids in school."

"Yes, Rick, it can be pretty lonely. I, I saw you talking to Sheeni Saunders in the hall today."

"She hasn't asked me to spy on you, Apurva. We're just friends."

"I, I didn't mean to imply anything, Rick. It's just that I'm, I'm so confused."

"Can I buy you a cup of tea?"

"What? Oh, I don't know . . ."

"Come on, Apurva. I'm pals with the waitress at Flampert's. Maybe she'll sneak us a brownie on the house."

No such luck, but Ida did provide free refills of hot water. We sipped our tea and discussed the challenges of teen life and cross-cultural marriage.

"Rick, you seem very empathetic for a boy," commented Apurva. "You must have a sister or two."

"How did you know?"

"I suppose they all have their troubles with boys?"

"Sure, but nothing we can't work out together. They value my advice."

Like Rick S. Hunter's mythical sisters, Apurva let down her hair and poured out her heart, filling me in on her sudden trip to Mississippi with Trent, the rift her marriage caused with her parents, her surprise pregnancy, and her distress over Trent's reaction to Sheeni's accusation of paternity.

"I don't understand you American boys," she complained. "Perhaps I should have obeyed my father and gone back to Pune. Why can't Trent deny that he is the father of Sheeni's baby? Is it because he wishes that it were true? I know he still loves her. He refused to do anything when she broke into our house."

"Oh, he's just trying to be a good sport, Apurva. Your husband's been brainwashed. He's sat through too many lectures by gym coaches on sportsmanlike conduct."

"But what about being a good sport to his wife, Rick? Doesn't she count for anything? He actually proposed that we adopt Sheeni's baby!"

"That was a noble gesture, Apurva. When you marry a fundamentally decent guy like Trent you have to expect them now and again. Would you rather he tried to shirk his every responsibility?"

"I suppose not, Rick. My Trent is very idealistic. I know he'll be a wonderful father. Of course, it's a great inconvenience having our first child so soon. We were very careful too."

More guilt for Rick. OK, I admit sabotaging those condoms was hitting below the belt.

"Apurva, I think this will turn out to be a positive experience for you both. Sheeni's cruel falsehood has opened Trent's eyes to the true nature of his former love. No affection can survive such a deception, especially one calculated to inflict so much pain. And you have witnessed another confirmation of your husband's essentially noble, if not always practical, character."

"That is very reassuring, Rick. You have given me new insight into my husband's mind. How can I ever thank you?"

"Just stay married," I replied, paying the check and leaving a not ungenerous tip for Mr. Whatley. "That's all the thanks I need."

I don't care what Connie says. I want Trent either dead or matrimonially cemented to a woman who's going to fight for him tooth and nail.

THURSDAY, April 15 — One good thing about being a fugitive from justice, you don't have to bother with filing an income tax return. Uncle Sam may be the sole interested party this year not grabbing a slice of my dwindling estate.

I had a nasty scare this morning when Sheeni and I came back to my place after first period. My Love opened her purse and pulled out a menacing revolver.

"OK, traitor," she said, pointing the gun at me, "what the hell were you doing talking to Apurva yesterday in Flampert's?"

I stared at the lethal-looking gun barrel and instinctively raised my hands. "It was just a friendly chat, Sheeni. We're in driver's ed together. We were discussing parking!"

"Yeah, I know the kind of parking you're interested in. I ought to plug your perfidious gizzard. And there's the little matter of Sonya. You've taken your last phone call from that dame, you, you chubby chaser."

"Sheeni, be reasonable," I implored. "Is that thing loaded?"

"You're damn right it's loaded. I'm going to make you crawl. Down on your knees, lover boy."

My heart pounding, my scrotum quivering, I sank down on my knees. "Sheeni, darling, what's come over you?"

My Love smiled slyly and lowered the revolver. "You must have a guilty conscience, Rick. I was only fooling."

I collapsed on the floor, but not from laughter. "Sheeni, that wasn't funny. Where did you get that gun?"

"I stole it from my father's dresser drawer."

"You brought a loaded gun to school this morning?" I asked, incredulous.

"Sure, Rick. Doesn't everyone? I brought my camera too. I want to take your picture."

Still shaking, I crawled up off the floor, and Sheeni handed me the gun. Its blue-steeled mass felt impressively weighty in my hand. "Is it really loaded?" I asked.

"I think so, Rick. There seem to be brass bullet-like items in the cylinder. You might want to keep your finger off the trigger. I'm not sure if the safety's on or off."

My Love snapped a half-dozen photos of me holding the gun in the same sexually suggestive manner as Jean-Paul Belmondo's famous pose on her beloved "Breathless" poster. I complied because helping a loved one fulfill a long-standing girlish fantasy can only strengthen the bonds between you. When Sheeni put away her camera, she refused to take back the gun.

"You keep it, Rick," she insisted. "If it's in my house, I know I'll wind up using it on my parents or myself."

"But what am I supposed to do with it?"

"Hide it somewhere. I don't care. So what besides parking were you discussing with Apurva?"

"How did you know about that?"

"I talked to Vijay. He's the only person my mother lets me take phone calls from—except for Trent, who never calls. Vijay saw you two together. Is she going to leave Trent?"

"Certainly not. Indians don't believe in divorce. And why do you care?"

"Why do you care, Rick, why I care?"

"Why do you care, Sheeni, why I care why you care?"

"I give up, Rick. Let's go in that other room and turn out the lights."

We did just that. It's even better following a severe jolt to the nervous system. I suppose the body must crave unbridled sexual release after dangerous gunplay.

After lunch, Sheeni left for school and I hurried to the post office, where I found a yellow slip in my box advising that a package had arrived. After an interminable wait in line, I retrieved my precious package and brought it back to my apartment, where I closed my ratty curtains and counted out the great wads of twenties, fifties, and hundreds. I came up with the same total three times:

$13,750. Just as I feared, my chiseler sister had shortchanged me. Someday I'd like to meet a Twisp I could trust.

I now had nearly $18,000 in cash in an apartment with dubious neighbors and a flimsy 1940s lock on the door. Thinking it over, I decided to rent a safe-deposit box—in a different bank from my previous one. The closest bank on my block did rent safe-deposit boxes, but only to account holders. So I grudgingly opened a checking account with $1,000 and stashed $15,000 in cold cash in my new safe-deposit box. The balance I'm hiding in the sofa with Sheeni's gun for emergencies. I've figured out how to set the safety so it won't go off and kill me if I roll over too hard in bed.

More parallel parking in driver's ed. I did a little better, but my heart still wasn't in it. Who cares how close you come to the curb, if you're just going to die making that next terrifying left turn? At least Apurva seemed in much better spirits. Her husband wants to meet me! She invited me to dinner next Monday in Carlotta's very own house; I accepted with alacrity.

When I got back from school, my phone was ringing. It was Connie Krusinowski driving home from college on a jammed L.A. freeway.

"I thought you never went to class, Connie?"

"I do occasionally, Rick. You can't really appreciate Spring Break unless you follow it up with at least one boring day of school. So what's been happening, guy?"

Connie thought it was great for my image that I was taking another girl to the dance, even if my date did have serious weight issues.

"I'm sure it's helping you appear to Sheeni to be The Person She Wants But Cannot Have," Connie said.

"But she's having me every day," I pointed out. "She had me three times this morning in just about every way imaginable."

"Reality doesn't matter, Rick. It's the impression that counts.

How are you staying in touch with Sheeni at nights and on weekends?"

"We're not, Connie. Her mother won't let her talk on the phone—at least not to me."

"But you've given her a secret cellular phone, right?"

"Uh, no."

"Rick, you're the guy here. Yours is the technologically oriented sex. I shouldn't have to point out these obvious steps to you."

"Sorry, Connie. I'll get right on it. How's it going on your end?"

It was only going so-so. Connie was pleased that guilt-wracked Lacey has yet to visit Paul in jail, but her dad got a bad scare from his lawyers on the potential division of assets that a divorce would entail. And paying his taxes this week hasn't left him in a very amorous mood.

"I can see Daddy needs help over the brink," Connie confided. "I'll have to work on getting Rita to file. It would help if things were going better with her and Paulo's father. Rick, you've got to get him to call my mother in Palm Springs."

"How am I supposed to do that?" I demanded.

"You'll think of something, Rick. I'm counting on you!"

9:25 p.m. Feeling semi-affluent, I had another lonely dinner for one at the Golden Carp. Steve the waiter had no illusions this time. He shuffled over to my table with weary disinterest and took my order as if I had insulted his ancestors. Somehow, it was all very reassuring. In an world of tumult and confusion, Steve's surly indifference is the immutable bedrock upon which I anchor my tenuous grip on reality.

FRIDAY, April 16 — Before I left for school I phoned the law office of Sheeni's father. As I had hoped, his efficient legal secretary answered.

"Elwyn Saunders, Esquire, please," I said in Rick S. Hunter's haughtiest falsetto.

"I'm sorry," she replied, "Mr. Saunders doesn't get in until after 9:30. Would you like to leave a message?"

I requested that he call Mrs. Rita Krusinowski in Palm Springs at the number Connie had given me, adding, "Please inform him that I've left my husband."

"Mr. Saunders doesn't normally handle divorces," she pointed out.

"Young woman, I don't care for your impertinent presumption!" Click.

Well, I've done my best to supply the connection. It's up to those two to rekindle the magic.

By now desperate for a shower (even if it did entail running a gauntlet of rowdy towel-snappers following 40 minutes of vicious basketball), I informed My Love I wasn't available for class cutting until after second period. I met her in a still-damp state at the Beaver Lodge cafe, where Sheeni sipped her virgin latte and complained her passport still hadn't arrived. Her spirits improved when I suggested a shopping expedition for his and her cellular phones.

We strolled to the local cellular and pager store, where I blew over $600 on tiny folding phones, spare batteries, service charges, activation fees, roaming options, extended warranties, and other miscellaneous telecommunications gougings. I was hoping My Love would chip in from her sizeable fortune, but she explained that she had only $12 in ready cash. Both phones were activated on the spot in my name, and both bills will be sent to you know who. At least they started us off with 500 "free" minutes.

Her shopping bug stimulated, Sheeni volunteered to help me look for a suit to wear to the dance tomorrow. As I was budgeting no more than $20 for the complete ensemble, we confined our search to Ukiah's fashionable thrift shops. My Love prefers the more upscale Cancer Society shop, where it seemed to me that you risked contracting a terminal case just breathing in all those stale and sickly odors. We searched through the racks of expired cancer-victim suits, but everything was sized for men with big appetites and unhealthy diets. Despairing, My Love asked an elderly clerk if they had any suits that would fit me. The woman removed her old-lady glasses and checked me out.

"Hmmm, he looks like a 36-short. We did get one in yesterday in that size, but it's rather unusual. It's still being priced. I'll see if I can locate it."

A minute later the clerk returned with a "rather unusual" suit made of some kind of crinkled leather. It wasn't tailored from large hides, but had been sewn together from many small, irregularly shaped pieces—all in varying shades of blue, ranging from a pallid turquoise to a bold indigo. The lining was a tasteful flaming orange color.

"Rather striking, Rick," commented My Love. "Don't you think?"

"What on earth is it?" I exclaimed.

"It's eelskin," explained the clerk. "Too bad the label's been cut out. The ladies in the back think it might be by some famous designer. I'm sure it was quite expensive when new."

"Try it on, Rick," urged Sheeni. "This I have to see."

The suit fit as if it had been personally tailored for Rick S. Hunter. Sheeni thought the rakish cut was very flattering and added inches to my height. She said the lines obviously were Parisian inspired. My Love quickly picked out a coordinating pale yellow shirt, wide paisley tie, brown shoes, and matching brown fedora hat. She even chipped in her last ten-dollar bill when the total soared to over $40.

"You don't think the suit's a little loud?" I asked as we were leaving the shop with my purchases.

"We were very lucky to get it, Rick," she replied. "And such a good buy too."

The suit may have been, but I was still leery of those used

shoes. I just hope the previous owner hadn't died from cancer of the feet.

Alas, no lovemaking today; My Love had to hurry back to school to take an English test. I stopped at a florist shop and ordered a budget corsage, then went home, chatted up Mr. Whatley as she got ready for work, and fixed a lonely lunch for one. As I sat down to eat, something non-scrotal vibrated in my pants. I took out my tiny pocket phone.

"Hello?" I said.

"Rick, is that you?"

My Love and I were communicating totally without wires.

"Where are you, Sheeni?"

"In the cafeteria. I think your friend Sonya is looking for you. Would you like me to give her a message?"

"Tell her I'm reserving all the dreamiest slow dances with her tomorrow night."

"You're such a slimeball, Rick."

"I can't help it, Sheeni. It's my French blood."

"Do you like me, Rick?"

"You're OK."

"You're OK too. 'Bye, darling."

"Good-bye, Sheeni."

Sheeni called me darling! But dare Rick S. Hunter employ a similar term of endearment with her? I must ask Connie if and when such flagrant exhibitions of affection would be permissible.

10:15 p.m. My Love called me three times tonight on her new phone. To avoid detection, she locks herself in her bathroom and turns on the shower. Now her parents are worried she's developing a cleanliness fetish. Is their repentant daughter trying to wash away her sins, they wonder? Sheeni experienced fresh passport disappointments this afternoon, but I assured her you can't expect neck-snapping celerity from the U.S. Government, even if you did specify expedited service.

"I wish we could spend the night together," she remarked during our last conversation.

"That would be nice."

"You could try sneaking into my house, Rick. I could leave the side door unlocked."

"And what if your parents discovered us together?"

"You could escape while Father was searching for his gun."

"We better not do anything suspicious, Sheeni. It's best to be patient."

"This time next week, Rick, we may be in Paris."

"Yes, Sheeni, that's quite probable," I lied.

"I think you should know, Rick, the Parisian girls are likely to go wild over you. Jean-Paul Belmondo is like a god to the French."

"I'm prepared for that eventuality."

"I hope superstardom doesn't go to your head, Rick."

"If it does, Sheeni, I'll always remember you fondly."

"God, Rick, you're such a cad. Well, I better not keep you. Sonya's probably due there any minute."

"No, she's scheduled third tonight. Bye-bye, Sheeni."

"Good night, darling. Je t'aime."

Sheeni actually said she loved me! But does it count if she thinks I don't know a word of French?

SATURDAY, April 17 — I slept in late after another night of raucous motorcycle racing in the alley. I would have slept even later, but Sonya phoned with a timely dance update. I was to meet Fuzzy DeFalco promptly at 7:30 at the garage housing his car. She gave me the address, which I pretended to write down.

"Isn't that where Apurva Preston lives?" I inquired.

"You should know, Rick. I hear you're pals with her. How come the only kids you've met so far are good-looking girls?"

"Search me," I replied, not pointing out that I had also made her acquaintance.

"I'd like to, Rick. See you tonight, honey. What color is my dress?"

"Uh, diesel-spill brown?"

"I hope you're kidding, Rick. It's lilac!"

11:15 a.m. I was polishing my cancer shoes when My Love checked in with her first cellular call of the day.

"Rick, something dreadful has happened!" she exclaimed.

My genes panicked.

"Sheeni, you didn't lose the baby?"

"No, unfortunately. And it's not a baby, Rick, it's barely a fetus. I just called my offshore bank to transfer some funds for our escape. There's a shortfall in my account of $54,000!"

"Really? Maybe it's just an accounting error, Sheeni."

"It's no error. Someone altered a check. Nick's sister is a crook! The entire Twisp family is one vast sinkhole of criminality. I can see that now."

"But isn't it Nick's money they're trying to get back?"

"Rick, why are you defending them? You know nothing about it."

"I suppose not, Sheeni," I sighed.

"The worst thing is I'm not in a position to complain to the authorities. But Nick will be in for a surprise if he tries to contact me."

"You'd turn him in, Sheeni?" I asked, alarmed.

"I think I should, Rick. I think it would be best for everyone. You don't know the guy, Rick. Nick would never let us alone if he found out we were together. I'm almost afraid that he's spying on us now. Oops, someone's pounding on the door. Got to go." Click.

I can only hope it's a temporary, pregnancy-induced hormone imbalance that is causing My Love to adopt such a censorious attitude toward her former love.

3:15 p.m. I just picked up Sonya's corsage. Boy, for twelve bucks you'd think you'd get more than one crummy flower and some half-dead greenery. On the way into the florist shop I passed Trent exiting with a snappy orchid number. I can't believe he's taking his own wife to a high-school dance. Is that done? It seems like it takes all the mystery out of wondering whether you're going to get lucky that night.

My Love just phoned from their basement. Her parents are restricting her to one shower a day lest excessive chlorine exposure harm the baby. She now sneaks down to the laundry room and switches on the dryer. I could hear it rumbling in the background as she reported breathlessly that her father suddenly has been "called away on business"—to Palm Springs.

"He just left for the airport," Sheeni added. "He says he's working on some big gas merger down there."

"He's working on a merger all right," I replied. I told her about Mrs. K's marital rupture and recent decamping to the desert.

"This may prove propitious," Sheeni remarked. "It could give me some crucial leverage over him. I didn't dare use the Mexican liaison against him because I didn't have any proof."

"Sheeni, I thought your father was devout and moral and born again and all that stuff."

"He claims to be, Rick. First he was born again and now he's entering his second childhood."

"Sheeni, if your parents' marriage goes on the rocks, maybe they'll cut you some slack and we won't have to go to France."

"Don't count on it, Rick. You don't know my mother."

"Well, I do—sort of."

"Not really, Rick. Believe me, the woman you met in Mexico was my mother on her very best behavior."

Now that is a truly scary thought.

7:00 p.m. I'm all dressed for the dance—the second such occasion of my high-school career. I'm still not taking the partner of my choice, but I do get to go as a guy this time. I hope the gym is well-ventilated. This clammy eelskin doesn't seem to breathe very well. At least my cancer shoes are already comfortably broken in. Evelyn the retired sawmill hand showed me how to wear my fedora tipped rakishly to the side. He says he had one just like it in 1943. It could be the same hat for all I know. He says he likes my suit, but hopes I don't get picketed by outraged eel lovers.

Well, I'm off to meet Fuzzy and The Date from Hell. Wish me luck, kids.

SUNDAY, April 18 — Herewith is an honest accounting of last night's events, slightly abbreviated only to lessen the trauma:

Fuzzy DeFalco in a new black suit introduced himself to me in his late grandmother's driveway and asked to see my driver's license. He was somewhat short-tempered from having to ask Trent to move his "damn Acura." I could tell my pal wasn't happy about turning over the keys of his beloved Falcon to a complete stranger.

"Boy, you don't look 18," he said, handing me back my fake ID. "How long you been driving?"

"Oh, for years and years," I lied, grinding unknown gears as I started the engine. We lurched out of the garage, down the driveway, and into the street.

"Are you sure you know how to drive?" he demanded.

"Relax, guy," I said to all parties in the car as I tried to rein in my hyperventilating lungs. I never imagined drivers could see so little at night. Why aren't cars equipped with vast racks of powerful floodlights?

"I guess you must like Sonya, huh?" asked Fuzzy, by way of making conversation.

"Of course not. But it was girls ask boys and she nailed me. Is that a dog over there?"

"No, it's a Volkswagen. And you just blew through a stop sign. Who told you it was girls ask boys?"

"You mean it wasn't?"

"Nope. Looks like you got duped, Rick."

"Damn! Well, now I don't feel so bad about spending only $12 on her corsage."

Fuzzy eyed my fading bouquet in its plastic wrapping. "Looks like they rooked you on that one too."

"How much did you spend on yours?" I asked enviously.

"Ninety-five bucks, Rick," he said, cradling the elegant ribbon-tied presentation box in his lap. "But the orchid stems are dipped in real 24-karat gold."

Lana and my date were waiting impatiently in the living room of Sonya's modest home, from which all parents had been banished to avoid embarrassing introductions or tedious photo-snapping. Like a modern-day Cinderella, Lana looked genuinely enchanting in strapless pink satin, now accessorized by the Tiffany of corsages. She smiled and said she liked my hat. She had highlighted her nascent cheekbones with rosy blusher, a beauty ploy Carlotta was never quite able to pull off. Less successfully made up in her customary purple tones (her eye-shadow actually glittered), Sonya appeared to have single-handedly cornered the world market in lilac chiffon. She frowned when she saw her corsage and my suit.

"Gee, you shouldn't have. Hey, Rick, this isn't a costume dance, you know."

"Peasants," I grunted to Fuzzy. "Some people wouldn't recognize a $4,500 Armani eelskin suit if it bit them in the ass."

"Don't get too close, Sonya," joked Fuzzy. "Those could be electric eels."

My phone rang as corsage pinning was in progress. Saved by the bell, I let Sonya finish the job while I took the call.

"Where are you now, Rick?" whispered My Love.

"I'm at Sonya's house," I replied. "We're about to leave."

"How does she look?"

"Well, I can't really talk now."

"Why not? Are you holding her hand?"

"No."

"Are you holding other parts of her?"

"That doesn't happen until we get to the dance. Thank you for calling. Good night." Click.

"Who was that, Rick?" inquired Sonya, attempting to straighten her wilting flower.

"Oh, just a friend—an elderly shut-in trying to relive her golden high-school years."

Piling into Fuzzy's Falcon, Sonya mashed herself right next to the driver, while Lana cuddled in the back seat with Fuzzy and produced a spliff the size of those giant novelty cigars. Fuzzy held a lighted kitchen match to its end while Lana puffed away madly. It was like trying to get a campfire started. Eventually, the aromatic log was ignited, and we passed it around. I took a drag and felt my brain engorge like an elephant's cock. I gripped the steering wheel and concentrated my expanding mind on the view out the windshield.

"God, how fast am I going?" I cried.

"You haven't started the engine yet, honey," Sonya replied.

"Right, I knew that," I said. "I was just testing you."

Fortunately, the school was only four blocks away. Somehow we made it there in one piece. I parked the car on an unoccupied shrub; the prodigious joint made one last circuit, then Fuzzy snuffed it out while Lana dispensed breath mints. The spicy sweetness overwhelmed my hypersensitive taste buds. I gripped Sonya's fleshy hand and loped giddily toward the gym entrance. "Dance!" my reeling mind raved, "Gotta Dance!" I felt like the klieg lights had been switched on in my soul, and I had stepped into a lavish MGM Technicolor musical. I was a young Frank Sinatra and Sonya was a larger-than-life Debbie Reynolds—OK, much larger than life.

Inside was another tour de force of the decorative arts. Tonight's theme was "Plenty Amid Privation." As we throngs of expensively garbed revelers jostled our way past the dateless ticket-takers and vigilant chaperons, we left the First World and entered a lovingly re-created Third World slum. Faux cardboard shanties lined the walls of the gym, and freshmen dressed as ragpickers scavenged through heaps of faux garbage. Or perhaps it wasn't so artificial after all; something sure smelled rank. I prayed it wasn't me in my eelskin suit. One of the ragpickers, I noticed, was Dwayne Crampton giving a not very credible impersonation of a starving peasant. On a low platform made of rusty corrugated steel, a live but diseased-looking grunge band was thrashing out "music" at a volume that rattled the fillings in my teeth.

"God, this place is a dump," I thought I heard Fuzzy scream.

"I want something to drink!" bellowed my date.

"Me too!" screamed Lana.

Fuzzy and I located a debris-strewn table, settled in our dates amid the trash, then made our way toward the faux tumble-down refreshment shack, scrawled over with angry "Yanqui Go Home!" graffiti. After waiting in a lengthy line, we were served four tin cans of red fruit punch ladled up from a 50-gallon drum labeled "XXX Herbicide." Among the servers were Janice Griffloch and Barb Hoffmaster, both dressed as blue-bereted U.N. relief workers. On the return trip we pushed our way through an irksome rabble of freshmen mendicants clamoring for alms. The pushiest beggar was authentic Third-Worlder Vijay Joshi, whose sandal-clad foot I managed to trod upon forcefully. That will teach the wanna-be plebeian to wear open-toed shoes to a formal dance.

Reunited with our dates, we sipped our watery punch and attempted conversation.

"What band is it?" screamed Lana.

"It's the Ringworms," shouted Sonya. "God, they're bad!"

I'm not sure, but I think that was intended as a compliment.

I felt my phone vibrate in my pants. All I could do was switch it on and let My Love experience the ear-pummeling sonic ambience. Conversation was out of the question; I switched it off when Sonya grabbed my hand and dragged me out on the dance floor. My hat I left at the table. We danced frenetically to discordant aural blasts that went on and on and on. The indefatigable Ringworms didn't play "songs," they generated nonstop malignant noise by the hour. Occasionally they would sing something into their microphones, altering the nature of the din but conveying nothing intelligible. Cole Porter had nothing to fear from these dudes. Nightmarish as they were, they did save me from my worst dread. The uncompromising Ringworms did not play slow songs.

I saw many familiar faces among the revelers, but no Bruno Modjaleski. Candy Pringle was there playing the field in a backless and strapless black sequined dress further enlivened by a plunging neckline. It was an all-time traffic-stopper and something that would never have gotten past the door in Miss Pomdreck's day. The dress was a hot topic in the boys' restroom, where the consensus was that its daringly disparate parts must have been glued to Candy's naked body.

My phone rang while I was on a break in that room.

"Hi, Rick. What are you doing now?"

"Oh, hi, Sheeni. I'm taking a leak."

"Is Sonya there with you?"

"No, this room provides a measure of sanctuary."

"I've never spoken with a fellow at a urinal before. Are there other guys doing it too?"

"Yes, I'm surrounded by a veritable Niagara Falls."

"Are you allowed to peek at your neighbor?"

"That's frowned upon, Sheeni. One usually studies the wall and contemplates life. There, I'm zipping up now. How's your evening going?"

"I'm not having nearly as much fun as you are, Rick."

"Don't bet on it, kid."

"Did Sonya like your suit?"

"Oh sure," I lied. "She can't keep her hands off it."

"And where are your hands, Rick?"

"Up to my elbows in lilac chiffon!"

My Love hung up. Some people can't take a joke.

Returning to the noise pit, I danced until the sweat pouring off my head made my eelskin glisten in the throbbing light. At one point, I found myself cavorting near Trent and his lovely wife.

"Nice suit, Rick!" Apurva shouted approvingly.

"Nice dress!" I shrieked back. I liked the way curving forms were moving rhythmically under the silken fabric of her scarlet gown. I hoped little Trent Junior was enjoying the agitation. Movement on a more massive scale was taking place close by under lilac chiffon, but I did my best to avert my eyes—though many around me seemed absorbed by the awesome sight.

Even the Ringworms have to stop eventually, if only to let their amps cool off, and before we knew it, we were tottering across the parking lot—our stunned senses still jangling—toward Fuzzy's car and its dormant spliff. Fuzzy lit another kitchen match, I started the engine, and soon I was navigating down dim streets through a cloud of vision-obscuring but sensory-expanding vapors. Fuzzy was charged with directing me to his house, but since he was preoccupied by Lana's reefer and ruby lips, I drove there unerringly on my own, as Sonya pasted her still-perspiring bulk to my right side and dug familiarly into my pocket to pull out my vibrating phone.

"Hello," she giggled, "Sonya Klummplatz here! Yeah, lady, the dance is over and, man, was it a blast. We got all hot and bothered with a bad case of the Ringworms, and now we're going to Fuzzy's to have a tiny bite to eat and cool off in his very own heated pool. Hey, Lana, pass me that puff. Oh, and don't worry, Fuzzy's parents are down in Millbrae at a conference on concrete. Sounds pretty boring to me. What? Sorry, you can't talk to Rick, because my guy's driving the car and I'm driving him to distraction. Maybe you should go to bed now and let us young people get on with it. Hey, Rick, your old lady friend hung up on me. And she didn't sound that old!"

Not great news, but possibly good for my image. Fortunately, nobody thought to ask how I had found my way to Fuzzy's imposing concrete mansion on my own. I squealed into the drive and slammed to a stop just inches from a cement retaining wall. We piled out and trooped into the darkened house, where an elaborate cold buffet was laid out in the poolside family room. Fuzzy popped some cold beers and told us to dig in. Needless to say, my date was first in line.

"Hey, Frank," I called, "what's that alien spaceship outside in your yard?"

"That's the bubble my dad has installed every winter over the pool," replied Fuzzy, handing me a beer. "They'll take it off next month for the summer. Say, how did you know my name was Frank?"

Bad slip by Rick. I better watch it.

"Oh, I think Sonya mentioned that. Why do they call you Fuzzy?"

"Search me, Rick. I guess it's a nickname."

We filled up our plates and toted everything outside to the gleaming silvery bubble. I could hear the hum of a small fan somewhere that kept it inflated. We passed through a zippered airlock and entered the giant cocoon. Wisps of steamy vapor rose from the luminous blue water—as the pool's underwater spotlamps illuminated the fabric dome with a wavering liquid light.

"Totally cool!" exclaimed Sonya, plopping down at a poured concrete table and motioning for me to take the cement cube beside her.

Fuzzy put down his food, grabbed a rope by the pool edge, and fished out a tethered floating thermometer.

"I had the heater on all day," he remarked. "Lana likes it like bath water."

"What's the temperature, darlin'?" asked Lana.

"96 degrees," he replied proudly. "A new world's record."

Nothing like a little light reefer to make a guy feel peckish. After two return trips to the house for snack refills, I sat back on a concrete chaise longue, belched contentedly, and sucked on my third beer.

"OK, swim time!" bellowed Sonya. "Everybody strip!"

I was the last guy out of his clothes, but then I had seen all the others naked before. Lana didn't scream when Fuzzy revealed his furry self, which led me to conclude she was no stranger to his intimate parts. A guy can't help but get a warm feeling knowing he's helped a pal secure a fulfilling sex life—especially with someone so nicely put together as Lana. My own naked date checked me out when I at last dropped my thrift-shop underpants.

"God, Rick, how do you stay so skinny?" she demanded.

"I burn a lot of calories hanging around gorgeous chicks," I slurred. The beer was getting to me.

Sonya shoved me playfully into the pool, and I nearly drowned in its soothingly warm water. It was like immersing one's entire body in a giant wet vagina. Not a bad way to go. Sonya pulled me up from the depths by my hair and kissed me as I coughed pool water into her eager mouth. What was that other odd sensation? Oh, I was being groped. This went on for a long time, then I heard Fuzzy and Lana climb out of the water on the other side of the pool.

"Good night, guys," called Fuzzy. "You can crash in the guest room if you want."

"Good night," I heard Lana say. "See you tomorrow."

The rest was a little hazy. I remember brisk towel-rubbing of parts public and private, Sonya pushing together some chaise cushions beside the pool, my stating that I had too much respect for her as a person to take advantage of the situation as someone unrolled a condom over my improbable T.E. I remember Sonya muttering something about not intending to remain a virgin forever and my being elected by unanimous consent as the deflowerer designee. Then she told me to lie back and pretend I was Trent Preston, which I remember thinking was a pretty low blow as a hand guided me to where enough of me wanted to go that I was able to function in an acceptable manner to all parties concerned until I heard my little phone ring somewhere in the distance and suffered a major sexual shutdown probably induced by guilt but maybe it was the beer and the reefer and my throbbing head. And then it was over and Sonya said it was a night she knew she would never forget. I may not either, but God knows I intend to try.

We got our clothes back on, I took Sonya home (no good-night kiss), and parked Fuzzy's car in front of Trent's house (his Acura was blocking the drive). The keys I dumped in Trent's mailbox. I got home in the dead-of-the-night, post-motorcycles quiet, and immediately blacked out.

5:50 p.m. No call from Sheeni. I carried my phone around all day too. I suspect she's mad at me. I'd call her to find out for sure, but I don't dare risk having her expensive cellular phone ring within earshot of her parents and get confiscated. Fuzzy called sometime after noon and asked if I wanted to come over and help finish up the buffet.

"Is Sonya going to be there?" I asked.

"No, sorry, Rick."

"Fine. I'll come over."

"You got a bathing suit?"

I told Fuzzy I didn't; he said he'd lend me one of his.

"You got wheels, Rick?"

I said I had a bike and would be there in 15 minutes.

Fuzzy looked surprisingly well rested in red swim trunks probably intended to coordinate with his russet body fur. I changed into some baggy tan swim trunks in my pal's guest bathroom, then he and I took our beers and plates down to the pool bubble.

"Where's Lana?" I asked, helping Fuzzy move the cushions back on the concrete chaise longues and taking a seat.

"Her brother picked her up at Sonya's. The story was she spent the night over there."

"Good thinking."

"Sonya's bragging she nailed you."

"Man, I wish she'd keep quiet about that."

"I found a condom by the pool, Rick, but it was empty."

"That's not surprising."

"I don't think it counts if you didn't come."

"God, I wish I could believe that, Fuzzy."

"I'm Lana's first real boyfriend, Rick. Sonya got jealous when Lana lost her virginity, so I guess you got drafted to even the score. Chicks are pretty competitive about stuff like that. But I don't think Sonya likes you that much."

"That's a relief," I said, sipping my beer.

"Sonya's stuck on this guy Trent Preston, but he's married. Lana says she walks by his house about five times a day."

"Really? That's sick."

I've never walked by Sheeni's house more than four times in one day.

"What do you think of Lana?" Fuzzy asked.

"She's very nice, Fuzzy. No offense, but I could stare at your girlfriend's naked body all day long."

"I feel the same way. She's not dumb either. She just talks that way because she's from West Virginia. I hear you're putting the moves on Sheeni Saunders."

"We pal around together."

"I better warn you a good friend of mine is totally stuck on that chick."

"You mean that kid who's wanted by the cops?" I asked.

"Yeah, Nick Twisp. He looks harmless, but the guy is pretty devious. If he finds out you're messing with Sheeni, he could make your life miserable in ways you haven't even dreamed of."

"I'll keep that in mind," I replied, flattered. "So what's the latest on this Twisp guy?"

"Not much, Rick. I got a call from him a few weeks ago, then zip. The cops haven't found him, I know that. Vijay Joshi thinks he might be dead."

"Sounds like wishful thinking to me."

"You kind of look like him, Rick," commented Fuzzy. "Your body, I mean."

"I'm sure I'm much more muscular than that wimpy guy."

"Maybe a little. It's funny, Nick had this mole on his left nut, and—not that she was checking out your package—but Lana says you got one there too."

"Oh, moles like that are very common," I insisted.

"Really? I never seen one besides Nick's—not that I spend much time gawking in locker rooms. But I am the manager of the football team."

"Oh, well, dumb jocks rarely have them. Moles on the scrotum are a sign of intelligence. That's a proven scientific fact, Fuzzy."

"You can call me Frank if you want. That's what Nick called me. I kind of miss that guy."

"He probably misses you too, Frank. Good friends are hard to come by."

Damn. I wonder how much a doctor would charge to take an acetylene torch to that incriminating blemish?

MONDAY, April 19 — The big story in today's paper was the $8.8 million wrongful arrest suit filed by indignant lumber executive George W. Twisp. If Dad wins, he'll have dinged every taxpayer in the county over a hundred bucks. Sure he may bankrupt local government, but what a valuable lesson for those rabid law-enforcement officials.

No sign of My Love in school today. I hope she's OK. I managed to dodge a certain chatty non-virgin and actually went to all of my classes. Some of my forgetful teachers had to be reminded who I was. In study hall I penned a nasty letter to my sister impugning her integrity and demanding an additional $1,250 in cash. Better late than never, we hit the road again in driver's ed. Apurva complimented me on dodging another logging truck, then reminded me of this evening's dinner engagement at her house.

"Would you like to bring your friend Sonya?" she inquired.

"I better not, Apurva. She's still madly in love with your husband."

"Oh, he has that effect on everyone, Rick. My boy is remarkably lovable. Even my father is starting to like him!"

That's odd, he never did a thing for me.

9:45 p.m. Wonderful aromas were wafting from Carlotta's kitchen when I arrived promptly at six to be greeted by a hug from Apurva and hostile growls from Albert and Jean-Paul. I bet it would surprise Fuzzy's late grandmother to know that her old yellow stove was now being used for the preparation of Red Lentils and Rice Khichadi. Many changes had been made in our former home. Furniture was rearranged, new pictures brightened the walls, an ornately patterned Indian cloth had been draped over my expensive sofa, Trent's sports gear was much in evidence, and Granny DeFalco's unsettling crucifix had disappeared from the bedroom wall. Her sanitized quilt remained on the double bed, which lately had witnessed so much after so many decades of so little.

I was helping Apurva grate cucumbers for the raita when Trent came in the back door from his after-school job. We shook hands, as this was his first formal meeting with my latest personality. The guy sure radiates a healthy glow. He must be in the 99th percentile of poets now for muscles. Maybe Rick S. Hunter should get a part-time job heaving around 80-pound bags of concrete-mix on sunny loading docks. Nah, I have enough trouble just doing Dogo's laborious exercises.

Dinner was delicious, not too spicy, and completely vegetarian. Apurva has decided that although she is married to an American, she can at least be true to her roots by eschewing meat. I'm sure it would discourage America's cattle ranchers to know that such ostentatious virility as Trent's could be sustained on a diet of lentils and sprouted mung beans.

As we sat down to dinner in the dining room, I couldn't help but feel more than a little envious. Here was Trent Preston, a guy with no marital ambitions, who was now enjoying blissful wedded life and dining on exotic cuisine with Ukiah's second sexiest teen in a nice comfortable home furnished at my expense. Meanwhile, I, who have forthrightly pursued an honorable marriage with the woman of my dreams, was hiding out from the cops under an assumed name and cooking my own budget glop in a slummy bachelor's apartment. Now I ask you, is that fair?

"I'll never understand you Americans," Apurva commented, passing me the basket of warm, aromatic naan. "I enjoyed the dancing last night, but don't you think it was cruel to make sport of less fortunate peoples?"

"That wasn't the idea, darling," replied Trent. "Miss Najflempt, the world cultures teacher, suggested that theme to the dance committee as a way of helping students realize that not everyone in the world is as fortunate as we are."

"All those students jeering at the beggars didn't seem very understanding," Apurva replied. "And someone deliberately stepped on my brother's foot."

"How deplorable," I said. "I saw Vijay limping today. He must be excited about becoming an uncle."

Apurva blushed. Perhaps that wasn't considered by Indians a proper subject for polite dinner conversation.

"We're all very excited," smiled Trent. "Of course, it was a great shock to discover I'm going to have a son."

"Not to mention a daughter," added Apurva.

"Oh, are you expecting twins?" I asked.

Faux pas by Rick. That comment by Apurva was a surprisingly sarcastic allusion to her husband's other acknowledged paternity. I was rescued by a vibration in my pants.

"Mind if I take this call?" I asked. "It might be important."

"Not at all," replied Trent, stifling a blush and not looking at his wife.

"Hello?" I ventured.

"Rick, you must really despise me!" declared My Love. "First you have sex with Sonya. And now you're having dinner with Apurva!"

Even for Sheeni she seemed remarkably well informed. Did my phone contain some undisclosed eavesdropping function?

"Call me back in a couple of hours," I said. "I can't talk now." Click. "These cellular phones are such a nuisance," I chuckled, returning it to my pants.

"Apurva wants one, but I think they're dangerous," said Trent. "The antenna generates a strong output right next to your ear. You can get a brain tumor!"

"Yes, but usually it's just a small attractive one you can work into your hairdo," I joked. "Have you thought of any names for your baby?"

"We are having a slight disagreement about that," said Apurva.

"I think our son should have an American name, but Trent favors an Indian name. What do you think, Rick?"

"Well, you could compromise and give him an American-Indian name. How about Geronimo? You could call him Gerry for short."

My phone vibrated again. God knows what kind of tumor I'm getting from the signal down there. This call I took in the privacy of Carlotta's old bathroom.

"Sheeni, can't this wait one goddam hour!" I hissed.

"I suppose it can, Rick. I just thought you'd like to know our trip is off."

"Off? But why?"

"My mother intercepted my passport at the post office. My perfidious friend Vijay snitched on my escape plans."

"That's terrible, Sheeni," I said, feigning distress. "But we still have the U.S. and all its territories to run away in."

"I don't think so, Rick, not now. That's not all my mother intercepted. She also got my latest bank statement. She called my father and had him fly back from Palm Springs. They're making me sign over my money to them."

I gasped as an electric thunderbolt short-circuited my nervous system.

SHEENI'S PARENTS HAVE THEIR FILTHY HANDS ON MY MONEY!

TUESDAY, April 20 — I didn't stay for dessert last night. I excused myself as soon as possible and wandered home in despair. I had a terrible night. It didn't help that the "painless wart remover" I got at Flampert's and administered to my privates started hurting like hell. It felt like my living testicles were being dissolved in strong acid. Big alarming sore down there this morning. Now my genes are even more insistent that Sheeni have our baby. It could be my one and only shot at a gifted child.

I taped up my bleeding part, but it was excruciating torture to walk, sit, or stand. I felt like staying home, but I forced myself to go to school in order to confer with My Love. No sign of her by her locker or outside her homeroom. I asked Coach Hodgland to be excused from gym, but he said I'd need a note from Nurse Filmore. No way I was going to have that woman poking around down there. I endured 40 minutes of relentless ball agony, then some towel-snappers in the shower spotted my sore and started chanting, "VD! VD! Rickie's got an infected wee-wee! Hee-hee, VD, he's gonna loose his pee-pee!" Real mature, guys. And these cretins are juniors?

I bailed midway through lunch when I concluded Sheeni was not on campus. I re-bandaged my now-swollen part, and spent the rest of the day flat on my back in bed. No calls from anyone. Life once again had reached a nadir. Things suck royally, but I'm not going to say they can't get any worse. I learned my lesson on that score.

WEDNESDAY, April 21 — My nut case is a little better. The swelling went down some overnight, and it stopped bleeding. Now I have a big gross scab. It still hurts to walk though. I went to school, but decided to cut gym without consulting Coach Hodgland. I was easing down into a booth at the Beaver Lodge cafe with my scone and latte when My Love walked in the door. Surprisingly happy to see me, she planted a juicy passionate one right on my needy lips. She ordered her usual virgin latte, then rejoined me in the booth. We kissed again and I clutched her warm hand under the table.

"You're not mad about Sonya?" I asked.

"Of course, I am, Rick. But I'm also a realist. French men are notoriously uncommitted to monogamy. This moral ambiguity is the foundation of French Literature. But remember, promiscuity is a double-edged sword."

"Uh, I'll keep that in mind, Sheeni. How's it going with your parents?"

"Terrible, Rick. But I've got it all planned out. We're running away together tomorrow night—assuming you can tear yourself away from Sonya and Apurva."

"Don't worry about that. I'll be ready to go."

"Good, Rick." She lowered her voice. "I found out what my father did with my passport. You've got to help me get it out of his office safe."

"Sheeni, why don't you make your father turn over the passport by threatening to inform on him to your mother about his affair?"

"I already tried that, Rick. He got very offended and said I was imagining things. He admitted that he saw Mrs. Krusinowski in Palm Springs, but claimed it was only to advise her on her marital difficulties."

"What a liar!"

"Well, he is a trained lawyer, Rick. And I have no evidence against him. We've got to get my passport."

"Why do you need a passport, darling, if we don't have the money to go to France?"

"Well, I'm not entirely destitute. And I thought we could use some of your motorcycle accident settlement money to get there, then we could both get jobs or live with your father's family. Rick, I'm desperate. I'll do anything you say."

"Anything?" I asked, thinking it over. Desperation in loved ones is often a very useful quality.

"Well, virtually."

"OK, Sheeni, I'll help you get your passport—on one condition."

"What, Rick?"

"That you agree to marry me."

"Marry you! Rick, you never impressed me as the marrying kind."

"Those are my terms, Sheeni."

She kissed me. "Of course I'll marry you, darling. Do you imagine I'd actually let you enter France without insisting you marry me first?"

"Really, Sheeni?" I asked, stunned. "Why's that?"

"Because it's the only hope I have of keeping my darling away from two million screaming French girls."

At that moment, a desperate-looking Vijay Joshi limped into the cafe. "Sheeni!" he called, spotting us. "I've been looking for you everywhere! I've got to talk to you!"

"Let's go, Rick," said My Love, standing up and cutting him dead. "The atmosphere in here has become quite intolerable."

The odious knave tried to block our way, obliging me to trod once again on his injured foot.

6:05 p.m. Sheeni wanted to go back to my place to celebrate our engagement, but my intimate injuries obliged me to decline. Even if my balls weren't painfully disabled, I knew I'd have trouble explaining that all-too-apparent (even in the dark) scab. My Love would suspect I'd picked up something contagious from Sonya and make me wear a condom for the next 150 years. What a drag to be officially engaged and celibate to boot. It was almost like we'd found religion or stepped back into the 1950s.

Sheeni returned to school to recruit Trent for her plan. I hope she's right about that poet's trustworthiness. I went to Flampert's and found an Easter Bunny mask on closeout. I'd prefer something more intimidating, but that was all they had. I also picked up some strong nylon rope and budget pigskin gloves for fingerprint prevention. I'm trying to concentrate on the incidentals and not think about what I'm supposed to do tomorrow night. I just hope these upcoming events don't put a permanent crimp in my relationship with my future father-in-law.

10:15 p.m. Sheeni just phoned from the laundry room. Trent is set for tomorrow night. He's going to tell Apurva he has to work late at the cement plant. To secure his cooperation Sheeni had to promise him that she wouldn't get an abortion.

"And do you intend to keep that promise?" I asked hopefully.

"Certainly not, Rick. Promises made under duress don't count."

"But haven't you promised under duress to marry me?" I pointed out. "How can I believe you'll keep your word?"

"Because you're making a very big sacrifice by helping me, Rick. I couldn't go back on my promise after you did something that selfless and brave. Besides, I want to marry you."

"Do you love me, Sheeni?"

"Of course, Rick darling. Do you love me?"

"Yes, I do. With all my heart."

Connie wouldn't approve of such a confession, but I feel honesty is important in a relationship.

THURSDAY, April 22 — Sheeni and I agreed we'd both skip school today to get ready for our escape. I found a backpack at a thrift shop to replace the one I'd lost to the L.A. cops. I went to my bank and sucked all the cash out of my safe-deposit box. The thousand bucks in my bank account I left as a reserve in case I need to write a check for some reason. Then I went around to more banks to change the $20s and $50s into $100s, so it would all fit in my money belt. People have started married life on much less, I suppose, but my imposing wad of hundreds is a big comedown from my former fortune.

2:15 p.m. Sheeni just checked in to coordinate the details of operation Flight to Marriage. She has packed her grip and hidden it in their old coal cellar. I am to leave for her father's downtown office (four blocks south) at 7:00 p.m. sharp. At 7:10 Sheeni is to sneak out of the house and make her way to my apartment, which I will leave unlocked. At 7:30 Trent will pull up and park in the alley behind the donut shop. If all goes well, we should reach Willits with plenty of time to catch the 9:30 bus to Grants Pass (with connections to Portland).

"Don't be nervous, Rick," said Sheeni, encouragingly.

I gulped. "You know, Sheeni, I know a fellow down in L.A. who could make you a first-rate counterfeit passport for only a few hundred dollars. And I'll pay!"

"How long would it take, Rick?"

"Just a few days, once he receives your color photo and the cash."

"I can't wait that long, Rick. I've got to get out now. There have been some ominous phone calls and whispered conversations. I think my parents are up to something. God knows they're capable of anything."

9:30 p.m. I am lying low in my apartment with the lights out and the curtains drawn. The only illumination is my laptop screen. I am typing this in a desperate attempt to keep from going insane.

As planned, I left here at seven o'clock. First hitch: the door to Mr. Saunders's office building was locked. I loitered by the entry for a few minutes hoping someone would come out. No such luck. So I walked around through the parking lot to the back of the building and tried the rear door. It opened. I scuttled up the back stairs to the second floor and located the door to suite 207. I slipped on my gloves and tried turning the handle. It appeared to be unlocked. So far so good.

I retreated across the hallway to a men's room, where I removed my gloves to perform some emergency leakage due to extreme nervous agitation. I zipped up, put on my Easter Bunny mask, and re-donned the gloves. I then took out Sheeni's gun and switched off the safety. I spent several minutes more composing myself—thinking of married life with Sheeni and reminding François he was one tough hombre who didn't shrink from a little gunplay. Finally, I took a deep breath, opened the door, and walked across the hallway.

Mr. Saunders looked up startled from his desk when I pushed open the inner door to his office and stepped silently into the room.

"Hands up!" I said in a quavering falsetto as I pointed the none-too-steady gun at his head.

"Is this some kind of joke?" he demanded, not raising his hands.

"Hands up or I'll blast you!" snarled François.

That threat got some action. He raised his hands and eyed my weapon. "Where did you get that gun? Did you steal it from my house? My God, be careful with it! The trigger has a very light action. What is it you want?"

"Open the safe," I snarled.

"Why?" he demanded.

"Don't ask questions. Just open it."

He didn't move. "I know who you are. You needn't try to disguise your voice. Do you actually imagine I'll let you take my daughter away from me?"

"Open the safe!"

"My wife chooses to believe that Trent is the father of Sheeni's baby, but you and I know otherwise, don't we, Nick? Can't you see it's your own child we're trying to protect?"

"Sheeni doesn't want it. And I want her. If you don't open the safe, I'm going to shoot you in the right knee. Then in the left knee. Then in your . . ."

"All right! I get the picture. The safe's in that cabinet behind my desk. I'm going to get up now and walk over to it."

"OK, but no sudden moves."

Mr. Saunders took three steps back and kneeled beside what looked like a two-drawer oak filing cabinet. He unlocked the top drawer with a key, and the entire front panel swung open on concealed hinges, revealing a gray metal safe. He quickly dialed the combination, pushed down on the handle, swung open the heavy door, and reached inside. His hand came out holding a black automatic. I was already ducking behind his desk when the room exploded with gunshots. Something impacted my mask, knocking it back so I couldn't see. I heard a cry of pain and a thud. My ears rang from the deafening noise and I smelled an acrid odor I guessed was gunpowder. No pain except a sharp stab in my sore testicles, pinched uncomfortably in my crouch. Or had I been shot? I tore off my mask and looked down. No sign of blood.

I listened intently. No sounds except normal traffic noise outside. Finally, I worked up the nerve to peer around the corner of the desk. Sheeni's father was lying on the beige carpet, now staining red under his right shoulder. A frightening smear of purplish blood also was discoloring his torn white shirt. He was unconscious but appeared to be breathing. Red bubbles gurgled from his nostrils. I couldn't believe my eyes. Had he shot himself? I looked down at my gun. My finger was still frozen on the trigger, now squeezed all the way back.

I struggled to remain calm. I flipped on the safety and placed the gun on his desk blotter. The mask with one ear shot off I returned to my Flampert's shopping bag. I stepped over Sheeni's fallen father and searched through the safe. I quickly found Sheeni's passport and also a large white envelope stuffed with cash. Slipping both into my bag, I returned to the desk, picked up the phone, and dialed 911. "Come quick!" I croaked, when the operator answered. "There's been a shooting!"

I left the phone off the hook in case the automatically retrieved address had not yet appeared on the 911 operator's computer. I left quickly with my bag and darted down the back stairs. I was barely a block away when I heard the first sirens.

My Love had heard the now multiplying sirens as well. She was alarmed when I ducked, ashen-faced, through my apartment door.

"Rick, what happened?" she demanded.

"Quick, Sheeni, we have to go!"

"Rick, you shot my father!"

"It was an accident, Sheeni. He was shooting at me and my gun must have gone off when I ducked."

"He was shooting at you!" she exclaimed.

"He had a gun in his safe. Let's go, darling! We haven't a second to spare."

"Rick, you killed my father!" she gasped.

"Well, he was alive when I left. He might be OK." I looked out the window. "Sheeni, Trent's here. Let's go!"

"I can't go anywhere, Rick. My father's been shot. Don't you see? I have to go to him."

"But, Sheeni, I got your passport. We can go away now. We can get married!"

"It's no good, Rick," she said, pushing me away. "You keep the passport. I'll get Trent to take me to the hospital. Oh, God, I can't believe you shot him."

"Sheeni, you won't tell anyone it was me, will you?"

"Of course not, darling. I'll deny any knowledge of the crime. If worse comes to worst, I'll say it was Nick. You stay here and don't go anywhere. I'll try to call you as soon as I find out anything."

We embraced and kissed. And then she was gone.

11:45 p.m. No call yet from Sheeni. I've burned the mask and gloves in the sink and flushed the ashes down the toilet. The rope I'm saving in case I have to hang myself. I hid the envelope of cash—uncounted—in my sofa. I thought of calling the hospital to check on Mr. Saunders's condition, but decided I couldn't risk it.

If he dies, I've decided to give myself up, commit suicide, or flee to Mexico. So far the last alternative sounds the most appealing, even if it means renouncing forever the woman I love. Perhaps I could live with lovely Angel after Dr. Rudolpho burns off my fingerprints with acid. Then I would be free of Nick Twisp for good, except for his incriminating DNA, and I'm not sure I've left any of that around for the cops to analyze.

To make amends for my missteps Rick S. Hunter could live a quiet, exemplary life as a law-abiding Mexican citizen. I could go on a spiritual quest like Paul and write virtuous books aimed at the moral uplift of troubled youth. I could acquire wisdom and probity and dignity. I would watch my smart mouth. I would be nice!

FRIDAY, April 23 — 1:52 a.m. No call. Sheeni must be too grief-stricken to phone me. That can only mean I am now officially a murderer. Considering my criminal record, they'll probably opt to try me as an adult. I could be destined for San Quentin and those last two choices they give you on Death Row: the menu for your final meal and the gas chamber or lethal injection. How prophetic that as a little kid I hated getting inoculations and was always thinking I smelled gas.

3:20 a.m. Sheeni finally called. Needless to say, I wasn't asleep. Her father is out of surgery. He has a collapsed lung and is weak from loss of blood, but is expected to recover. Though he was still somewhat groggy, the doctors let him speak briefly with family members and two Ukiah police detectives. He told the cops his guns went off accidentally while he was putting them away in his safe! The investigators were pretty skeptical, but the doctor wouldn't let them ask any more questions. My Love speculates that her father is covering up the truth to prevent her being charged as an accessory to attempted murder.

"I never thought I'd say this, Rick," she confided, "but it's a good thing I'm pregnant. I'm sure my father wouldn't be nearly so understanding and forgiving otherwise. I've learned one thing though."

"What's that, darling?"

"My father is braver than I thought. Even if he is a lawyer."

"He tried to kill me, Sheeni. Your father is a homicidal maniac!"

"He was only defending himself, Rick. The situation is not at all comparable to Nick's bloodthirsty mother. It's the Twisp family that carries the bad seed, not mine."

That could be, but given their genetic heritage we might want to keep our gifted children away from firearms. Even François can see the wisdom in that. Me, I'm going to bed.

3:40 p.m. I am trying to convince myself that yesterday was just a terrible dream. I dragged myself out of bed this morning feeling much the worse for wear and made it to school almost on time. No sign of Sheeni, of course. Though I was feeling none too clean and a long showerless weekend loomed ahead, I cut gym to take my customary morning break at the Beaver Lodge.

The shooting of a prominent Ukiah attorney merited a brief story at the bottom of page one of the local paper. You could tell the reporter was frustrated by a paucity of facts. Elwyn Saunders, 53, was reported to be in serious but stable condition. Police were investigating the "mysterious circumstances" of the incident, but would say no more. They declined to speculate whether Mr. Saunders had been attacked by a "disgruntled client." That sounds like a good possibility to me. Lawyers always have plenty of dissatisfied clients, especially after they send out those onerous bills.

I was rereading the newspaper story for the fifth time when vile Vijay Joshi walked in the door and limped straight for my booth.

"What lies have you been telling Sheeni Saunders about me?" he demanded.

"Are you addressing me?" I inquired with a simulacrum of politeness.

"I want to know what slanders against me you have been spreading!" he shouted.

"Sounds to me like you have some sort of personal problem," I replied calmly. "I don't know what you're talking about."

"You do!" he insisted. "You have been plotting to turn her against me!"

"If any injury has been committed, it is by you against me. You have been spying on me. Don't try to deny it. You better just leave us alone."

"No, it is you who had better leave Sheeni alone!" the foaming Indian raved.

"I can hardly do that, Vijay. We're engaged to be married."

"Engaged! That is a lie! She just met you. You barely know each other."

"I don't choose to discuss my personal affairs with obnoxious strangers. Go away and leave me alone."

My red-faced adversary flexed his unintimidating fists. "Let us go outside and settle this like gentlemen."

I looked at him in disbelief. The twit was threatening me with violence. "Go away, Vijay. I don't pick on guys who are smaller than me."

The brute grabbed me by my shirt and knocked over my latte. I saw red, lashed out, and to my surprise landed a hard kick square on his population center. He doubled over in pain and went down—raking his nails along my bare arm in the process. The guy fights like a girl. So we both got ejected by the cafe manager, and now I'm banned from the Beaver Lodge for life. But it was worth it. François had been itching to boot Vijay in the goolies practically since the day I met him. The deed was long overdue!

Nurse Filmore swabbed disinfectant on my bleeding arm and told me I shouldn't play basketball so rough. I assured her I would take it easy in gym from now on. At noon I split for home and crashed on my bed for three solid hours. I feel better now, though I smell like something the cat barfed up.

6:05 p.m. Sheeni just checked in by clandestine cellular phone from the laundry room. She and her mother had spent most of the day at the hospital. Her father was doing very well. He even got out of bed and circumnavigated the corridor twice.

"I was in his room, Rick, when the detectives returned to question him. My father insisted that I be permitted to remain."

"What did he say, Sheeni?" I asked eagerly.

"He stuck to his story, thank God. Of course, the cops had some very pointed questions for him. They wanted to know how it happened that he managed to discharge both guns accidentally. They also pointed out that his wound was not consistent with a gun having been fired at very close range, as such accidents usually entail. And they wondered why the weapon that delivered the bullet had no fingerprints on it, even though he wasn't wearing gloves."

"Tough questions," I admitted. "What did he say?"

"He was very lawyerly in his replies, Rick. He just kept repeating that he couldn't remember any details from last night. Finally, the cops got disgusted and left."

"That's great, Sheeni!" I exclaimed.

"I have even better news, Rick. As I was assisting my father on his walk, he confided that he's changed his mind about forcing me to have the baby. And he promised to get my mother off my back. So now I don't have to run away!"

My genes didn't like the implications of that news and neither did I.

"But, Sheeni," I protested, "what about our getting married?"

"Oh, Rick, I love you, but we're really much too young."

"But, darling, you promised to marry me if I got your passport."

"You're right, Rick, I did. But I didn't know you were planning on practically murdering my father. That changes everything. And what's this I hear about your attacking poor Vijay?"

I straightened her out on that score, then hung up. Connie's right. I should never have told Sheeni I love her. Things were going fine until I decided to open up and share my feelings. What a chump!

SATURDAY, April 24 — The sponge baths weren't doing it, so I broke down and actually climbed into that dank bathtub. No hot water, of course. I hope my still-healing balls don't get infected and fall off. Part of my gross scrotum scab did come loose in the towel. Looks like the joke's on me. The damn mole was still there.

The whole bathing experience was so disgusting I came back and counted the money I swiped from Sheeni's father. It came to $16,500, nearly doubling my net worth! With a chunk of change like that, maybe I can look for a decent apartment. All that cash on hand was making me inordinately paranoid, so I headed straight to my bank and stashed it (plus the wad from my money belt) in my safe-deposit box.

François's unsolved crime got a brief mention on page three of today's paper. It reported that the hospital had upgraded Mr. Saunders's condition to satisfactory, and noted that the police were "stymied" in their investigations by "alleged inconsistencies" in the victim's statements. It's not just the police who are suspicious.

If you ask me, $16,500 is a lot of cash for a lawyer to have stashed in his safe. Back in business math class we learned about the "time value" of money. Say you have $20 that's not earning interest. One week later it may be worth only $19.99. And you've missed out on several cents of interest too. All those penny losses can add up fast. That's why astute people don't keep around big wads of cash, unless they're fugitives like me or crooked in some major way. So maybe Mr. Saunders isn't clamming up from a noble desire to protect his daughter, but to cover his own sleazy bribe-taking or tax-cheating ass. That lawyer could be even more of a hypocrite than his daughter supposes.

4:20 p.m. Fuzzy invited me over for another swim in his pool. Too bad he didn't call earlier to spare me that revolting bathtub wallow. Pools are great for the shower-deprived because the heavy chlorine dose cuts down radically on your b.o. worries—at least for a day or two. On the ride over I swung by the hospital on the off chance I might run into My Love. No such luck.

Fuzzy's scary Italian dad and oversexed mother (who once tried to seduce me and shoot my father) were both in the house, so we cut out fast for the pool bubble. My pal was excited because he thinks Nick Twisp may be back in town.

"Er, what makes you say that?" I asked, attempting to float on my back.

"Well, Rick, you know Sheeni's dad got blasted?"

"Yeah, I hear it was an accident."

"It was no accident, Rick. I'll bet you anything it was Nick."

"Do you have any proof, Frank?" I asked, flailing for the pool edge. No way 20 pounds of meat on a skeleton can float.

"Not exactly. But it's pretty suspicious that a guy could accidentally shoot himself with two guns. Sonya thinks Nick is back in town and on the warpath. She thinks he's pissed off and gunning for everybody who ever crossed him. I just hope he has his facts straight and doesn't think I ratted on him to the cops."

"Well, I doubt he suspects you, Frank."

"I hope not, Rick. I just thought I should warn you. And your fight with Vijay might not have been such a smart idea, even though the creep deserved the pounding."

"Why not?"

"Because if Vijay turns up dead, you'll be a prime suspect. And it would be just like Nick to kill two birds with one stone."

That was such a good idea François almost wished he'd thought of it.

7:48 p.m. No check-in call from Sheeni. I hope My Love is OK and not taking me for granted because I once foolishly called her darling. I did, however, get an irate call from Connie.

"Rick, why exactly are you trying to kill my mother's new boyfriend?" she demanded.

"How do you know I was involved, Connie?"

"Let's not be coy, Rick. Are you trying to sabotage my carefully laid plans?"

Sighing, I filled her in on my armed quest for Sheeni's passport, her father's homicidal response, and my tragic near-miss in the marriage market. Connie was flabbergasted.

"Rick, do you mean to tell me that you actually got a Saunders sibling to agree to marry you?"

"Uh-huh. We were officially engaged for not quite 56 hours. She even told me she loved me."

"Rick, this is a tremendous breakthrough. Sheeni impressed me as even more averse to marriage than Paulo. This could be a very hopeful sign for us both. Mind you, your girlfriend is pregnant. The prospect of a husband may be slightly less oppressive to her in that condition. I wish Paulo could get pregnant. I don't see why all the burden has to fall on us women. Did I tell you Lacey dumped him?"

"Really, Connie? I'm amazed."

"I had to write the letter for her, of course, but she signed it. I convinced her it wasn't fair to string him along. I gave it to Paulo this morning."

"How did he take it?"

"Like a man, naturally. The guy is so emotionally together. And he looks so sexy when grief-stricken. I felt like dragging him under the table right there in the jail visitors' room."

"I know what you mean," I said. "I feel powerfully attracted to Sheeni whenever she's especially distraught or heartbroken."

"We're a couple of rescuers, Rick. People should thank their lucky stars we're around to pick up the pieces!"

SUNDAY, April 25 — My cellular phone vibrated in my pants while I was doing my morning Dogo exercises.

"Good morning, Sheeni," I said cheerily.

"Who is this?" demanded a voice. It was Sheeni's 5,000-year-old mother!

"Expectant mothers' help line," I replied, disguising my voice. "How may we assist you?"

"Stay away from my daughter!" she screamed. Click.

Damn. My Love should have been more careful. Now she's lost her expensive cellular phone, cutting off a vital communications link. Her busybody mother must have pressed "redial" to find out with whom Sheeni had been conversing. I just pray Mrs. Saunders doesn't start using that phone to make free long-distance calls around the world at my expense.

6:30 p.m. I spent most of the day apartment hunting. It was pretty discouraging. Landlords take one look at me and think wild parties at 3 a.m., irate neighbors, broken plumbing fixtures, holes knocked in the sheetrock, and bounced rent checks. Treating teenagers with contempt may be the only form of housing discrimination that's still legal.

I did find one place I really liked in Fuzzy's neighborhood. It's a nicely private in-law apartment over a garage; the rent is a semi-affordable $525 per month. It had a real bathroom with actual hot water. I told the lady renting it that I was looking for a place for me and my mother, who was away right now on combat duty in the United States Marine Corps.

"Your mother is a Marine?" the woman asked.

"Yes, she's a major," I replied, "and boy is she strict. She makes me go to bed at nine o'clock and keep my room as neat as a pin. The only music she lets me play are Frank Sinatra tapes turned down low. I guess it's for my own good though. I'll probably be going away to Stanford anyway next year. I'm in the accelerated program at Redwood High."

The lady let me fill out an application, but she seemed pretty skeptical. I wrote down Mr. Frank DeFalco and Ms. Lana Baldwin as my references. I trust they'll give me a glowing recommendation.

9:45 p.m. It's been two whole days since I've spoken with My Love and incalculably longer since I've held her in my arms. These separations are unendurable. I'm looking forward to some extensive class-cutting with her tomorrow. I've washed my sheets and may even shower in gym for her. Another painful sacrifice for love, but I'm used to it.

MONDAY, April 26 — No sign of My Love in school today. I'm hoping she had another routine doctor's appointment in Santa Rosa and hasn't had to maintain a bedside vigil at the hospital because her father took a sudden turn for the worse. I'd call the hospital to find out his condition, but those nurses can be such snoops.

Too depressed to write much. Got a nasty letter from my sister accusing me of miscounting the money she sent and berating me for not calling our mother in her time of need. Right. We could compare notes on how it feels to shoot people.

I went to all my classes except gym. Started a maple breadbox in wood technology class. Hope Sheeni likes Early American kitchen accessories. Saw Vijay the Vile in the hall and we both ignored each other. His sister was pretty frosty toward me in driver's ed. She must have heard a one-sided account of the fight from her brother. I informed her that I merely had been defending myself against attack, but apologized anyway. Apurva said she thought it was unfortunate that Sheeni Saunders felt the need to keep every intelligent boy in town in a state of constant agitation.

TUESDAY, April 27 — My Love was absent from school again today! I haven't heard from her in four days. In desperation, I called the hospital. Mr. Saunders had been discharged yesterday, they said. The guy is definitely on the mend. So why isn't his daughter in school?

9:27 p.m. I broke Sonya's record. I walked by Sheeni's house six times today. No sign of My Love. I strolled by twice tonight and both times her bedroom window was dark. This is not good. I am getting a very bad feeling about this.

WEDNESDAY, April 28 — When I saw My Love wasn't in homeroom this morning, I immediately dialed her home number from a school pay phone. Her mother answered.

"Hello, Mrs. Saunders. This is Vijay Joshi," I lied.

"Oh, hello, Vijay," she replied, unenthusiastically. "I think your sister should know that if she persists in this unnatural union with Trent Preston, we're prepared to file suit against her. My husband is an attorney, you know."

I pretended to take seriously this blatant bluff. "Please don't do that, Mrs. Saunders! I'm certain she'll listen to reason in time."

"Time is something we don't have a lot of, Vijay."

"I understand, Mrs. Saunders. I am somewhat concerned about your daughter. She hasn't been to school this week."

"She's fine, Vijay. You needn't worry."

"Would you like me to bring over her homework?"

"That won't be necessary, Vijay. Sheeni has been withdrawn from Redwood High School. My husband sent them a letter yesterday."

Total panic.

"And where will she be going to school?" I croaked.

"You needn't concern yourself about that, Vijay. And I wouldn't bother calling us anymore. Sheeni isn't here."

Panic on top of panic.

"Oh, where is she?" I asked as nonchalantly as possible.

"She's away. And don't worry. She's being well taken care of." Click.

Nightmarish anguish and despair. My One and Only Love has been ripped from my arms and sent to God knows where!

THURSDAY, April 29 — Too depressed to write, to think, to hope. No call from my hoped-for landlady either. Now I understand why they say April is the cruelest month.

FRIDAY, April 30 — François's had enough. He told me to get off my butt and find out what the hell is going on. So at lunchtime I sought out Ukiah's best-informed teen gossip queen—Sonya Klummplatz. I swallowed my pride and took a seat beside her at the zaftig's table. She didn't seem very pleased to see me.

"Hi, Sonya," I smiled. "Where have you been keeping yourself?"

"Oh, it's the standoffish and stuck-up Rick Hunter. You must want something."

"Just the pleasure of your company, Sonya," I lied. "I had a great time at the dance."

"That's some late-breaking news. What has it been, two weeks?"

"Are you busy tomorrow night?"

"Maybe. What'd you have in mind?"

"Well, I thought we could go to the movies. There's that new teen sex comedy in town."

"I don't know if I like those, Rick. I was in one myself—about two weeks ago."

"Sorry about that. Do we have a date?"

"I'll think about it. Are you sure you didn't come here just to ask me if I know where Sheeni Saunders is?"

"Of course not."

"That's good. Because I know where she is, and I'm not going to tell you."

"Why not?"

"I have my reasons."

"I bet you don't even know where she is," I scoffed.

"I do so too. My mother is friends with Mrs. Tondo whose sister cleans house for Sheeni's mother. I got the whole story, which Vijay Joshi has already tried to pry out of me without success."

"Why won't you tell me, Sonya?" I whispered. "I mean, we're practically lovers."

"We are lovers, Rick. Or were you too drunk to notice? OK, I will tell you this: Where Sheeni has been sent, the people who are holding her prisoner have been instructed to be on the alert at all times for certain teenage boys. So you can forget about rescuing her. What time are you picking me up tomorrow?"

"Sorry, Sonya. I just remembered I have a previous engagement."

"Who with, rat boy?"

"With Nick Twisp. We're planning a few murders."

"Liar!"

4:15 p.m. Seventh period found me loitering outside the girls' gym, from which Sonya and Lana emerged in a freshly showered state. This looked good on Lana, who I knew was still alluringly moist and pink under her clothes. Sonya may have been sopping under hers for all I care. I managed to separate Lana from her jealous friend for a private hallway chat. Lana told me all she knew, which, as usual, wasn't much.

"Well, Rick, from what Sonya says it's like this combination home for unwed mothers and Christian prison camp for problem girls. Sonya says it's real strict. I guess Sheeni's like totally locked up."

"What's the name of the place, Lana?"

"Oh, what's the name? She told me too. Oh, I remember, it's the Ingenious Home."

"The Ingenious Home?" I asked skeptically.

"That's right. Kinda funny name, huh?"

"And where is it, Lana? Is it around here?"

"Oh, Sonya wouldn't tell me that, Rick. She knows too, but she ain't sayin'. She's gonna be mad at me anyways for talkin' to you. I wish you two were gettin' along better. Don't you like her, Rick?"

"A guy can't like someone who keeps secrets from him, Lana."

"She's only doin' it 'cause you been ignorin' her, Rick. I bet you could win her away from Trent if you tried. You already slept with her and that's the hard part."

You can say that again.

6:48 p.m. No "Ingenious Home" in the phone book. I also entered the name in a half-dozen Internet search engines, but turned up no prison camp for unwed mothers. Those Neanderthals must not have a Web presence. Why should they? Probably most of the parents they deal with don't even have computers because they're not sanctioned by the Old Testament.

Seeing no other alternative, I phoned Trent Preston and asked for a big personal favor.

"You want me to call Sonya Klummplatz?" he asked doubtfully.

"I'd appreciate it, Trent."

"I don't know, Rick. I'd hate to encourage her. I think she may be somewhat, uh, unstable. She has pictures of me pasted up all over the inside of her locker. It really bothers Apurva."

"Trent, I wouldn't ask if I thought there was any other way to get the information."

"Maybe Sheeni's better off in that home, Rick. They'll take care of her until she has her baby."

"I think so too, Trent," I lied. "I just want to know where she is so I can write to her."

"OK," he sighed, "but my wife's not going to like it. Apurva has a thing about Sheeni."

Gee, I wonder why.

10:15 p.m. Trent just called sounding stressed. Sonya's agreed to tell him where Sheeni is, but only if they discuss the matter in person.

"That's great, Trent," I said. "When are you getting together?"

"I'm picking her up in front of her house at 11:30 tonight, assuming my wife doesn't brain me first."

"That's good, Trent. One piece of advice: I'd take her someplace public for your chat."

"I intend to, Rick. I want bright lights and lots of people around."

"The Burger Hovel?" I suggested.

"That's a possibility. Or maybe the lobby of the police station."

MAY

SATURDAY, May 1 — 1:15 a.m. The ringing telephone just jolted me awake. It was a worried Apurva calling to say her husband had not yet returned and she was thinking of alerting the police. I told her not to panic and just to be patient.

"But, Rick, my boy is out in the middle of the night with another woman!"

"He's performing a valuable counseling service," I pointed out. "You should be proud of him, Apurva."

"I shall never understand you Americans," she sighed, hanging up.

4:30 a.m. I just sent Trent home in a taxi. He washed up here about a half-hour ago stoned out of his mind. He was crashing about in the corridors with his clothes askew and waking all my neighbors. No sign of Sonya. She must have used a few of Lana's giant spliffs on him. I fixed him some coffee and tried to make sense of his antic blubbering. Most of it had to do with obscure topics like the sanctity of marriage, but mixed in with the gibberish were two critical words: "Crescent City."

My Love is being held prisoner in Crescent City, California. Fear not, darling, I'm on my way!

11:25 a.m. On the bus, heading north on Highway 101. I had a fortifying early donut binge downstairs, then loaded up my backpack, and re-sucked all the money out of my safe-deposit box after the bank opened. From the frequency of my visits to her vault, the bank manager must figure that's where I'm stashing my dope. My money belt is now stuffed to capacity with over $30,000 in cash. The overflow I had to hide in my pack. I'm literally awash in hundred dollar bills, a comforting but also nerve-wracking condition. All my recently acquired household goods I left behind in my apartment, along with my bike, suicide rope, eelskin suit, cancer shoes, and flashy fedora. Who knows if I'll be returning?

I'm not sure what the plan is when I get to Crescent City, but I'll think of something. François wishes I hadn't left that handy gun at the scene of his last crime. I don't know, those things have a way of going off precipitously. I'd rather not subject my nervous system (not to mention my conscience) to another attempted homicide.

I've never been to Crescent City, but I know it's the last town on the north coast before the Oregon border, and the weather is supposed to be the pits. A nice summer day there is 55 degrees with a blowing fog. I seem to recall that most of its downtown got wiped out in a big tidal wave from an earthquake in Alaska back in the sixties. I hope My Love is safely away from the shore. They have a prison there at Pelican Bay where the nastiest dudes in the state system chill out. I may know it intimately someday, though I hope not within the next week or so.

I hope Trent takes my advice and lies through his teeth about last night to Apurva. What a wife doesn't know can't hurt her—or her husband. An obvious truism, yet damning confessions dribble out of guys all the time. And if anyone is prone to leak like a sieve, it's Trent. You'd think this trait would have been bred out of humans by the failure of honest guys to achieve reproductive success. After all it's a known fact that women are most attracted to rogues and rascals.

6:42 p.m. Crescent City was not living up to its reputation

for bad weather when I arrived. It was sunny and fairly pleasant. Even the frigid Pacific was doing its best to appear a beneficent blue. From what I can see, the town's main activities are lumbering, fishing, clipping tourists, and incarcerating the dregs of California's criminal class. Lots of motels clustered around the forlorn post–tidal wave, low-budget downtown. On the recommendation of the bus-depot clerk, I got a room at the Fog Horn Motel. Pretty clean and only 28 bucks a night. The first thing I did was use up $27.50 worth of hot water taking the world's longest shower. Then I checked the town's comic-book-sized phone book for "Ingenious Home." No such listing. Damn! It's occurred to me that New Orleans, Louisiana, is also known as "The Crescent City." But would the Saunders send their only daughter to a prison camp halfway across the country?

10:20 p.m. On my way out to dinner at a nearby Chinese restaurant, I stopped in at the motel office and asked the sari-clad Indian woman behind the counter if she knew of any local homes for unwed mothers. This question didn't seem to phase her.

"You would be wanting the Eugenia Home," she replied. "That is the big green house over on Walrus Street. It has quite a tall fence around it."

"Ah yes, the Eugenia Home," I said, greatly relieved. "And which way's Walrus Street?"

"It is three or four blocks north of here, but you can't go to the home after dark."

"Why not?"

"At night they have a pack of vicious attack dogs roaming wild over the grounds."

"Oh, I see. Well, thanks for the information."

Ten minutes later I was ambling past the Eugenia Home. I had to cross over to the other side of the street to quiet the half-dozen assorted slobbering German Shepherds and Rottweilers lunging at me through the eight-foot-tall chain link fence. Set on at least an acre of mangy grass, the sprawling old house once must have been some rich pioneer's imposing mansion. It had been stripped of its Victorian finery, re-windowed with cheap aluminum sliders, and slathered in dingy green stucco. A stark two-story dormitory-like structure had been grafted onto the back with a notable lack of architectural finesse. There were lights in some windows, but all the blinds were pulled down tight.

What heartless sadism, to cage my sensitive darling in such a grim and forbidding place. Now I wish François had done a little more damage to Sheeni's father—at least blown off an arm or two. He deserves it!

SUNDAY, May 2 — A quiet day in a quiet town. Even the seagulls were looking subdued and contemplative. I walked past Sheeni's prison before breakfast, but saw few signs of life. In the early morning sunshine Eugenia Home appeared, you'll pardon the expression, fairly impregnable. All the gates were chained and padlocked. A businesslike strand of razor wire looped along the top of the encircling rusty fence. No guard towers, but it wouldn't surprise me if the jailers inside had a shotgun or two at the ready. Perhaps I'll have to purchase a used armored truck and storm that fence at breakneck speed.

After breakfast at a downtown greasy spoon, I went back to my motel and called the Eugenia Home. Eugenia Fairchild herself answered the phone. I told her I was a concerned father looking for a facility for my sixteen-year-old daughter Deirdre, who unfortunately was in "the family way."

Eugenia was brisk and all business. "We do have a vacancy at the moment, sir. Our rates are $1,800 per month, payable in advance on the first of each month. That covers everything except clothing, personal items, phone calls, and medical fees. I'm a trained midwife, but most families choose to use our local hospital. They have an excellent obstetrics department."

I said that sounded fine, but confessed that my "rambunctious" Deirdre might be reluctant to stay there.

"We can handle her," Eugenia replied. "In our 23 years we've only had two attempted escapes, and both girls were picked up by the sheriff within an hour. There's just the two highway routes in and out of town, you know."

"That's comforting," I lied. "And when do you permit your charges to leave the grounds?"

"We don't, except for medical checkups. And we accompany them on those."

"They don't even leave to go to church?" I asked.

"No need to. My husband Waldo is an ordained minister. He's conducting Sunday services right now. They're compulsory, of course. And we give our girls two hours of nonsectarian religious instruction every day. We like to say we're strict but loving."

"I see. If I were to phone ahead and request that my daughter be permitted to meet me downtown, would that be allowed?"

"No, sir. We'd ask you to pick her up here in person. You have to understand we sometimes get boyfriends trying to pull stunts like that."

"Really? And are you armed for such occurrences?"

"My Waldo's a Vietnam veteran and a crack shot. But don't worry, we keep all our handguns and rifles locked up. We're very security-minded."

"Yes," I sighed, "I can see that."

3:20 p.m. A depressing afternoon in a depressing town. I strolled by Eugenia Home again after lunch, though I realize I can't continue doing this without raising suspicion. Crescent City is not a town of pedestrians. On its deserted residential streets I stand out like a sore thumb. I did spot some obviously pregnant girls sneaking smokes behind the ramshackle carriage house (now used as a kennel and garage), but my tobacco-eschewing love was not among them. François wanted to call them over to the fence, but I decided they were too far away.

I'm beginning to realize I have very little aptitude for prison breaks. Tunneling under the fence doesn't seem very practical. Swooping down from the sky has a certain brash appeal, but how do you go about obtaining a helicopter and a sufficiently impetuous pilot? I thought of renting a policeman's uniform and trying to arrest My Love—perhaps on a morals charge—but decided Eugenia probably is acquainted with all the local law. Besides I doubt if I look old enough to be in possession of a badge.

9:47 p.m. I have a plan. It may not be a great plan, but at least it's a plan. I cooked it up in consultation with Connie, who I called in desperation on my cellular phone. She was up on the subject because she has spent a lot of idle time lately daydreaming about springing the other Saunders sibling from his prison. I have many things to do tomorrow, the most pressing of which is to buy a car. I'm getting my first set of real wheels! A momentous step in any man's life, especially as I have to obtain a vehicle with sufficient horsepower to elude the police.

MONDAY, May 3 — God has switched off the tourist-friendly weather. Crescent City was revealing its cold and misty true grim self. It was the kind of weather that makes you want to retreat to your rundown trailer and gulp a few methamphetamines. No doubt some locals were doing exactly that as I bustled around town after breakfast. I got most of what I needed before noon, except for my wheels.

I couldn't shop at the local used car lots because dealer sales get you involved with the Department of Motor Vehicles (where my mother used to spin red tape before her indictment for attempted homicide). But buying a car from a private party, especially in a rural area, is a challenge if you lack transportation. You almost need to own a vehicle in order to shop for one.

I phoned up about two cars advertised in the paper, but both sellers were located way out in the boonies and neither was willing to drive into town—even when I said I had the cash and was eager to buy. Either they'd already been burned by that ploy or they knew their budget-priced vehicles wouldn't make it that far. All the other advertised cars were either wimpy subcompacts or out of my price range. I hope I don't have to unleash François to steal a car.

2:15 p.m. I saw My Love! Or at least I think I did. As I strolled past Eugenia Home on the one daylight perambulation I permit myself, I spotted some inmates hoeing a patch of bare earth near the carriage house. I was pretty far away, but one girl resembled Sheeni—though it's hard to believe my fashion-conscious darling would tie up her hair in a bandana like that, or be seen in public in such a dowdy dress. I considered heaving a mash note over the fence, but decided I couldn't risk it falling into the wrong hands.

8:45 p.m. I was washing my underwear and newly purchased wardrobe in a laundromat when I spotted this handwritten notice on the bulletin board: "Body man's dream! 1983 Ford Escort. Big V-8 motor, Hurst shifter. Rad stereo. Won't smog. $800 obo. Call Cass."

Cass turned out to be a lanky guy a few years older than me with long stringy hair, bad skin, and worse teeth. He boomboomed into the laundromat parking lot ten minutes after I phoned him—the thumping bass of the "rad stereo" heralding his arrival from several blocks away.

"Cool stereo, huh?" he said, easing himself out of what had once been an orange-colored Escort, now rapidly fizzing away from the corrosive sea air. It looked more like a body man's nightmare. The worst cancerous patches had been bandaged over with duct tape and then spray-painted with gray primer.

"What's that giant lump in the hood?" I shouted.

Cass thankfully killed the noise. "That's your air scoop for the motor," he replied, proudly raising the hood. "My cousin dropped it in. It's a big-block 390."

"390, huh?" I said, trying to sound knowledgeable. "Is that the compression ratio?"

I could tell this question had cost me some status with Cass.

"390 is the cubic inches," he grunted. "It's got a hot cam too."

"Good. I was hoping for a hot cam," I said, inspecting the muscular engine. I didn't know much about cars, but even I could tell something was missing. One could gaze right down into the bore of the carburetor. "Uh, Cass, shouldn't there be an air cleaner?"

"Don't need one with a motor this big. The crap just blows right on through. It runs like a top, Rick. I'm only sellin' it 'cause I want to get a dirt bike."

Agreeing to a test drive, Cass drove down the highway like a lunatic to demonstrate his car's performance features. That ratty little Escort could fly all right, but I was leery of its non-automatic transmission. I confessed that I had never driven a stick shift.

"No problem," Cass assured me. "Your motor's got so much torque, you could start out in fourth if you want. Plus, you got your genuine Hurst shifter. Four on the floor, man! The babes go for that."

Cass could tell I was ready to buy, though he was severely offended when I offered only $400.

"Man, Rick, the stereo alone's worth more than that!"

"I suppose," I conceded, "but I'm not that interested in damaging my hearing. The interior's a wreck, the tires are balding, and, as you admit, it won't pass a smog test. How about $450?"

We settled on $550, I counted out the cash, and Cass handed me the greasy keys.

"Do you have the pink slip?" I asked.

"Not really, man. You want one, huh?"

"Oh, I suppose not."

Cass gave me a quick lesson in shifting, then showed me how to spray starter fluid down the naked carburetor to assist with engine starting on "damp mornings." As a goodwill gesture, he tossed in the three cans of fluid rattling around on the floor behind the front seats.

"You want the tape too?" he asked, pointing a grimy finger at the stereo. "It's the Young Dickheads."

"OK," I replied. "I'm supposed to like them."

We shook hands, Cass loped off into the mists, I piled in my clean laundry, and drove back to my motel in my new car. I only stalled three times trying to start out in diverse mystery gears. And you really do need to remember to push in the clutch if the aging brakes are to have any hope of halting your rapid progress toward the wall of your motel. But what a feeling of raw power. I've got wheels!

TUESDAY, May 4 — I spent the morning becoming acclimated to my new car. I pulled out the dipstick and discovered my engine was full of a brown foamy goo. Oh well, it ran "like a top" once three blasts of the ether-like fluid got it started. And the battery at least looks fairly new. I drove around town and practiced my shifting. Not too hard, but I can't imagine why anyone would want to bother. This is not the era of the Model T, after all. Face it, guys, the automatic transmission is here to stay.

I found a pair of woman's panties in the damp, moldy trunk (in lieu of a spare tire), and a long machete-like knife stuck under the front seat. Cass must have kept it in reserve for road-rage confrontations and to defend his right to subject large areas of the countryside to his musical tastes. Nothing in the glove box except a few empty food-stamp booklets and some soiled tampons (unused). The radio doesn't work (Cass neglected to mention that), so I'm limited to the Young Dickheads. Perhaps I can employ them to keep the police at bay should I find myself surrounded.

Fuel-efficient my big engine is not. I drove 38 miles and burned through more than a quarter-tank of expensive premium gas. Every time I accelerated I could sense a Saudi Arabian somewhere was smiling. I topped off the tank after lunch and drove slowly back to my motel to get ready. Operation Baby Bust Out begins tonight.

I pushed the intercom button on the front gate of the Eugenia Home at 7:45 p.m. —about 15 minutes before the dogs customarily were released. Clutching a small overnight bag, I was outfitted in teen polyester fashions gleaned from the ladies' departments of several Crescent City thrift shops, augmented with the necessary brown bouffant wig, budget cosmetics, flashy dime-store earrings, and excessively feminine glasses. Carlotta, or at least her ghost, had returned.

"Who is it?" Eugenia's voice inquired over the crackly intercom speaker.

"It's me. Deirdre," I replied, chewing my gum. "I'm here!"

Eugenia emerged from the house, sauntered down to the gate, and inspected me through the grillwork. Dressed in a baggy sweatshirt, jeans, and leather house slippers, she was a stocky 45 or so, with short graying hair, mannish features, and hard gray eyes.

"I'm here," I repeated. "I walked all the way from the bus station and do I have to pee!"

"Where are your parents, Deirdre?" she demanded.

"My mom's in heaven and my dad had to work. He sent me here by myself."

"He shouldn't have done that, Deirdre. He hasn't signed any paperwork. What's his phone number?"

"Dad's workin' now. He works nights. They don't have a phone out at the fireworks factory on account of the possible sparks. But Dad's comin' here tomorrow."

"I can't let you in, Deirdre. I can't accept the responsibility."

"You can't?" I gasped, shifting from foot to foot. "But I got to pee!"

"I'm sorry, Deirdre. You'll have to come back tomorrow with your father."

"Boy, is that a bummer. Dad will be so pissed. Oh well, some nice man down at the pool hall offered to buy me a motel room. I guess I'll go back to him."

"Wait, Deirdre. Did your father give you any money?"

"Yeah, $65, but I gave all but $3 of it to this cute boy I met on the bus."

"Oh dear. I can't believe he let you out by yourself. I don't suppose, Deirdre, that you do very well in school?"

"Well, I got a C once in geography, but I had to do something nasty to Mr. Grelsome's private parts. Gee, I gotta pee bad."

Eugenia reluctantly drew a chained key from the large ring jangling on her belt and unlocked the gate. She said I could stay the night, but warned if my father didn't arrive by 10 a.m. with a check for $1,800, she would turn me over to the county.

Inside, the Eugenia Home was just as funereally dismal as the outside. After I paid a quick pretend visit to the downstairs bathroom, Eugenia took me into a cramped untidy office, where I was grilled mercilessly by her and Waldo. Tall and grizzled, the Reverend Mr. Fairchild had shifty dead eyes and an even shiftier Adam's apple. He clearly was dismayed at the prospect of extending Christian charity to a girl in distress. He and his wife asked lots of prying questions about my family, my background, my pregnancy, and my father's income. This they especially zeroed in on. Deirdre, however, was somewhat vague in her replies.

"Well, what kind of car does your father drive?" demanded Waldo in exasperation.

"Dad drives a brand new Cadillac," I replied. "All big-time fireworks men drive Cadillacs on account of the dangerous occupation."

"Then your father owns the business?" asked Eugenia hopefully.

"Uh-huh," I confirmed. "With Uncle Harry. Dad works nights and Uncle Harry works days. That's why I'm lacking supervision and got in the family way. But Randy's mom made him join the Navy, so here I am. Do you have TV?"

They had no TV, but I had arrived in time for evening prayer service. My interrogation concluded, I followed my hosts into the back parlor, where the assembled inmates were lounging on metal folding chairs and wondering what the holdup was. Most of the two dozen girls were obviously expecting and a few appeared as grossly overdue as my sister. I scanned the bored and bloated faces and felt a surge of panic. MY LOVE WAS NOT IN THE ROOM!

Following her husband's lugubrious prayer service, Eugenia introduced me to Peggy, who was to be my roommate for the night. She was so big I was surprised she didn't require a forklift under her abdomen. We said "hi" and trailed after the other girls filing through the rear of the house into the attached cinder-block dormitory. Peggy and I were to occupy a small second-floor cubicle just big enough to hold two narrow beds and a particleboard dresser. I looked around the prison-like cell and pretended to settle in.

"Better get your clothes off, Deirdre," said Peggy, shedding her maternity top. "Lights out in five minutes."

I quickly turned away, but not before glimpsing a stark white brassiere and something truly frightening below it. Was she expecting quintuplets?

"Uh, which way's the bathroom?" I asked, keeping my gaze fixed on the ceiling.

"End of the hall. But you better make it snappy. Eugenia does a bed check before lights out."

I found the bathroom, took a fast whiz, and tossed my

nightgown on over my dress. Peggy was a blanket-surmounted volcano in her bed when I returned. I slipped into the other bed and switched out the light. Thirty seconds later Eugenia opened the door, shined a flashlight in our faces, said "Good night," and closed the door.

"Peggy," I whispered, "is there a girl here named Sheeni?"

"Nope. And we're not allowed to talk after lights out."

"Did any girls arrive in the last week?"

"Just Sherry. She's totally stuck-up."

"What's her last name?"

"We're not allowed to tell each other our last names. I guess we're supposed to feel ashamed, but I don't."

"Is Sherry pretty with chestnut hair?"

"I don't think she's so pretty. Eugenia paddles us if we're caught talking."

"Why wasn't Sherry at the prayer service?"

"She's disobedient, Deirdre, like you. She's confined to her quarters. She called Waldo a pious degenerate."

That sounded like My Love all right.

"Where's her room?"

"Ground floor, in the front, on the right."

"Thanks, Peggy. Now let's go to sleep. We don't want to get in trouble."

"Too late," she sighed. "I got in trouble about eight and a half months ago. Big trouble."

You can say that again.

WEDNESDAY, May 5 — I didn't think I would be able to sleep a wink, but Peggy's sonorous breathing soothed my flayed nerves and I soon dropped off. Fortunately, the electronic chirpings of my tiny alarm clock roused me at 3:45 a.m. without waking the slumbering volcano. I rose in the darkness, removed my nightie, extracted a miniature flashlight from my purse, and slipped stealthily down the stairs. The house was as still as a tomb. Creeping along the narrow corridor, I came to the room I guessed was My Love's and opened the door. I could just make out two beds, both occupied.

"Oh, excuse me," Deirdre announced. "I was looking for Sheeni Saunders."

I closed the door and waited in the hall. Twenty seconds later my own precious darling emerged wearing extremely unbecoming pajamas.

"Who are you?" she whispered. "What do you want?"

"It's me, Sheeni. Rick."

"Rick! What the . . . ?"

"Shhhh. We haven't much time. Let's go."

We slipped into the downstairs bathroom, closed the door, and switched on the light. No lock on the door, naturally, and not even a mirror on the wall.

"Don't kiss me, Rick," protested My Love, "I haven't brushed my teeth. And don't look at me either. I don't have any makeup on and I know I look terrible. Why are you dressed like that?"

"You look great, darling. It's a long story. We don't have much time."

I took two red felt-tip pens from my purse and handed one to her. "You do me, Sheeni, and I'll do you. The idea is to apply a fine red rash extending down the face from the hairline."

"Accomplishing exactly what?" she demanded.

"We're attempting to simulate German measles," I said, setting to work disfiguring My Love.

"That's brilliant, Rick," she said, going to work on me with equal enthusiasm. "The highly contagious Rubella virus can wreak havoc on a developing fetus. But will this fool anyone?"

"All we can do is try, darling."

We spoke in low tones as we dotted away.

"Oh, Rick darling, I'm so glad to see you. However did you find me?"

"It required some enterprising investigative work."

"You should have finished off my father, Rick. He betrayed me! He only pretended to be on my side so I wouldn't run away before they could stick me in this fascistic hell-hole."

"Parents suck, Sheeni. They're not to be trusted."

"You did a nice job on your makeup, Rick, but my friend Nick makes a better-looking girl. Your features are a bit too masculine. Oh, I never noticed you had pierced ears."

"Uh, yeah, I had a girlfriend once who liked that look on men. Please excuse the cheesy earrings."

"Who are you supposed to be?"

"I'm Deirdre. She's not too bright."

"No girl's very bright if she winds up in this place."

"Don't worry, Sheeni. Just play along with everything I say."

Our faces now done, we applied the red rash to our necks and chests, enabling me to cop a cheap feel for old time's sake. My Love didn't seem to mind. When we finished, we stepped back and checked each other out. At least to a couple of laypersons, we looked decidedly unwell.

"That's great, Sheeni. Now try to raise your temperature."

"How do I do that?"

"Think about your deceitful father. And remember to puff out your cheeks so you look like you have swollen glands."

Ditching the pens in the tank of the ancient toilet, I sent Sheeni ahead to rouse the Fairchilds while I lurked in the hallway. I heard a commotion of voices from their bedroom, then a moment later My Love returned looking ill but happy.

"I have to get dressed," she whispered. "Eugenia's taking me to the hospital. Waldo went out to bring in the dogs."

I gave her a thumbs-up sign, puffed out my cheeks, placed

a weary hand against my feverish forehead, and shuffled down the corridor to the front entry where a grim-faced Eugenia was tossing on her coat.

"Ooh, I don't feel so good," I moaned.

"Not you too!" she exclaimed. "Damn, I better go check everyone. You stay here."

Five minutes later My Love and I were hurtling along the deserted, still-dark streets in Eugenia Home's large rusty van—an angrily muttering Eugenia behind the wheel. For being so devout, the woman sure can sling the profanities. Waldo stayed behind to supervise the preparation of the morning gruel.

Despite the earliness of the hour, the emergency department of the hospital was bustling with disease and distress. After waiting what seemed like an eternity, but by the clock was only 20 minutes, Sheeni and Deirdre were summoned to the counter and asked a lot of probing medical questions by the admitting nurse. Then we had our temperatures and blood pressures taken, were handed green hospital gowns, and were escorted down a corridor to adjacent examination rooms, where we were directed to strip and put on the gowns.

Since Sheeni was the actual paying client, Eugenia accompanied her. I sat fully dressed on the cold examination table in the sterile room and forced myself to count slowly to one hundred. Then I dashed into the room next door, where my feverish love was clutching the open-backed gown to her naked torso and a glum Eugenia was sneaking an illicit cigarette.

"Mrs. Fairchild!" Deirdre exclaimed breathlessly. "Your husband just phoned! Your house is on fire!"

Eugenia turned a pleasant shade of Arctic White. "Oh my God!" she gasped.

"You go on ahead," I said. "We'll be OK here."

"Don't you dare leave," she warned.

"I'm not going anywhere," moaned my puffed-out love, playing her part wonderfully. She lay back on the examination table in a swoon as Eugenia snuffed out her cigarette on the floor and rushed from the room. I watched as our guardian paused to speak to a nurse, then hurried out through the double exit doors.

"OK, let's go." I said.

"Wait, Rick! I have to put on my clothes."

"No time, Sheeni," I said, grabbing her neatly folded stack of frumpy Eugenia Home raiments. "You can dress in the car. Let's go."

I peered out the doorway, saw that the coast was clear, and waved her to follow me. We headed up the corridor away from the nurses' station, and went through a door marked "Authorized personnel only. No admittance." This put us in a room full of buzzing medical machines. We crossed the room, went through a door, darted down another corridor, and came out in a hospital ward, where we were stopped by a beefy male nurse.

"Where do you think you're going?" he demanded.

"A man in the emergency room!" I shrieked. "He's got a gun!"

The alarmed nurse raced off in one direction; we fled in the other. Down another corridor, through two more doors, into some kind of locker room, out the employees' entrance, up a concrete ramp, and we were in the parking lot. Ducking low, we wove our way among the parked cars, traversed a landscaped expanse of grass, crossed the street, turned a corner, and darted up a side street. There, still parked at the curb where I had left it, was my rad Escort. I could have kissed its rusty essence. I even found my keys in Deirdre's purse and the door locks still worked. Feeling optimistic, I shoved in the clutch and turned the key in the ignition. Futile grinding noises.

"Rick, it won't start!" exclaimed My Love.

"Don't worry," I said, shifting the stick into neutral and grabbing a can of miracle fluid. "When I give the signal, you turn the key."

I opened the hood and fed my hungry carb a big gulp of starter fluid. Then, just to be on the safe side, I sprayed a second generous spritz. At that moment I heard the starter click over and a billowing red cloud of flame erupted from the carburetor. It seemed like I had forever to contemplate its fiery roilings as it rose up, expanded, grew progressively nearer, and then inexorably engulfed my face and head. I felt an echoing eruption of pain as my flesh seared, my glasses melted, and my polyester wig ignited. I knocked off the smoldering glasses and clutched my hands to my raging face; someone screamed nearby and I felt a hand pull off my burning wig.

"Oh God, Rick!" My Love exclaimed. "Are you all right?"

I was not all right. I flung open the passenger door, reached inside, found Sheeni's folded dress, and pressed it against my tormented face. The raging pain eased slightly.

"Oh God, Rick, should I go get some help?"

"No, Sheeni!" I slumped forward in the passenger seat. "I'll be OK. You'll have to drive." At least my sadistic engine was idling like a top.

"But, Rick, I've never driven before!"

I heard a siren in the distance.

"It'll be OK, Sheeni. Shut the hood and let's get out of here!"

My Love climbed in behind the wheel. I told her to press in the clutch, as I shoved the gearstick into what I hoped was first. It wasn't. The engine stalled when Sheeni released the pedal. Fortunately, the engine had warmed up enough that it restarted on the second try.

This time I pushed the stick over further to the left. "OK,

Sheeni, ease out on the clutch as you press down on the accelerator."

My nervous love tried her best but seriously over-revved. We burned rubber as the car lurched forward. Sheeni swerved just in time to dodge the car parked in front of us; we barreled down the street at some improbable RPM as her right foot froze on the accelerator. Fortunately, I had guessed right this time and we were in first gear.

"Oh God, Rick, we're coming to a stop sign!" she cried. "What'll I do?"

"Just press in the clutch. Now step on the brake."

Miraculously, the car stopped without impacting anything.

Though it hurt like hell, I eased the cloth aside enough to peer out with one eye. Good news: I wasn't blind.

"OK, Sheeni, we have to turn left here and go down to the main street. There's no other way. Take your foot off the brake, ease out on the clutch, and don't press on the accelerator so hard."

My Love followed my instructions to the letter. We progressed slowly down the street in first gear and stopped at the intersection with the main highway. We turned, accelerated, Sheeni pressed in the clutch, I shifted into second, she released the clutch, and we were chugging along at a legal and respectable 25 miles per hour as Eugenia's van passed us going about 85. She was headed back toward the hospital.

"Do you think she recognized us, Sheeni?"

"I don't think so, Rick. It's pretty dark and she was going too fast. Oh God, it feels like I'm going to sideswipe the cars along the curb."

"You're doing fine, Sheeni. Just stay in your lane. That's why they paint those stripes on the road."

I had a mild heart attack as a deputy sheriff's car roared by, followed a moment later by the Highway Patrol. It looked like all the law in the area was converging on the hospital. Better that they should be looking for a madman with a gun than two runaway girls with measles. I pointed this out to My Love.

"You're such a genius, Rick. I thought you had seriously miscalculated when you said that to that nurse. But the cops will be looking for us soon enough. Where exactly are we going?"

"It's not much farther. We turn left at the next intersection."

Feeling a new confidence in her driving, Sheeni made her turn without yielding to the giant oncoming semi. I heard a blast of diesel horn, saw a pair of blinding orange headlights rushing directly at me, and witnessed through one horrified eye as the skidding truck jackknifed across the highway and flipped its trailer over, sparking and grinding across the asphalt and missing us by the width of a hydrogen atom.

"Sorry, Rick," said My Love, accelerating up the road. "Shouldn't that truck have stopped?"

"I'd say the guy was in the wrong place at the wrong time. But now the cops will be after us for sure. Are you ready to try third gear?"

"Let's do it."

We did. We barreled up the winding road at speeds I felt certain took several years off my life span. I was almost thankful for the distracting facial agony.

I knew exactly where we were going; I had driven it on two practice runs the day before. The eastern sky beyond the black forested hills was warming to soft pink as we successfully pulled in at the small local airport. We parked in the deserted lot, and Sheeni helped me retrieve my pack, laptop, and other gear from the trunk. She led the way toward a compact twin-engine business jet—its wing lights flashing brightly—that was idling on the runway. I kept my free eye open to see where I was going and got a nice view of My Love's divine ass through the open back of her hospital gown.

Connie came down the foldout steps to help us aboard.

"Rick, what happened?" she exclaimed.

"Got my face a little charred," I replied. "Have you been waiting long?"

"You're right on time. We just landed a few minutes ago."

That talented deviate Dogo Dimondo was at the controls. He wasted no time in getting us airborne. Everyone kept their eyes forward as Sheeni went back to the third row of seats and changed into a fashionable ensemble Connie thoughtfully had provided. A swab of cotton dipped in nail polish remover cleared up her rash.

I decided to stick it out as Deirdre with the measles until my face felt better. I discovered that by removing the cloth from one small area of my face at a time, I was able to tolerate the stinging torment. By the time we were beginning our descent into cloud-shrouded Grants Pass, Oregon, the cloth and the worst of the pain were gone. Connie checked out my savaged face.

"Well, Rick, you lost your eyebrows. And you toasted your nose and forehead. But it doesn't look that bad."

"He was very brave," said My Love, squeezing my hand.

"Sheeni, you didn't wait for my signal before starting the car," I pointed out.

"Poor communication, Rick," she replied. "You didn't specify the signal, so I had to use my own judgment. What will happen to your curious car?"

"With any luck," I replied, "the guy I bought it from will be charged with felony hit and run."

"My Rick thinks of everything," said Sheeni. "Where exactly are we going?"

"Our ultimate destination is Mississippi," I confessed.

Sheeni smiled. "You've been talking to Apurva, Rick. OK, darling, I've always wanted to see that state. I hear their marriage laws are shockingly lax."

"That reminds me," said Connie. "I have some wonderful news. My mother filed for divorce yesterday."

"Congratulations, Connie," I said. "You have successfully broken up your parents' marriage. It is the modern child's ultimate revenge."

"Not hardly," scoffed My Love. "I almost had my father killed."

Let's hope our own gifted children act more charitably toward us.

The flight plan Dogo filed in Los Angeles listed Grants Pass as their destination. With any luck there will be no record of their brief stopover in Crescent City. While our plane was being refueled in Grants Pass, Dogo filled out another flight plan for a cross-country jaunt to Atlanta. My three companions grabbed a fast breakfast in the airport snack bar, while I changed out of my Deirdre clothes and sneaked into the men's room to wash my mutilated face. I hope I haven't done any permanent damage to Rick S. Hunter's Gallic good looks. Soap alone did nothing to remove my measles, so I had to resort to Connie's caustic chemical. More racking torture, and I still came out looking like a recent atomic holocaust survivor.

8:45 p.m. It was late afternoon when our plane touched down at a deserted rural airstrip somewhere in the wilds of Mississippi. All the snow had melted and it was hot as blazes. Dogo, at least, seemed to know where we were. Unloading our gear, he told us to walk down the dirt road to the highway and catch the next bus south to Yazoo City. After thanking our benefactors and assuring Connie that if we got caught, her assistance would never be revealed (kidnapping is a federal offense), we waved farewell as their small but fleet plane soared off toward the east. I put my arm around My Love and contemplated the alien green landscape.

"This is kind of scary, Rick."

"Don't worry, Sheeni. You'll feel better after we're married."

"Somehow, Rick, I don't think that's the solution to all of life's problems."

We trudged out to the highway, the bus eventually came, we found a motel in Yazoo City willing to rent us a room, we ate dinner in a Chinese restaurant, and now I have to feign extreme fatigue in order to prevent my amorous love from discovering my still-lingering scrotal scab. I'll also have to change into my pajamas in the bathroom because numerous bright lights outside our window are blazing in through the too-sheer drapes. This is not a motel room conducive to premarital modesty.

I'm not complaining. Hallelujah, brother! I've reached the promised land at last!

THURSDAY, May 6 — American motels always have such oversized mirrors. They must think we're a nation of traveling narcissists. Not good when you're missing your eyebrows, and the skin on your nose and forehead has turned brown and scaly. I had to brush my teeth this morning with my back to the sink. At least my facial impairments provide an excuse for economizing on wedding photos.

First stop after Dixie donuts was the local hospital for blood tests. We passed. The intern said my burned face was looking OK and asked Sheeni if she knew she was pregnant. She said isn't that the usual reason people get married in Mississippi?

We paid our $35 at the courthouse, and through some clerical fudging got in just under the waiting-period wire for their Saturday afternoon wedding special. We're scheduled at 1:30 after two other couples. I used my fake driver's license for my ID, and My Love used her genuine passport—grudgingly brought along by me from California only for that purpose. To throw off Mr. Saunders's bloodhounds we both made slight misspellings in our last names on our license application—crucial errors the chatty clerk didn't spot. As far as Mississippi knows, Miss S. Heridan Sanders is wedding Mr. Rick Shunter.

After lunch we went shopping for nuptial necessities. Hundred-dollar bills were sucked out of my money belt like condoms from a high-school vending machine. I now have a southern-style poplin sport coat and a 14k gold wedding band. Sheeni has a very pretty azure dress ("not bad for Mississippi," she commented), matching shoes, lots of gauzy underthings, an executive luggage set, and the companion ring to mine.

Despite the brightness of our motel room, the balance of the afternoon was devoted to passionate lovemaking. I was able to indulge in this activity because I'd soaked off the last of that pesky scab in my morning bath. Sheeni finally got a good look at Rick S. Hunter's scrawny bod, though I kept my mole-bearing nether regions under the sheet as much as possible. Her only comment was to express puzzlement over my absence of disfiguring motorcycle scars. I said they must have faded away in the beneficent Ukiah climate.

FRIDAY, May 7 — My last full day on the planet as a bachelor. Lest anyone think I'm rushing things, let me note that I am nearly fifteen. When Gandhi was my age, he had already celebrated his third wedding anniversary. I hope his kids behaved well at the party.

While showering this morning, I felt such a sense of joyous anticipation that I found myself warbling a medley of Frank Sinatra's greatest hits. Sheeni complimented me on my excellent singing voice, but Rick S. Hunter must guard against such obvious Twispian displays.

Having exhausted genteel Yahoo City's limited sightseeing opportunities (and finding the heat and humidity oppressive), we spent a good part of the day in our air-conditioned motel room's king-size bed. Sheeni has taken to Southern Life by flouncing about in her slip and talking like Blanche Dubois. When she's not pining away for a mint julep, she's mewling for "those boys" who are ever calling out to her from the dark. So far, at any rate, the only boy doing that is me—though she has been causing a stir among the teen redneck crowd on our walks to the nearby Chinese restaurant.

SATURDAY, May 8 — Sheeni and I were married this afternoon in the chambers of Judge Josephine Jackson. My Love thought it was very progressive of Mississippi to provide us with an African-American judge. I was much more nervous than I had been at Trent and Apurva's wedding, but I managed to blurt out the words, slip the ring on her slender finger, and kiss the bride.

We celebrated our union with a gala wedding dinner at Yazoo City's most elegant downtown restaurant, a dimly lit eatery specializing in Southern Cuisine. I sat beside my wife in an intimate booth and reveled in my good fortune.

"How is your catfish, darling?" I inquired.

"It appears to have been thoroughly deep-fried," she replied. "And how are your chitterlings, dearest?"

"From what I can tell, they're extremely authentic. Darling, since we're married now, I thought we might consider having your baby. I could help."

"How generous of you to offer, Rick. How about if I carry it for the first four and a half months, and you carry it for the final four and a half?"

"I would, Sheeni, if I could."

"Rick, do you have any idea how much work it is caring for a baby?"

"I do, Sheeni. I had some experience with it recently. But I'm told you don't mind nearly so much if it's your own kid."

"But it wouldn't be in your case, Rick." My darling sipped her virgin mint julep. "Or would it?"

I choked on a chitterling.

"What, what do you mean, Sheeni?"

"I've been studying your ears, Rick."

"Really?" I asked, suddenly feeling very self-conscious. "What on earth for?"

"When my friend Nick got his ears pierced, he put up such a fuss that the hole in his left lobe wound up decidedly off-center. I couldn't help but notice that yours is similarly misaligned."

If you can't be honest on your wedding day, when can you be?

"I wasn't putting up a fuss, Sheeni. I was writhing in agony."

"Oh my God!" my wife exclaimed. "My worst nightmare has come true. I'm married to a Twisp!"

I squeezed her warm hand. "I hope you don't mind too much, dearest. And please remember that I endured my ordeal of plastic surgery just for you. I'm sure it was much worse than recovering from a motorcycle accident. But I promise not to be too clingy. If it's any help to you, I'll try to keep my declarations of love to a minimum."

"Well, that's a start, I suppose."

"I thought, Sheeni darling, since we have to live on my money, that we might move to Topeka, Kansas. I understand the cost of living is very low there."

"Well, Rick or Nick or whatever your name is, it is true that my parents seized my Cayman Island funds, but I was not so foolish as to keep all my eggs in one basket."

"You mean . . . "

"Yes, darling, I have several more accounts in Liechtenstein and elsewhere. The total comes to nearly half a million."

"Sheeni, that's marvelous! We're in the chips!"

"Well, Nickie, at least one of us is. So there's no need to economize in Kansas. We leave tomorrow for Paris."

I gagged on a chitterling.

Oh, no! Not France!

It's my worst nightmare come true.

ABOUT THE AUTHOR

C.D. Payne is also the author of the novels *Youth in Revolt, Civic Beauties, Cut to the Twisp, Frisco Pigeon Mambo, Young and Revolting,* and *Revoltingly Young.* He lives in Sonoma County.